THERE IS NO SUCH THING AS A LITERARY AGENT

A New Orleans Mystery

Jane Stennett

HILLIARD HARRIS

HILLIARD HARRIS

P.O. Box 275
Boonsboro, Maryland 21713-0275

This novel is a work of fiction. Names, characters, places and incidents either are the product of the author's imagination or are used fictitiously. Any resemblance to actual persons, living or dead, events, or locales is entirely coincidental.

There Is No Such Thing As A Literary Agent Copyright © 2006 by Jane Stennett

All rights reserved. No part of this book may be reproduced or transmitted in any form or by any means, electronic or mechanical, including photocopying, recording, or by any information storage and retrieval system, without the written permission of the Publisher, except where permitted by law.

First Edition-September 2006
ISBN 1-59133-173-0

Book Design: S. A. Reilly
Cover Illustration © S. A. Reilly
Manufactured/Printed in the United States of America
2006

To 'Officer Darren-Darrel" who knows who he is! This book is a result of his generous spirit and information about how detectives and police stations operate.

Acknowledgements:

Thanks to Rosemary and Joe James of the Faulkner House Books in the French Quarter and the extraordinary opportunities inherent in the yearly Faulkner Society's Competitions. My attendance of the reception at the famous haunted house inspired this novel.

In 1831, the lavish Lalaurie House was originally the home of Delphine McCarty Lalaurie and her husband. Supposedly, Madame Lalaurie tortured slaves locked in an attic and the spirits of these slaves haunt the mansion.

I am grateful to Jay and Miggy Monroe, the current owners, for opening their home to all of us 'tortured spirits' known as readers and writers. A warm thanks goes to Bill Wiegand and my daughter, Stephanie, for nurturing me with expert editing and generous critiques. I am indebted to a certain officer in the Jefferson Parish who advised me while giggling at my exaggerations.

CHAPTER 1
UP the ATTIC STAIRS

THE EVENT WAS going well–all things considered. The Faulkner Society's literary bash for Ronald Well's newest novel had drawn radio and TV personalities, patrons of the arts, and New Orleans' posh literary activists as well as hoards of hopeful writers. Amid the luscious strawberries and Creole cream cheese, champagne and conversation, Mona Wright, gifted writer of nine years past, felt rejuvenated. Her dry spell had ended at last. It had been many years since she could respond to the infuriating comment, "I just loved *Playhouse for Dreamers!*" followed by the inevitable question "And what are you writing now, Mona?"

What could she do except smile too brightly and say, "Oh, I've got a few things in progress that I'm excited about, but we'll have to see what develops." She had just finished the masterpiece of her sporadic literary career. Riding on the fifteen minutes of fame of her one and only bestseller had worn out the artistic community including her ludicrous husband who took a walk when the money well ran dry. She had married the stupid son of a bitch on the rebound when she was a roll of human Glad Wrap so hadn't cared when Julien Montz bailed out on her. He said it was due to playing second fiddle to her fame as a radio psychologist plus her damn bestselling novel, but she knew differently. Julien had strutted around in his worn seersucker suits making like he owned her house in Aububon Place. The asshole had the gall to call himself a member of the landed gentry. He even tried to bully her into using his name, but she rebelled at the thought of being called Dr. Mona Montz. It sounded like a character off of "Saturday Night Live"!

Jerk-off Julien had packed his duds in 1999 and had made off with everything that wasn't nailed down, which included her laptop, as well as cleaning out all the cash in their checking account. She bit into a strawberry about the size of a lemon and thought, *good riddance-bad rubbish*!

Nonetheless, being on the dark side of forty and single again was the pits. But she could reconcile herself to the single life now that her writing juices had begun to flow again. Plus now-days, there was a lost love blooming on her horizon—amazing how passion can re-blossom from what seemed an another lifetime ago. As a psychologist, she could testify to the power of that first deep love, how the remarkable pull of it alters our lives. At any rate, he was back in her life and it was useless to let the past fester—besides she no longer felt she could live forever. She knew she looked younger than her years; she didn't feel old either. For a moment her mind dwelt on her finances—she bristled at the thought. God, things were going fine except for ready cash. Maybe her literary agent in New York would fill in the money gap, but there was a hitch developing around rights to her new novel, *Skiing the Rainbow*. Seems another writer was claiming he wrote it. Both manuscripts arrived on John Warren's desk on the same day…curious coincidence? Mona doubted it. She drained her wineglass quickly. Hell! She needed that advance.

The crowd of grazers was moving from the food into the library to listen to Ronald Wells reading passages from his book, *Intimacy and Pain*. The title was certainly fitting. Ronnie had written a book about the spooks that supposedly rattled around in this very house. The new owners claimed it just 'tain't so,' but it didn't slow Ronnie down for a minute. Supposedly, Madame Lalaurie had tortured slaves locked in the attic and the spirits of these slaves still haunted the house. Later Delphine Lalaurie became an early victim of yellow journalism and was forced to flee for her life. The house was certainly lavish and could easily house a ghost or two.

Mona skillfully ducked a drunken fan that pestered her at every opportunity. The woman called herself Ms. Incognito and the pseudonym suited her to a tee. The dame pulled her shoulders up into a rigid blocking stance. Mona thought the fan could have been wearing football pads under her shirt. Suddenly, the woman twitched, thrust out her jaw, and shrugged as if her tendons were directed by will alone as she elbowed her way around the table to attack the pate like a famine victim. At present, she was chugging down white wine and stuffing tortilla chips into her mouth by the handful. One chip hung out of her lips like a rusty tongue.

Meanwhile, Ms. Incognito's male companion was busy trying to stick his wineglass in his suit pocket.

Mona reached the grand doors to the library, an attractive room with walls of blue stripped back to the original plaster. The centerpiece of the room was a marble fireplace, and over it, a moody fresco of a Louisiana landscape showing the world of swamps, cypress, and Spanish moss. A thick-legged mahogany table had been placed in the center of the room directly under an interesting eighteenth century Venetian glass chandelier. It was here that the book signing ritual was beginning. There was a limited capacity for all the eclectic gathering of dilettantes trying to ooze up to some potential benefactors. She found herself crunched between a houndstooth wool jacket reeking of mothballs and the houndtooth's bosom buddy in a pair of dilapidated jeans topped with maroon jersey, breasts protruding like a balcony. The vapors of camphor made it hard to focus on what was being said. She decided to solve her dilemma by taking a breather on the patio.

She escaped down a black and white marble hallway running through the center of the spatial first floor. On her right, lovely bedrooms opened on to a glassed inner-courtyard resembling a Japanese Zen garden. Her eyes roamed around the tranquil scene, evaluating the intriguing use of the space. Her eyes lingered over the delicate crosshatching of the evening light. Now here was something she liked. The right selection of trees and flowing water created the effect of a fine screen painting–stark, vivid, dramatic. A tiny sparrow fluttered gracefully from one slender branch to another. She watched the little feathered creature flutter between the branches and mused *that's how I feel about my past and future: unanchored, floating between the known-too-well and the unknown.*

The oriental effect was refreshingly unorthodox for most Southern gardens—different from the usual camellias and azaleas at this time of the year. It was so picturesque and pristine as to be a peaceful feast for the eyes. Mona stood with her hands on her hips as she watched the little bird hop from limb to limb. She felt secluded–untroubled–as if she were being given another chance to get on with things. It was a pleasant sensation.

Her peaceful interlude was interrupted when an obnoxious woman in an equally obnoxious black hat with a bulbous, screaming fuchsia rose flopping over its brim clumped through the sliding door. Mona eased toward the side door to the patio just as the woman waved both hands and tittered, "Is this where he's gonna read?"

Mona twitched her face out of shape and shot the woman a cross look. She wanted to tell the broad to get lost, but decided not to answer. She wasn't getting paid for this kind of encounter so she retreated once again through a door that admitted her into a wide expanse of paneled hallway. A flight of elaborate white stairs took all the space they needed to curve gracefully up and to the left like a swan craning its neck. She could hear rock music banging and echoing along the paneling on the landing of the second floor. The stairs didn't stop there. They rose for at least two more stories. She mused aloud, "Jesus, this is one hell of a house. I can't believe they could build this in the French Quarter in 1831. Must have used slave labor and some of them got lost up there and still hang around!"

A male voice came from behind her, "Fascinating, isn't it?"

She jumped as the question resonated along the curved walls. She turned to face a man with the map of Hibernia written in the lines of his face. The bottle-green eyes were moving up and down her body with undisguised admiration of her still youthful figure. She gave him a confused look. "Oh, Christ, you startled me!"

"Thought I was one of the family spooks, did ya' now?" the tall stranger purred. He was very fit and tanned in a green shirt that matched his eyes perfectly—unbuttoned lower than was necessary to display a broad chest and a great deal of curly red hair matching what was left of curls forming a halo around his receding hairline. He held a wineglass in his large right hand and a stack of white napkins in his left. "I don't believe I've had the privilege of meeting you in person. Ya' just might be the famous author of *Playhouse for Dreamers*, Dr. Mona Wright-Montz. Am I correct in my assumption?"

Mona winced at the name. "You are partially right. My name is Wright! It is not right to call me Wright-Montz! Hell, what I mean to say is—how did you ever decide I'd taken that bastard's name? How did you—"

The man flushed a bit and interrupted her sentence, a habit of some people that Mona found annoying.

Reading her expression and not liking what he saw there, he frowned, "Oops, time for a little damage control! Then I take the Montz part back and beg your pardon, I just assumed—"

Mona interrupted him this time. One good interruption deserves another! "Well, you assumed wrongly! Julien Montz is long gone—to hell, I hope!" She resented feeling at peace and then having Julien sprung on her.

Her unwanted companion stiffened. He looked puzzled as if something flashed before his eyes. He took a sip from his wineglass and stuttered, "I—I never meant to offend you." He glanced upward for an instant. "You just looked lonely out here. I don't like crowds much myself so I thought I might play tourist and wander about a wee bit. Would ya' be wantin' ta explore the upper reaches of this haunted castle? I'm a literary agent and—uh, also a music agent for Irish rock bands and I heard some interesting music from above. Do ghosts like rock, I wonder?"

She hesitated then asked haltingly, "Are we permitted to go upstairs, Mr....?"

"The invitation read 'Open House,' didn't it?"

"Yes, but I'm not sure how 'open' that was meant to be." She was aware of being chatted up and it felt rather nice. "I didn't catch your name."

"Michael O'Shea. My friends call me Irish Mike." His brogue sounded as if he had just landed from Killarney.

Mona laughed, "I bet they do! Is all that broughy talk real or just to impress the gals?"

His eyes went hard for a second. They reminded Mona of shards of broken glass. She felt odd to have noticed it.

The look quickly passed and was replaced by a seductive twinkle and a grin from his almost feminine lips. He inspected her from head to toe before reaching his hand to her. "Uh-huh. I think I've had enough of people for now, how 'bout you? Come on up the stairs, fair Colleen. Irish Mike will lead you to your destiny. After we pop in on the rock concert, I'll whisk you away to the attic for a scary visit with the ghosts of New Orleans Past."

Mona had to admit to herself that this fellow had his act down pat. He wasn't quite handsome but he smelled nice—the distinctive masculine cologne reminded her of fields of heather and old leather saddles. She was a writer and writers are always a susceptible breed. Why not tag along? If they were reprimanded, she could always blame the intrusion on this overly zealous music agent, Irish Mike.

His eyes sent out one more admiring glance. His movement radiated vitality as he held out his arm in one final appeal.

She curtsied broadly and placed her hand in his. Smiling, she hoped, infectiously. "Ah, a trip to by-gone days would be nice, kind sir." They did a Rhett-and-Scarlet-sweep-up-the-stairs thing.

On the second floor, the first door was open to display a vast unimpeded back window view of the ancient roofs of the Vieux Carre and the sparking Mississippi River. It was as romantic as the set for the artist's garret flat in Paris as seen in her favorite opera, *La Boheme*. A solid wall of antique windows glimmered with the spring sunlight. The music was not grand opera, however. Limp Bizkit scorched the air. A lanky youth had his back to the doorway and was gyrating in front of the windows. His slender shoulders kept time with the crashing sound. She put her hands to her ears. The Irishman entered and tapped the young man on the shoulder.

The boy swung around, his outstretched arms colliding with Irish Mike's chest. Irish Mike yelled above the thumping sounds, "Whoa thar', Boyo!"

With that, the zit-faced kid with hair sprouting in a hundred different directions stopped his long-limbed gyrations and stared at them. He had a mouthful of the Brooklyn Bridge and jutting from the middle of the braces was a lit cigar. He hastily removed the stogie and held it behind his back. "I thought you guys were my parents." He barked, not a little belligerently, "What 'cha want, *Dude*?"

Irish Mike bantered amiably, "Oh, your Da won't miss one Cuban. Smells grand, I can tell ya! We're interested in this palatial mansion you get to call home. Your maw said there was an oil panting of Madame Lalaurie in the attic. She invited us to take a wee peek at it because there was a striking resemblance between my lady friend here and ole' Delphine herself." His Irish cadence was at full tilt.

Mona shot her companion a quick frown and her lips were ever-so-slightly disapproving. She was amazed at his facility for lying.

Irish Mike winked at her and continued, "That's fine sound equipment ya' got there, laddie." He breathed in and then out importantly, then he shouted over the volume. "I'm in the rock and roll music business meself."

The tall, wiry boy with the straw-colored hair and intense gray eyes ignored Mike's invitation for a rap-session concerning his tweeters and thumpers. Not deigning to answer, he continued to glower at them.

Suddenly Mona's purse began to ring. Her cell phone could barely be heard through the reverberating guitars. She unzipped her purse and fumbled for the phone.

The lad cackled nastily, smirked at her, and sniped sarcastically, "Don't you know that just because it rings doesn't mean you have to answer it?"

Mona was so taken aback by his wisecrack, she ignored her phone call. She stiffened with a befuddled laugh and zipped her purse. "You have a point there. I'd never thought of it that way." His wise-crack made her feel rather old.

"Oh, knock yourself out." Without any desire to continue the conversation, the kid raised one hand in what could be interpreted as a gesture of dismissal.

She felt a little foolish as they beat a hasty retreat. Mike nudged her up the stairs while he shouted in her ear, "Youth is great, isn't it?"

Mona retorted, "Uh-huh, leave it to the young! They deserve everything they get! This is a bit of a climb round and round." She glanced down at her high heels and groaned, "I have on heels, not climbing boots."

At the top of the stairs she turned to look down three floors. The view was spectacularly beautiful if a bit daunting to a woman who didn't care much for heights.

Mike sighed, "Nice, very nice," and added, "no people and rock music."

"Deafening, ain't it? I don't see how you stand the friggin' stuff." Mona couldn't shake the edginess she had felt with the boy. Her colorful companion's lie about some picture looking like her wouldn't go away. She couldn't figure out why the lie was so intensely irritating. Why had the kid gone so silent about music? You'd think he would jump at the chance to talk to a real music agent. Kids have an uncanny sixth sense about lies and con artists. She'd seen enough teenagers in her psychology practice to realize he was at the age where he exaggerated everything—and they had caught him smoking. Still, something perturbed her.

The pair regarded each other for a moment then Mike nodded his head; a strange little smile slid across his face. "Oh, I can stand lots of loud rock today." He turned and tried the door. It opened with the creak of rarely used hinges. He stood to one side and bowed, "Let's go. Ladies first."

Bad idea, she thought as she eyed the small, low entryway. "Wait, I'm tall and the door is short. Folks used to be shorter in those days." She grinned sheepishly at her own discomfort then bent to slip off her shoes. "I'll just ditch these spikes. Leave them out here."

Mike picked the heels up by the sling straps hooking them to his little finger beneath the napkins. A patronizing grin broke his face.

"Oh, no, Cinderella, I'll hang onto 'em. It maybe rough on your hosiery."

Already having second thoughts, Mona ducked her blonde head and hunched down to step gingerly over the threshold. Mike followed her though the opening and pulled the door after them.

There was an unnerving smell of dust, old fabrics and mildew. Drawing a short intake of breath, she wheezed, "Whoa, leave that door open. We need the light, not to mention some air up here."

He didn't reply.

A tension had settled between them, uncomfortable and gnawing. She sat her purse down beside the door as she looked around in the gloom and quipped, "There isn't much to see—no chains or whips." The gloomy space was no small jewel. It was smaller than she had imagined it would be considering the size of the house. The high ceiling was exposed bargeboards and slate, the walls appeared to have been whitewashed at one time. Two dormer windows were painted over with peeling flakes of gray paint.

The man entered behind her and didn't say a word.

Mona completed her inventory and declared, "Just a big old aquarium–at least a fifty gallon one. It probably sprung a leak—more's the pity, no famous painting here." She was re-assessing the wisdom of this trip, shaking her head but still smiling. "I think I've lost my appetite for spook research." She pursed her lips and asked him quizzically, skeptically, squinting in a way that indicated her discomfort. "Did you plan all this? Is this a scheme? Why did you have to make up that *shtick*? I'll bet the kid didn't believe you. You Irishmen are always kissing some blarney stone! Maybe we ought to head back—"

She was ready to laugh and ignore it when suddenly she heard a crash followed by the tinkle of falling glass on the floor. She lifted her head as she turned to face him. The shattered remains of a crystal wineglass sliced though her throat. Irish Mike calmly stepped to one side as her blood splattered against the closed door in a machine gun spray of red streaking upward to the ceiling. Her body slammed backward across the rim of the dry aquarium. Mona Wright would never know if her bestseller would ever be published.

Avoiding the fountain of blood that shot toward the ceiling, her assailant unzipped his pants and dragged out his penis. He threw back her skirt, ripped though her pantyhose and jerked down the flimsy lace panties. As her head collapsed to her chest, blood pumped into the aquarium. Without touching her, he proceeded to rape her still jerking body. Then he carefully wiped the stem of the wineglass and violently shoved it deep into to her vagina. He wiped his hands, zipped his fly, straightened his clothes, wiped the straps of her shoes before he dropped them beside the corpse, and moved through the door. Using his remaining party napkins, he carefully swiped the edge of the door facing and the knob. He folded the bloody side inward before he carefully tucked the napkins in his pants pocket and descended the circular stairs to join the party.

YOUNG WILLIAM ST. Denis turned off his sound system at midnight. He was puzzled by what he imagined was the ringing of a cell phone from above his room. He thought sleepily to himself, *probably just my ears drubbing from all my music. What the heck, it sure drowned out my folks' dorky party good enough.*

Jane Stennett

CHAPTER 2

AT BREAKFAST THE next morning, William brought it up. "Say, y'all, I gotta' be having hallucinations. I keep hearing a friggin' phone ring in my ceiling. Drove me bonkers all last night, but the buttheads were making so much noise I couldn't tell for sure. This morning it woke me up first thing."

His father put aside the paper and eyed his fourteen-year-old son gravely. "Well, it's about time something worked to wake you up. The alarm clock certainly doesn't!"

William shot his dad the finger under the table and rolled his eyes. "Yo, wicked! I can get up whenever I want to. It's spring break, Dad." He turned to his mother. "Say, do we have some stuff stored in the attic?"

"Nothing but that old aquarium you insisted on keeping."

"No old pictures of that lady who lived here? The weirdo who whipped her slaves to death?"

"That's just a myth, Billy. No, we restored Madam Lalaurie's portrait. It hangs with all the others in the library. Why do you ask?"

"Well, yesterday afternoon while you guys were boozing it up with literary dweebs, a frigin' geek and some lady wandered upstairs to listen to my music. They said that there was a picture up there."

Janice St. Denis thought a minute then waved her hand in the air. "Oh, it was probably just a ploy to get to see the attic. Everyone is curious about all that ancient history. I don't see why blood and gore fascinates the public so much. Eat, then go enjoy your holiday. Your dad and I think you spend too much time in your room. Why don't you call a friend and take in the Quarter?"

Billy frowned at her. "Why can't you just leave me alone?"

Robert St. Denis, well-educated attorney with effortlessly good manners, shook his paper and raised his eyebrows at his son. "And why don't you stop being an obnoxious teenager and knock off being rude to your mother."

"Dur! Bite me, dude! I'm gonna go up to the attic and find that cell phone. It must be up there somewhere." The flaxen-haired youth swigged down his orange juice and loped out of the breakfast room.

His parents exchanged meaningful looks. Robert just shrugged his shoulders and returned to his newspaper. Janice shook her head as she reached to answer her own cell phone that lay on the table. After checking caller ID, she recognized the caller as a close friend, Rebecca Webster. Janice chirped, "Hi, y'all."

After asking how the party went and complimenting the St. Denis,' Rebecca asked if either of them had seen Mona Wright.

"The reception went fine, but God, it was hectic! I'm exhausted. My housekeeper bailed on me at the last minute. Yes, Mona was here around sevenish. Robert talked to her about some screw up with her new novel." Janice glanced at her husband. He frowned and shook his head as he put a finger across his lips. She waved her hand at him and shrugged helplessly. "Oh, he's going to give her legal advice. You won't believe this—some schmuck has challenged her authorship. The imposter sent the exact same manuscript to her agent, John Warren, in New York. She was beside herself with shock! It's so sad after all those years to get a new book out. Robert says it may tie her up in court for years. It's no wonder she couldn't write with her carpetbaggin' husband telling everyone at the Pickwick Club that her first book was lousy—"

At the sound of her husband clearing his throat, she turned to face him and delivered a broad wink. "Uh-oh, Robert is giving me the 'Don't ask, don't tell sign.' I know I'm talking out of school, but who would listen to Julien's malarkey?" Another pause and she laughed, "Apparently Mona *listened*—which explains how she got stuck with him!" Janice listened. "I know, he's slow poison." She paused to listen again. "What? Why doesn't she just divorce him? It's not that simple?" She continued, "Oh no, not because of the church–church smerch! No, because she failed to get a prenup agreement and this is a community property state, my dear! She's a smart lady, so I can't imagine how she let it happen. You'd think a psychologist would know better! Robert says if the skirt-chasing cockroach ever shows up again, he's apt to get half of her grandfather's mansion on Audubon Place. It's very discouraging."

She listened then grinned at Robert then stuck her tongue out at him. Nodding her head, she said to the caller, "Yes, I agree, life should be on the up and up! She's one tough cookie! Mona may have to take care of him the rest of her life while Don Juan's off screwing every attractive woman he meets!" Janice listened. "No, I don't remember seeing her leave. Maybe Robert does." She glanced at her husband.

He stopped buttering his croissant and shook his head. "No, he has no earthly idea, but we do know that she was dressed to the nines. That woman has the best taste in clothes. Saks made a bundle off of that cream-colored Ralph Lauren. I've never seen a fitted jacket and silk tulle tulip skirt done so well. She looked very *now*— so chic, like a fashion model. Maybe...what's her name, the one with the gap between her front teeth? Who? Yeah, Lauren Hutton, that's the one. You can tell her next time you two get together." Janice listened for a moment as she ran her hand though her hair, newly colored ash blond and done in a stylish bob. "Yeah, let's do lunch at the club. Invite Dr. Mona Wright when you catch up with her. Don't tell her, honey, but I bet she left with some new guy just to make Brian Herlihy jealous!" Janice giggled, finished the conversation, and folded her phone away.

Robert had been more amused than annoyed at his wife's womanly gossip plus her fashion commentary on the famous Dr. Mona's taste in clothes. With a wry grin, he was about to make a crack about what a lucky duck Janice had been to have married the right person so she didn't have to experience unwelcome surprises when the racket of feet came thundering down the stairs. It sounded as if a diesel truck was rumbling towards them.

The couple looked at each other askance. Robert turned in his seat and shouted, "Ahm...Billy, corral that herd of elephants!"

Billy was breathing hard, his eyes bugging out of a white face.

Janice laughed at her son. "You look like you've seen a ghost!"

"Come–come quick! The lady's dead and my aquarium is full of blood!"

His mother frowned. "William, don't joke around about things like that!"

William screamed at the top of his lungs, "Jesus, Joseph and Mary! I'm not joking! No joke, Oh God, no joke!"

After a quick inspection of the grotesque scene, Robert St. Denis called the police. William hid out in his room. Janice wrung her hands and stood guard outside her son's door.

The detective who arrived with the police homicide unit was Brian Herlihy. Brian was a burly, six and a half feet of maleness. Many of his friends had laughed when the one and only heir to a New Orleans' plumbing company had decided to become a Catholic priest, but they laughed even harder when he abandoned the church for the New Orleans Police Department. They scoffed and commented that what was known as plumbing's finest had become God's finest and now one of New Orleans' finest.

Detective Brian Herlihy swung up the circular stairs two at a time causing the massive ancient structure to groan and creak beneath his feet. Robert St. Denis, as grim as death itself, stood at one side. An officer held the door open. The small passageway filled with Brian's bulk as he stepped over the threshold. Uniformed policemen and the coroner joined Robert on the landing and stood in hushed silence. This was not a time to push their way inside. Every man respected Brian's right to go in first. But this was neither respect for his rank or his size. They all knew that this was the door to hell for the officer they affectionately called "The Big Guy."

His adoring fans thought the athlete's entire life was an absurd irony. Most of the city was familiar with the much publicized affair between the hard drinking Big Guy and the beautiful uptown heiress to a four generation red bean fortune who had become a best selling author plus a nationally known radio psychotherapist. Nobody dared speak of their present relationship—or the one that preceded this one. It was common knowledge that Brian and Mona were a hot item through their high school years. They were the perfect couple, above all the teenage angst, destined for happy-ever-after. After graduation, they both left for Louisiana State University. She had sat in Tiger Stadium for four years and watched as Number Seventy-two, the star who's teammates had given the moniker of "Big-Un," blocked and tackled his way to All American. It was in all the news when "Big-Un" sidelined his football career and abandoned both his steady girl and football in the spring of his senior year.

Tiger Stadium was referred to as Death Valley. That season it lived up to its name in more than one way. It was certain death to Brian Herlihy's romance with the lovely Mona when he announced that he felt compelled to enter the priesthood. All hell broke loose. Rumor had it Mona married the charming Julien Montz on the rebound. Supposedly, these events culminated in a heart attack killing Mona's father and the mental breakdown of her society-minded mother. After Mona's flaky husband engaged in several bar brawls and gambled away her family's fortune, he took off for Las Vegas.

Five years before Jules hightailed it out of Dodge, Brian had changed his mind about God's will for his life and turned to police work. He rose quickly though the ranks—partially because his football fame made great press, but mostly due to several highly publicized cases. While a rookie, Brian succeeded in getting a description of a killer from a reluctant eyewitness. The traumatized witness was a seven-year-old girl who had watched her mother be beaten and stabbed to death. Then, low and behold, two days later, Officer Brian Herlihy created his second piece of sensational press when he single-handedly apprehended the accused. It seemed that Brian had been on his way home when he went to the assistance of an automobile stalled on the railroad crossing on Jefferson Highway with a freight train barreling down. Officer Herlihy recognized Harry Benjamin Keller from the girl's description of his car and his mug shot. The young officer literally smashed his police car into the stalled car and shoved it off the tracks—then proceeded to arrest his suspect. The sick joke of the press was to refer to Harry Benjamin Keller as 'Heller-Keller.' Keller struck a plea bargain with prosecutors to avoid a trial on second-degree murder charges, which carried an automatic life sentence upon conviction. Harry "Heller-Keller's" sentence for manslaughter started at fifteen years and ended at forty years.

The promotions came rapidly after Brian was the only member of the New Orleans Police Department to enter the alligator-infested Maxent Canal to pull a woman's body out of the water. At least four alligators were seen swimming nearby during the recovery operation. With the press fueling the scenario with all the drama at their disposal, Brian "Big-Un" Herlihy was commended by the mayor for his acts of bravery.

Much to the community's surprise, Mona welcomed Big-Un back, but their new relationship never produced any announcement of long term plans. Everyone recognized Brian was devoutly Catholic. Dr. Mona was still a married woman—at least there had been no annulment or divorce. Even though there was no "see you in court," the "Dr. Mona Wright clan" plus the entire city continued to relish every scrap of news concerning their tragic princess and her long lost prince charming. The couple's envious following conceded that sometimes, once in a while, there were even happy endings—not always, however.

CHAPTER 3

Detective Herlihy stood staring down at the crumpled heap. His heart felt as though it was being ripped from his chest. The blonde hair he loved to run his fingers through was dangling over her face, shining tendrils soaked in her blood. The head was bowed, as if in obeisance—bent awkwardly over her bosom, obscuring the wound that had released the fatal hemorrhage. But he didn't need to see the slash to know it had gone deep, to the carotid and the windpipe. He was already familiar with the aftermath of such a wound, and he imagined her final moments—the artery spurting, the lungs filling up, his love aspirating through her severed windpipe. No matter how many crime scenes he walked into, that first sight of blood shocked him. But this was Mona's blood, a comet's tail of arterial splatter that shot across the wall that had trickled down to dry like streamers. The source was the love of his life. Her chest was heaved up on the far side of an aquarium, shoulders smashed against the inner glass sides, her arms flung out as if trying to catch her balance. Her hips rested on the nearest rim. Oh God, her skirt was flung back with her long legs splayed outward on either side of her crotch. She lay bent in half—stretched out—entirely exposed with the base of a wineglass protruding from between her slender white thighs. Brian fought back the rage rising within him, felt it like bile in his throat. He couldn't get his breath. He put trembling hands over his eyes to block out what he was seeing. There were no tears—this death was too horrible for tears. His mind buzzed and snapped with pain. *They are going to photograph her. Oh God in Heaven, they are going to take pictures. I can't even cover her. Bastard*! He unleashed a howl of anger and bitterness so intense everyone on the landing jumped.

Outside the room, the two morgue attendants who had gathered with the crime unit heard the Big Guy's curse. "God Damn Bastard!

Mother Loving Son Of a Bitch! You shit faced animal! I'll cut your prick off and stuff it in your mouth!"

Officers ducked their heads and someone snarled, "Amen!" The coroner echoed, "Amen, you tell the SOB, Big-Un!" Actually, they hadn't yet viewed the carnage, but no one doubted it was bad. Their resident priest had just delivered the final rites in such a way that they all choked up before they even knew what was in the room.

Time passed. Robert St. Denis, nonplussed by the detective's behavior, whispered tersely to the nearest officer. "What's he doing? We didn't touch anything but this doorknob. Billy didn't do anything except find her, and now my son is a basket case. We called immediately. He doesn't think we disturbed the crime scene does he? Do we need a lawyer? Why doesn't he come out?"

The officer held up his hand and said quietly, "Now, see here, Mr. St. Denis, just calm down. None of your family is suspect. You did the right thing, but by law, you shouldn't be up here." He jerked his thumb down the stairs. "Why don't you go down to the kitchen and join your family? Just give Detective Herlihy some time to cope. He knew the victim well—real well. Y'all are new in the city, and this thing goes way back."

The Orleans Parish coroner for the last twenty years, Andre Villere, moved up the narrow stairs to join the medical examiner. He paused to allow St. Denis to pass, but his mind was whirling with the matter at hand. Villere was a gaunt man with slightly stooped shoulders. There were threads of silver streaking his dark hair. Maturity carved deeply sober lines into what was still a strikingly handsome face. His green eyes were unreadable behind a pair of half glasses perched on the end of his nose, but he was having a considerable amount of personal feelings about this particular homicide.

It was unusual for Andre Villere to come to a crime scene, but he had a lengthy history with the detective. He attended St. Patrick's church along with Brian's family. Like everyone else, he had followed the career of the boy known affectionately in the parish as their "Big Un." He, too, had sat in Death Valley and cheered their hero on the gridiron. He, too, had been entranced with the glowing couple. He, too, had been shocked by Brian's decisions. He, too, had enjoyed the muffled amazement and had shared in the gossip surrounding the rekindling of the old flames. He shook his head, *Ah, he thought, New Orleans is the heart of romanticism for the whole nation, and this couple had been their best soap opera.* He, too, had awaited each episode, but not this one.

Andre looked at his watch. He knocked softly at the door facing and spoke gently but firmly to the hunched giant blocking the view. "Detective Herlihy, Brian, you gotta' let us in. Anything you could have done is in the past. Let us take care of business." He heard a sob, then a loud coughing.

Brian worked to control the overpowering urge to kick the door, a longing to drive his fist through the wall or the window, to feel pain as much as cause it. Even though his head felt like it was about to explode, he forced himself to back away. He forced himself to breathe and said irritably, "Okay, okay, I've seen all I can stand. Take care of her for me, Doc. Tell the damn crew to be fast and cover her up. You guard those photos with you life, ya hear?"

His bear-like body in a shirt drenched with sweat began to back out of the small doorway. As he emerged, Brian's voice was as tense as a fishing line holding a shark. "Bag her hands and roll her over easy. Don't let anyone make those crappy jokes. She doesn't deserve that smut mouth stuff—not now, not ever. Are we clear on this? I don't want the pictures to circulate. Tell the camera jockey I'll have his balls if any shots get passed around. Just get them to my desk after you do your job. I sure as hell don't want to see them." He choked back rage he couldn't afford. "Is Gracie here? Tell her to take over. I gotta' go puke."

Everyone crowded to the side as Detective Brian Herlihy exited the room. His face was as white as chalk. His pulse drummed at his temples and it was painfully obvious that it was taking everything he could do to sound calm. He nodded grimly, waved everyone off, croaking, "Just cut me some slack—I'll be back. Where is the nearest bathroom? I'll need a drink of water and a place to sit...like in the kitchen. Don't evacuate this house. Don't want the press to get wind of this. Tell St. Denis I'm gonna' need the guest register for the Faulkner Society shindig." He grunted past a raw soreness, "Tell him I request that they keep this homicide quiet out of respect for Mona, Dr. Wright. No phone calls or visitors—nobody in or out. That includes household help. If they need anything outside of this house, check with an officer. Now, where's that bathroom?"

The Big Guy grabbed the railing as he lumbered down the curving stairs. A herd of sympathetic eyes watched him go. At the second floor, Officer Grace Reme moved from beside the boy's closed door and began her ascent to the attic with its lifeless contents.

Joyce St. Denis led the way down the hall and knocked on Billy's door. "Honey, time to unlock this door. The detective really needs to use your bathroom. It's okay. Nobody blames you. Let Mother in."

The door was jerked open by a red-eyed boy. Billy burst into tears and threw himself across the room and on to his tumbled bed. His mother rushed to sit beside him. Brian hardly noticed them as he hurried past to the bathroom. His own grief and anger required his immediate attention. He slammed the door, knelt to embrace the bowl, ducked his head into it and threw up. Afterwards he straightened, gasping, and turned on the faucet, tugging a towel from a rack and wiping his mouth and face. "Sorry...sorry..." He tried to settle down, but it was as though a cloud had filled his brain, his lungs, and he couldn't get his heart to slow its racing.

LATER, THEY TALKED and the guest book was thoroughly gone over. No one recognized any name that fit with the stranger who had called himself Irish Mike O'Shea. There was no such name and no such talent agent listed.

Brian congratulated the St. Denis family and especially the boy. He was intensely interested in the incoming cell phone call Mona hadn't bothered to answer in her brief conversation with Billy. "Good, Bill, real good you caught that detail. There will be a record of the call and whoever was continuing to ring her number after...uh, what happened...uh, happened." He was shivering. He made himself calm down before he continued. "You got really sharp ears and a good memory. We could use you on the force."

Billy raised his head. His face looked molted, like strawberry skin. His nose began to dribble as he heaved a breath and moaned, "What if she had answered her cell? I made a stupid crack...real wise-ass stuff. She didn't answer it. What if she had gotten a call that made her have to leave the party? If she had then she'd still be alive. I caused it. I know I caused the whole thing." He broke down and put his head on the table.

Brian felt the tears starting to ache behind his own eyes. He realized that the boy would relive the nightmare of what had happened to her and see the scene in the attic for the rest of his life. Clearing his throat, he resisted the urge to pat Billy on the shoulder. His mother was doing enough of that. "No, Bill. You didn't cause it. No use for you to do all that what-ifing, either. Listen to me, Bill. I know what I'm talking about. If that...that animal...Irish Mike O'Shea—provided that is his real name—was determined to kill Dr.

Mona, he'd have done it sooner or later. Naw, it wasn't your fault. You were just a cog in the wheel. We're going to keep a close watch on you because you're the only person who actually saw them together before he lured her to the attic. It could happen to anyone at any time, don't forget that. When you're not so bummed out, do you think you could remember him well enough to describe him to a police artist?"

Oh, heck! Do I remember him? I didn't like the dork one bit. He *sucked*—all swarmy and blowin' about Irish rock bands." He hissed, "I scoped the scumbag out right away. I should'a told that jiggy liar to kiss off—just called the nerd a liar to his frigin' face!"

His mother gasped. "Oh no, Billy! He might have killed both of you right there in your room!"

Brian continued to stare at the kid. His lips seemed to form words that were somehow not connected to his thoughts. Then he nodded and said, "Your mother is right. You could have made matters a lot worse. Now, I gotta' go back…upstairs. You just stay put. Don't leave your parents or this house for any reason."

The detective collected his strength, preparing himself for what was to come, horrified by its necessity, alarmed by the degree of emotional resolve that this required, like dredging the black muck of a swamp. He knew that department procedure was going to want to replace him, but that wasn't going to happen. Not now, not until he found the killer.

SOMEHOW THE MORNING passed into afternoon. Mrs. St. Denis fixed coffee and sandwiches, but Brian couldn't eat. Finally, the team was finished and the body was removed. Yellow police crime scene tape draped the banister from Billy's room up to the attic. It looked as if a grisly Mardi Gras parade had assaulted the stairway. Brian walked to his car and collapsed over the steering wheel. His big hands grasped the wheel and pounded. His cell phone rang. Clearing his throat, he answered in a limp voice, "Herlihy here."

The call was from the ever-present press. He knew it was vital to stall any news leaks. Even though he raged silently, Brian deliberately forced himself to keep his voice light. "Oh, hi, Darrel." It was his old college buddy from three lifetimes ago, the former L.S.U. quarterback, Darrel Pitts. The detective liked the African-American who currently covered all the police news in the precinct. Yes, Brain and Darrel had seen each other through some interesting times and had developed that easygoing smart-assed way of dealing with each other that men adopt when they don't know how to show affection. Trouble was Darrel was as effective at connecting all the dots while nosing out disturbing news as he had been when passing to his receivers on the football field. He was adept at being the first reporter to cover any crime scene, but he could be nasty, brutal and his stories banged around like shutters in a high wind. The reporter showed little mercy regardless of the status or race of the individuals involved. He was determined to waltz into a Pulitzer on the backs of white folks. Brian supposed the reporter's disturbing fury was racial, but never dared to comment on this aspect of his friend's coverage. "Top 'o th' mornin' to ya! What can I do you for?"

Pitts wasn't put off by the clichéd quip. The voice on the phone sounded eager. "Hey, Big-Un, no Hibernian *shtick!* I figured I was gonna have to call 911 in order to get through to you. What's all the flapdoodle on Royal Street? Everyone in the Quarter get mugged?"

"Nuh-uh," He continued by electing to use the moniker the adoring public had given the quarterback, "Darlin' Darrel, we got things under control. Do me a favor and hang loose on this one. I figure you know who is involved, so I've got to ask you to lean back. These folks have been blasted out of their wits. It involves their son and the St. Denis' need some recovery time. And I need some lead time."

He moved the phone away from his ear as the reporter exploded. "Listen Big 'Un, I ain't your patsy! It's my duty to get this story! Jesus, you sound so chipper—"

Brian listened to the resistance and rolled his eyes. "Yeah, well it's an act, I assure you."

"Really bad? Pretty pissed off, huh?"

"Listen, I gotta get a leg up on this thing and I won't be pumped for personal stuff. Can't afford any feelings or I'll be jerked, and God forbid, I sure can't talk about it with you."

The voice on the other end of the line held a snarl, "Ha! Ya' mean *especially* with me, don't cha?"

"Look, Darlin', make nice, ya' heah? I can't stress this enough! It is absolutely vital the whole story not break too soon. We're not dealing with a moron here and can't afford to spook him. The perp has to think we're still in the dark. Will you just improvise and report that Dr. Mona Wright is missing?"

Pitts paused. When he finally spoke, his voice was guarded, "Is she…missing permanently?"

Handling the press was one of life's little challenges, but Darrel Pitts was no little challenge. Even though his head felt like it was about to explode, Brian tried to make his voice sound light and slightly carefree, "Oh, Darlin,' you're the Pitts! It's don't ask, don't tell, okay? But I will give you this much. When we find out the answers, you'll get the poop first. I concede Dr. Mona is the victim, but don't make this any worse for her and the St. Denis family than it already is."

'Darlin' Darrel Pitts was not amused. He was perplexed and retorted impatiently, "Promises, promises!" Then the reporter sneered, "Shit, Brian, ya' got balls! Okay, I'm cool with stalling—for now. I'll report her missing, but you owe me one. How about I hold folks at the paper off by doing a profile on her and make her disappearance into a mystery? But I won't chase you—you chase me! If I don't get the full story from you in twenty-four hours, you dis' me, and the freedom of the press takes over, y'all heah?"

"Thanks, Buddy! I need some running room. You'll get it as soon as I get a line on a suspect."

"Look, Herlihy, I'll hold off for old times' sake. You saved my arse, more than once. Cut the razzle-dazzle. And if you are lyin' to me, we'll never be able to darn this sock!"

"Yo, don't be a prick! Over and out!"

Brian signed off and headed for the coroner's office. *Twenty-four fucking hours until the nation knows!* He was having trouble dealing with the rape part. Was it someone she knew? It couldn't have been Julien. She wouldn't have given the scuzz-bucket the time of day, much-less adjourn to the attic with him. What was the connection? Someone she had just met? A relative? No, she had no close kin other than her pitiful mother in a convalescent home in Mandeville. Maybe a loony fan? God knows she had plenty listeners—sane and crazy. Where to start? He couldn't shake an overwhelming feeling of helplessness.

His thoughts turned to an episode one afternoon early in February, the fourteenth. He recalled the day because it was Valentines' Day, when some unknown admirer sent a dozen long stemmed American Beauty roses to the radio station while Mona was on the air. In his head, he began to replay her telling of the events. She had been puzzled by the card because it was blank, but she wasn't foolish enough to say anything about the bouquet's arrival over the air. After her show, she was cautious enough to have the mail clerk take them to the side of a car near hers and leave them there like a poisoned Christmas gift. She had watched from the elevator to see if anyone was hanging about. Perhaps the sender didn't know what she looked like.

Brain parked his car and sat reflecting on the evening after the flowers were delivered. They had made dinner and opened a bottle of her father's precious wine. After dancing around her living room, they had headed upstairs. He had propped her up on the pillows and rubbed her back while he warned her that Inmate "Heller-Keller" was blustering around the prison swearing he'd fix the S.O.B. who put him away. Brian recognized that such prison rantings were not unusual, but he had felt he should reinforce his warnings when she told him about the roses. Mona had retorted that the roses were bloody unsettling, but so was his attitude. Then she had rolled over on the pillows, assumed her radio voice and proceeded to give him a five-minute lecture on the personality disorders of incarcerated anti-socials including their self-defeating habits, paranoid outlook, narcissistic grandiose fantasies, uncontrolled anger and impulsive self-damaging escapades, such as gambling, promiscuous sex and spending binges.

He remembered making a sardonic crack about the description sounding like her ex, Julien Montz. She had been so surprised that she had responded as if it were a joke, arching her eyebrows at his sarcasm before making a crack of her own—something about conversation wasting valuable time for which they could find a more rewarding use. He remembered laughing and kissing her, long and deep. When they came up for air, she had solemnly assured him that she intended to be careful, but she pointed out it was pretty certain that no accomplice of Keller's would recognize her these days. Harry had been locked up for more than five years. Sure, her first bestseller was published the year Brain dumped Harry Keller in prison. Sure, the book had her picture on the back, but that was an old picture from years before when she wore glasses and hadn't bleached her hair. If someone was doing Harry's dirty work, why hadn't he jumped her in the parking garage? Brian recalled shrugging at her and grumbling that perhaps the jerk just wanted to get a look for future reference. Then he had pointed out the obvious, what would be easier to spot than a tall, blonde woman carrying an armload of red roses?

She had said nothing, just rubbed her leg against his. And then there was that moment he'd felt before when she would begin to gather herself up. He could feel the hardening of her resolve and held her closer, gently kissing the side of her neck.

That had been the end of the conversation. Mona hadn't wanted to go on talking about it or thinking about it. But that was the way she was, always fluffing things off that got in her way. He remembered that she had squirmed around in the bed to be closer to him and nuzzled on the left side of his neck and nibbled. He had turned off the light and made love to her.

Provoked with himself, he shuddered and rubbed his eyes as he tried to shut down that side of his mind. He thumped his forehead hard against the steering wheel and sat without moving. That conversation was only months ago. Nobody *had* materialized in that damn parking garage, but what if Keller's pal had followed her home? Naw, that wouldn't do the nutcase much good. Audubon Place was the snazziest closed community on St. Charles Avenue, maybe in all of New Orleans. It would take a mother of a stalker to get past the guards at the gate. It was highly improbable since Tom Cruise was now leasing a house within the confines. Brian had a sudden image of the fury and contempt in Harry Benjamin Keller's eyes—something about those roses was uncanny, but what?

CHAPTER 4

Andre Villere met him at the entrance. It was obvious to Brian the coroner was taking pains to take care of him. He was glad because he needed some special care. They went to Villere's office, not to the morgue. Andre gestured to a chair.

"I'll stand, thanks."

"No, God damn it! You'll sit down! You look as if you'll fall down at any minute. Sit, Boo-Boo, sit!"

Brian sat heavily and grabbed the armrests with both hands. After taking a deep breath, his response was swift and businesslike. "Give it to me."

Villere paused to clean his glasses, then, with a long melancholy face, he began to speak in the quiet tone that he used to prepare folks for bad news. "Brian, she was dead all night, rigor mortis had set in. I estimate the time of death somewhere between eight and midnight. The attack was sudden. Mona was dead by the time she hit the side of the aquarium. Seems he was right handed and severed the left carotid artery and the trachea with a single deep gash. The jugular vein was completely severed as she turned to face him because the arterial spray shot up not forward as she fell backwards. Her perp must have stood to the left because on the ceiling and right wall were dense clusters of small circular drops flowing downward, characteristic of an arterial spray as well as exhalation of blood from the trachea. Her blouse was saturated from downward dripping, but if it's any comfort, she didn't live long enough to know she was dying. Mona was actually twice dead. The metal lip of the aquarium broke her neck. The fall smashed the spinal column and completely paralyzed her. He raped a corpse that couldn't even twitch." He paused, struggling to phrase his words with the most delicacy possible. "There was no pain after the first shock. I doubt she even knew what hit her."

Brian gripped the desk with both hands, fighting to contain a sudden surge of nausea. Then he banged white knuckles against the desk in front of him. His jaw was set in stone. Through gritted teeth he snarled, "Cut it out. So she was twice as dead? You can't make it pretty, no matter what you say. Maybe there was no struggle, but that just means no skin under her nails. I want evidence, by God. Get me some evidence!"

Andre held up both hands in a gesture of mock surrender. "Okay, he didn't use a condom so we have trace evidence—minute amounts of semen on her undergarments—none in the vaginal swab. Either the alcohol contained in the wineglass did its work or perhaps he got limp prick and was incapable of doing much of a job. She was probably already dead when he tried...uh, what he tried. I know how painful this is."

Brian stiffened and responded grimly, "You have no idea how painful. Get it over with!"

Drawing a deep breath, the coroner continued, "Uh, to do penetration with the physics of the situation, her body sprawled in such an awkward position and due to lack of time, and of course, we must consider the precautions he took to avoid...uh, getting messed up in her blood. Can't determine some details on such short notice. It's shaky and we're running some more tests, but it is strange there isn't more fluid. Uh...none in her...uh...her oral cavity so there was no hankypanky goin' on. No contusions or abrasions, so he either got friendly post-mortem or it was consensual— which we know it probably wasn't. It doesn't appear they even kissed. Her lipstick would have been smeared or there would have been traces of foreign spittle. Or...er...something in her mouth." His eyes darkened. "Brian, brace yourself for this. It is a little too early to be sure, but he left a calling card. It takes weeks after exposure for certain viruses to become positive but half a minute to check a live sample. Lab reports won't be in for days but preliminary findings from the postmortem examination suggest the perp's HIV positive. The test is a quickie and not a hundred percent reliable, but we can assume that had she lived, Mona would have been exposed to AIDS."

Brian's face stiffened in disbelief. "Oh, God—she would have had AIDS?"

"Not necessarily, but a possibility. We'll have to do more tests, but it would have been mighty risky exposure to the virus. He wasn't careful on that score, but he was careful in other ways. The glass shards on the floor revealed nothing, so the prick must have wiped everything down. No fingerprints on her shoes and nothing on her purse except her prints."

"What about the door?"

"Tech guys came up with a few partials—probably the kid's. Mona's killer had to have planned it all because there was enough blood to cover him from head to toe. He couldn't afford to return to the crowd covered in blood. If he were a cat burglar and she surprised him trying to steal something, he'd be a guy who was in a hurry to leave." Andre gave a tired sigh. "Strange that he did a good job of cleaning up after himself, even wiped down her shoes, then gets rambunctious and makes the worst possible mistake and leaves his sap? It doesn't make sense, but even the smartest screw up." Andre pulled nervously at his mustache and waited. "I can stop anytime if this gets too rough for you."

They regarded each other for a minute. Andre Villere felt a twinge of shame that he could even suggest that this was the work of a common thief.

Brian shook his head and grimaced. "Bullshit! This is no bungled burglary. They talked to the kid on the way up. There's more here than meets the eye. Maybe he was in her circle of friends and admirers, but she obviously didn't know him well. The kid said she acted surprised when the perp bragged about being an agent for Irish rock bands. Mona would have picked up on that. She's just finished a novel about Ireland. Besides, she was pretty hip with the media work and had plenty of hip guests. I'll get Gracie to get a list of her recent interviews and go through her professional correspondence. Shit, it's gonna be difficult. Bet we'll be missing plenty. Julien lifted her computer when he took off." He rubbed his face. "I think we've ruled out passion. That being the case, there seems to be only two possible motives—money or revenge." He flashed on Harry Keller, but elected not to mention his suspicions. No use to bring up old business or the recent threats with Andre. The fewer people who made a connection with Keller, the less pressure for the brass to replace him on this case. His voice became sarcastic. "We'll check AIDS clinics with his description, but who knows if the SOB sought treatment or counseling or if he did locally. The rape might be an attempt to cover up some other motive. Maybe he wanted us to believe it was purely a sex crime—that's why he was so brutal."

Andre leaned across the desk. "Yeah, and that explains why blood didn't flow when he pierced her with the remains of the wineglass.

Dead bodies don't bleed—at least they don't bleed much. All the blood was on her upper torso or in the goddamn fish tank."

The detective stood and paced the floor like a wild man. "Well, it's not much, but we gotta' go with it anyway. Our perp isn't as cracked as he wants us to believe. He's too skillful. I figure he's a hired hand."

Andre continued, "And there's one more thing. We found two crinkly pubic hairs other than her own behind her left thigh near her buttocks. They are reddish-blonde and one has roots we think. With any luck at all in about three days, we will be able to match DNA. You find him and we've got him!"

"No, if I find him, I've got him!" Brian's eyes glazed with a determination to make himself completely numb.

Villere looked alarmed. "Whoa, Brian! Don't let this take on a life of its own. Do everything by the book, you hear? You got a hellava Irish temper and sometimes working with you is like living with a Rottweiler. You're not after the facts. You're after vengeance. It's written all over you. You should see your face. You're white to the lips. Hand this case over to someone with no personal involvement. If for no other reason than you loved her. There're plenty of good detectives who will do it right because they *know* you loved her!"

Turning sharply, Brian stomped out of the office flinging his words over his immense shoulder. "Nobody will do it righter than I will! Let them try to take me off this case! I got some favors to call in on the force," he seethed. "Two things are sure. The chief won't replace me, and we got less than twenty-four hours before the bastard Paddy knows we've found her. Fax your report to Gracie ASAP, but use my private number, not G.Q.'s. That's like putting it in the morning news. We may have a leak to the press."

CHAPTER 5

Officer Gracie Reme had adored Brian "Big Un" Herlihy ever since she had laid eyes on him. She recognized her crush as partially hero worship and partially romantic slop left over from their childhood. Her father had been a plumber in Brian's dad's company for forty years. She and Brian used to go on jobs with her dad. They'd play in lawn sprinkler and sit in wet clothes in the plumbing truck while listening to the radio. Or they'd go get snowballs together. She'd lick his and he'd lick hers—snowballs, that is. She hoped he remembered those summer days before he'd gone to Newman School then Jesuit and L.S.U. She went to Dominican High School and University of New Orleans. They had lost touch, especially when he became the property of the uptown princess, Mona Margaret Wright. A little envy there, she had to admit. Gracie stored him away with all her fairy stories of unrequited love without him even knowing it. She had felt a faint surge of hope when Mona married and Brian shucked his priest nonsense. But that fantasy was over. What chance did a plain, husky, black-haired Cajun plumber's daughter have anyway?

For five years on the force, she had chosen to suffer in silence, content with being his unofficial office wife. She deliberately downplayed her attractiveness by wearing an uncalled for uniform jacket and dark skirt or pants. The dull clothes weren't necessary in her position, but she had determined that she needed the vague look of a uniform as a shield of protection, a barrier against the messy and dangerous affection she had for him. She needed to feel safe and in control to survive as a cop, but the garments never flattered her stocky frame, and her hair was a careless mop of black curls. Forget makeup, she was who she was, and you either accepted it or you could go to hell. Her's was an okay life—at least she could be around him. Besides, it beat issuing parking tickets. She recognized her interest had as much to do with hormones as it did police business.

Oh, she could list all the reasons why working with him this closely wasn't a good idea, but it was a job. As much as she hated the thought, she felt a tiny bit of personal relief about Mona's death plus a mother-load of guilt about the merciless event that improved her own chances.

Biting her lower lip, she felt disgusted with herself for allowing such feelings to overwhelm concerns for the victim and her family. She was a damn fool to think that way! *Focus on the dead woman and how she got that way*! Nevertheless, her heart went out to the Irishman. His life was such a mess. She turned sharply to the tasks ahead of her.

She had returned to the precinct to start a check on VICAP. Maybe they could get a hit. But she suspected they wouldn't. This perp was obviously skilled, but was he an imported visitor and not a national? INTERPOL would be a different matter. VICAP, the Violent Criminals Apprehension Program was a national data base of homicide and assault information from cases across the country. Killers often repeated the same patterns, and with this data investigators could link crimes committed by the same person with the same MOs.

That search set in motion, she started tracing the idiot husband, Julien Montz. All the records indicated Montz thought he was a hotshot who had numerous careers including stockbroker before the '87 crash hit. There was a SEC investigation into some junk bond deals Montz had put together. It eventually cost him his broker's license along with whopping fines that Mona paid to keep him out of bankruptcy court. There were all sorts of complaints filed against him. Most were minor misdemeanors—running the old razzle-dazzle shell game, disturbing the peace, verbally assaulting an officer in front of a strip joint on Bourbon Street, a citation for public drunkenness at a gay bar called the My-O-My Club. She found a couple of civil actions concerning unpaid debts that Mona had settled out of court. There was a raft of parking violations and a D.W.I. She noticed the last of the moving violations was issued just before he split. Officer Reme stood silent for a moment absorbing this information. She thumped an index finger on her chin and thought perhaps it was coincidental, but the car he was driving was not registered in his name or any member of Mona's family. She frowned. It didn't fit. This auto was a 1998 silver Saturn registered to a Ruby Ann Higginbotham.

Gracie sipped a lukewarm Coke and tried the phone number listed on the citation report, but it had been reassigned to someone else.

The new party had never heard of either Julien Montz or his buddy, Ruby. The address on the report was a Camp Street flophouse off Lee Circle. When she called, the manager remembered the couple but said they had moved out in December of 1999. The clientele at the hotel believed Julien and his tart were off to Las Vegas. Usually he didn't give a hoot where folks went, but this time he had tried to track them down. He complained that the couple had left him with a fat unpaid room rent and requested that the police do something about it. The manager recalled that Ruby bounced her jugs at a strip joint named The Insider located in the adjacent suburb of Metairie known as Fat City. The surly gentleman also volunteered the information that Ruby Ann stripped under the name of The Silver Saturn. He chuckled wickedly when he told Grace that Ruby sprayed her whole body silver. Her trademark was the rings of Saturn tattooed around her shaved pubic mound. Gracie wondered how he got the tidbit of lewd information, but knew better than to ask. She then placed a call to the Metairie police only to learn the club had closed down.

She called the Las Vegas police and requested any information they had on the Saturn or the owners of same. She stressed the urgency and underscored the seriousness of the crime. A murder investigation gets everyone's attention.

Brian entered the office. Gracie looked at him questioningly.

Answering what she didn't ask, he cleared his throat and mumbled, "Well, I'm still on the case. The powers that be have agreed that I can handle my feelings about the victim." He laughed harshly. "I told them either I was on it or they would have to suspend me."

"Huh?" She grumped.

He arched his eyebrows and snarled, "What does that mean, 'Huh'?"

"Forget it! No way. You can't do it!" She stared at him like a child trying to connect all the dots.

He frowned, reading her expression and not liking what he saw there. "What's that look? You have a problem?"

Gracie leaned forward and gripped the edge of his desk with both hands, fighting a sudden surge of emotion. There was panic in her eyes. "Brian, you are making me your accomplice! Are you listening to me?" She rolled her eyes with one of her long-suffering rolls intended to convey fond exasperation. "This is too painful. You'll never be able to be detached and objective." She added in a hoarse whisper, "In case you've forgotten, the *victim* is Mona, for Christ's sake!"

Had she raised her voice, had she said it with hostility, he might have responded in kind. But she had said those last words quietly, and he could not muster the necessary outrage to fight back. "Trust me, it is my case *and,*" he pressed, "we're not going to talk about this! You got a problem with the way I do things? I can handle it with or without you. You'll either be with me or stand by and watch—so what'll it be?"

Her mouth had gone dry. Her gaze dropped to the sloppy folders scattered in front of her. His desk looked like chaos central. She had little tolerance for his sloppiness, and her files were always organized into two neat stacks. It took a few seconds for her to process what he had just said. She stiffened and took an uneasy breath, rolled her eyes upward and looked at him skeptically. "I wouldn't say this to just anyone, but I think you're one of the good guys. So, sure, just be an asshole and get your heart reamed out. Whatever! But you're really pissing me off. You know I can't stand by and watch even if it has nothing to do with me. You always need my help, and by the way, I think they were using Ruby Ann Higginbotham's silver 1998 Saturn."

He pushed back in his chair and eyed her for a minute then grunted his thanks. "Where are we with the Saturn, then?"

"Still at it," she replied. "Nearly two thousand 1998 Saturns in Vegas alone, not to count those in Miami and here."

"Fine work, Gracie, I've always admired your quick mind."

She chewed the right-hand corner of her lower lip in an unconscious parade of anxiety and tried again. "Oh, for heaven's sake, you're taking too much on your shoulders. You're not the only policeman responsible for what's going on out there."

"Right! Easy for you to say." The detective's eyes were like shards of topaz. "Any idea when the loving couple met?"

"Nope, not yet." Gracie hesitated then spread her hand, palm down, and made a rocking motion. "Who knows? I have a hunch it was right after the jerk married Mona and was flush. They apparently took off in Ruby's Saturn in the late autumn of 1999. That's the last of his parking and moving violations at any rate. They probably celebrated his newly acquired wealth and freedom along with the Millennium in Vegas.

"Oh, yeah, you got a call from Rebecca Webster in the last ten minutes. Jason Cox is on the desk. He said she's called about five times this last hour. You reckon she has found out some way?"

"Oh, yes, Darlin' Darrel Pitts saw to that. He probably called her the second he hung up with me. He'll have to be content running a vague story about our local psych-jock's mysterious absence from WGSO radio. I'm sure he smells the worst and telegraphed his concern in uppercase, bold type to Becky. He's probably pumped her and is frothing at the bit to involve the St. Denis family. It's a small enough price to pay to keep him busy for a while. Give Ms. Webster a call and ask her what she wants to tell me. I got bigger fish to fry than to talk with Mona's hysterical friends."

"I did call her back to check on Mona's cell phone records. Rebecca's number was on the call back, but she refused to talk to me. She said I'd have to arrest her first."

He scoffed beneath his breath. "That's not a bad idea."

Gracie put a hand on his arm. "Big Un, don't say I didn't warn you. I know this hurts a lot, but you need to talk to Webster. I'm calling Vegas again and ask them to check out recent high steppers with HITS, Homicide Investigation and Tracking System. I traced Montz and Ruby Ann to a prior address—a flophouse on Camp Street. No forwarding address on either of them, but the manager told me that Ruby Ann uses the stage name The Silver Saturn. She paints her body silver and completes the effect with rings around you know what!"

Brian locked up his feelings again and grimaced, "Well, it's a lead—better than calling herself The Black Land Rover, I guess. I figure Julien is hiding from possible charges of theft of Mona's computer and a lot of family antiques. He isn't likely to use his real name, especially if he sold her stuff to pay someone to bump her off." He patted Gracie's hand in a gesture that was unusual for him. "Thanks, Brown-eyed Buddy, I can handle it. It's just a hunch, but let's check the whereabouts of any of our old friends, Harry Keller's known associates, while you're at it. Run his mug shots by that manager and the residents. Could be some connection if anyone he hung with lived there at any time. Stay on Vegas to trace that Saturn and check any title transfers. It's a long shot, but maybe Julien got her to sign it over to him. We might be able to pick up some falsified identification if he's using another name."

Grace wiggled her lips to avoid tearing up and turned away. It had been a long time since he had called her his "brown-eyed buddy." She cautioned herself against crossing the line between business and personal issues. It occurred to her that even though he was supposed to have a ferocious Irish temper, she had never, since she started working with him, seen him really blow up. Even with Harry Keller. When he was truly pissed, he was the ultimate poker player. His face became a mask as he closed up, quiet-like. Only his eyes showed anything. His eyes did the thinking. They became alert and feral. Otherwise his attitude was typically Irish: either "Don't sweat the small stuff" or "Don't get mad, get even!" She considered his eyes to be alert and feral right now.

He added, "Check with the AIDS treatment centers." Not waiting for her reaction, which he figured he couldn't handle at the moment, he turned to dial Rebecca's number. His stomach soured. There was no way he was prepared to talk to the bitch.

REBECCA WEBSTER PICKED up immediately. It was obvious she had been waiting by the phone. Without ceremonial greetings, she whispered in a deadpan voice, "Brian, meet me in Audubon Park. I'll be at the parking area next to the zoo. Park over by the Audubon Tearoom and walk across the park. Be sure you are not followed. I don't want that snoopy reporter to see us together. You can never be too careful—he may have my phone bugged. I'm leaving my house this red-hot minute. Over and out!"

The dial tone hummed in his ear. He expelled air from his cheeks in exasperation. Becky Webster was such a ditz!

Gracie stuck her head in the door. "News from Vegas. Our gal, The Silver Saturn, worked in a dive famous for the availability of crack. Guess what the club was named? You'll never guess. It is called 'Swelled Elegance.' Isn't that revolting?"

Brian shrugged. "Not as revolting as Julien Montz."

"Speaking of Montz, Ruby Ann and Mr. Revolting Montz lived with her sister."

"What was her sister's name?"

"Her stage name was Roxy Rocksoff."

"Not her stage name, Dodo, her real name."

"Oh, real name—Angela Higginbotham."

"How do you know all this?"

"Well, Angela ain't no angel. She was apparently practicing her bumps and grinds on top of Julien when The Silver Saturn came home from a hard night's work. Police report was pretty vague about who bashed whom first. Julien swore it was self-defense on Angela's part. He testified that The Silver Saturn, Ruby Ann, started it but ended up with her head busted by her beloved sister. The hospital report actually took up for poor Ruby Ann. Autopsy says her sister didn't die from the blow to her head. Ruby Ann Higginbotham, alias The Silver Saturn, had ODed. There seemed to be some question about how the cocaine was administered when Ruby drifted off to na-na land—self inflicted or otherwise. They're sending all the records, but it appears they were also involved in porno and drug trafficking."

She waited to see how this impacted him. No reaction. "Report says that Julien was a real dork, roughed up both gals pretty regularly. Police think he may have been their pimp. No other witnesses and nobody pressed charges, but Angela, i.e. Roxy, and Julien were detained for possession. Police couldn't make it stick so Julien and his new main squeeze were released on February 10, 2001, and took off for Miami. Angela and Mona's hubby had to notify the Vegas police before they could leave Nevada. Seems she had priors on the books—solicitation and possession with intention to distribute."

Brian flashed back, "Stop using the term 'hubby,' will you please?"

She looked confused then shrugged her shoulder. "Sorry, Brian."

He rubbed his chin as something flashed in his brain: *February 10 of this year...roses delivered February 14...sounds about right.* He nodded at Gracie. "Let's get this thing moving, check AIDS clinics and hospitals with his description, in Vegas and Miami and here."

Gracie couldn't prevent a sharp intake of breath. "Why AIDS?"

Brian considered for a moment before answering. "Villere thinks the SOB had AIDS. We're still missing plenty. Maybe the attempted rape was his idea of some horrible joke."

Gracie muttered, "AIDS? He doesn't have much to lose."

"Tel-Ex Florida's Motor Vehicles for the Saturn registration in Florida. It's a long shot but maybe Angela was a good girl and registered it. Also, run citation and ticket checks on Irish Mike O'Shea and Julien Montz. It's a long shot but we need a break. Have Simmons run defense with Darrel Pitts and the other press vultures. Brief him on what to give them: as little as possible and no mention of any details of...oh, hell you know what. Get me a plane ticket to Miami. Notify the authorities to pick up Montz and crew. I'm off to Audubon Park to meet Ms Webster."

Tech Sergeant Paul Simmons entered the office. The officer looked younger than his thirty-three years. In fact he was so boyish, the force had nicknamed him "Junior" and called him their resident Boy Scout. Junior was beaming. "Big Guy, don't leave just yet. I can shed some light on the subject of Dr. Mona's cell phone. We traced the calls. At 5:28 PM there was an incoming call from Rebecca Webster that went unanswered. Hold onto your shorts. At 8:00 PM on the dot, a call from an aerobics studio called The Amazon Center. Guess where it's located—Miami Beach! The calls during the night were varied—a couple from Rebecca Webster and one from the same number in Miami. The last call is Webster's at 7:40 this morning then her battery went dead."

Gracie threw Brian a salute then followed Officer Simmons to the doorway. She turned back to ask, "Detective Herlihy? You're about to go off half cocked and you know it. How long since you ate something?"

"Dunno...breakfast this morning, but I lost whatever it was rather suddenly."

"Some advice: pain is better taken on a full stomach. Stop and eat something before you get even more hurt."

"Gracie, stop snapping at my heels like some bitchy bulldog and go do something! If you don't, you'll find yourself assigned to another case."

She stood her ground. "Holy smokes, you can be a real prick!" then she shook her head. "Fine, lie to yourself, and while you're at it, pull rank and be done with it!"

He growled, "Right! You control freak. All I know is that I have one nerve left and you're getting on it." He shrugged, "I'll swing by Mother's and grab a po-boy on my way. Just what I need, a prick-picnic in the park. Now, go work too hard!"

He got up and left without a backward glance.

CHAPTER 6

It was dusk and a light drizzle had begun to fall by the time Brian parked where the live oaks towered overhead like the walls of a great green tunnel. Even with the rain, the heat of the day still radiated off the blacktop. It would be another rain-soaked, uncomfortable night. An ambulance slid past the entrance to the park, lights flashing. He thought of all the women who were going to sleep tonight in their fine houses, oblivious to the night's evils. He wolfed down the roast beef poor boy and sipped a Coke. Then he took a deep breath, as though to draw in the courage to interrogate Mona's best friend. Pulling a wrinkled trench coat from the back seat, he headed across the park.

Rebecca sat in her Mercedes 500 SL convertible and was glad she had thought to put the top up. It was the beginning of the spring monsoons in New Orleans. She had parked under the canopy of live oaks. The dry, brown resurrection fern was soaking up the moisture, and, replenished by the rain, had sprung to life making the limbs of the host oaks look mysteriously furred in the failing light. She mumbled to herself, "You mighty oaks are beginning to need a shave." Suddenly the rain came down like a temper tantrum. She watched the lumbering man hunched in the rain as he leaped the rapidly accumulating puddles in the black gumbo soil. "God, you're big, Brian, my love."

He opened the passenger door and wedged himself into her car. His knees jammed against the dashboard. He searched for a lever under the seat to adjust it. "Rebecca, this car is a cracker box. I can hardly fit. Can you move this seat back some?"

She did the best she could, but his knees were still buckled. She shifted in her seat and faced him. "That's as far back as it goes, Big Un." She tittered as if an afterthought, "You'll just have to make it hunky-dory—get it? *Hunk*-y-dory?"

He wadded the trench coat beneath his knees. "Okay, big f'in whoop! Now, what's all this cloak and dagger stuff?"

She was in a confined space with a man who took up too much of it. His shoulder nearly touched hers. Something about him was so big and so vivid and so direct, it drew her in. Rebecca felt his closeness and smelled the rancid sweat made worse by the dampness of his clothes. She purred, "Brian, I don't know what to say or where to start. I was stunned when Darrel Pitts called me. It's just terrible, isn't it? Mona was such a dear heart, and to have something like this happen to her...I told her not to mess with that loony bunch of radio listeners, but she could never see it coming. I can hardly think about it."

His blue eyes narrowed. "Think about what was coming, Rebecca?" *Maybe she wanted to forget a trip to the attic.* "What do you know about Mona's disappearance? Be quick, I got a plane to catch."

She could hear from his tone, despite his effort at control, that something wasn't right. Her voice faltered. "I was hoping you could tell me. I only know she's missing. Man, it's too weird, I can't get her to answer her phone messages and I've stopped by the house a zillion times. She's either gone off somewhere or she's dead in there. That house is so big. God, it's like living in a moldy mausoleum. Just the upkeep must kill her! I told her to sell the damn thing, but she is too sentimental about her family history. Besides, it's actually good, estate-wise. She couldn't stand the thought of Julien makin' off with anything more than he did. She sought comfort in what was left to make up for what the fancy-pants had already bamboozled her out of."

I know where this is headed, he thought, and gave a tired sigh. "Rebecca, I don't have all night. Skip to the bottom line." The air was thick and humid. His head was pounding and the sandwich weighted a ton in his belly. He took a deep breath and tried to straighten out his cramped legs. To make matters worse, Rebecca lowered her window a bit and started to shake out a cigarette. "Don't light that! Tell me what you can tell me! What's so secret you couldn't tell Officer Reme? What were you doing when you called Mona at the party last evening? Janice St. Denis said you told her the next morning you were trying to locate Mona."

Rebecca's face fell into a pout. She didn't like the edge to his voice, but she ruefully placed the cigarette and her gold lighter on the dashboard in front of her. She put five slender fingertips onto the glass windowpane and began tapping softly, then she looked over at him and trilled in a little-girly voice. "Rains slowed—is it okay to leave the window open for some fresh air? I'm getting to it, but it's awful painful, Inspector Clouseau! I thought you detectives always worked in pairs. Where's your partner?"

She turned and looked at him seductively through her held up hands as she fanned out ten very long, very red fingernails. "This is what I was doing—my nails. I planned to meet Mona after the Faulkner bash. I called to see if I could take a taxi down and hook up with her. She has a perfect parking space at the Royal Orleans, so I wouldn't have to find a place to park in the French Quarter. You know what that is like? I wanted to hitch a ride home." Her voice trailed off as she bit her lip and gave him a wispy smile. "Honestly, that's all there is to it. So I just did my nails...and waited..."

He made a mental note. *So Rebecca knew about the parking space the radio station provided for Mona, and it would be easy for her to share the information about Mona's whereabouts that evening.* Brian ignored her smile and observed her while waiting for her to continue. Rebecca was one of those people who never aged or maybe never grew up. She was perilously close to forty-two but actually looked younger—twenty years younger, in fact. She looked exactly the way she had looked when they had been at L.S.U. where she had been quite the party girl. Becky was one of LSU's Golden Girls and had been rumored to put out. All he knew for sure was from bitter experience with the renowned flirt.

At present, her auburn hair was slightly frizzed from the constant moisture outside. She had hazel eyes set wide in her slightly pointed face, glowing skin, a soft mouth slightly too thin, yet appealing. There was a certain Southern bubbly way about her that was brought out by a few drinks. Rebecca was quick witted and impulsive, small and thin, too thin even in her clothes. She still dressed like a teenybopper. Oh, the outfit she was wearing was expensive enough—short white cotton sweater revealing a fair amount of freckled skin and ample cleavage but stopping short of her belly-button and a tight black skirt. Her straw espadrille wedges added inches to her diminutive height.

Rebecca turned back to the darkened scenery and seemed to be talking to herself. "I never was one of those girls who had working for a living in my life's plan, but Julien thought he had married a cash cow. But perhaps..." It seemed she couldn't finish the painful sentence. "What I'm trying to say is, since...if Mona's gone, maybe we can be friends again, you and I. We were inseparable once, Brian, the three of us. Mona won't be a problem." She looked over at him and suddenly widened her eyes at the enormous implications of her last statement. "I mean, it wasn't your fault...Mona would like us to be friends again. Maybe she could see the two of us and it would seem like it used to be back at LSU. She never understood why you turned against me and wouldn't even speak." Now that she'd started talking, she couldn't stop.

She is talking as if she knows Mona is dead. Why? The killer left her to rot in an attic. We haven't broken the news. Darrel Pitts may suspect it, but did he share his speculations with Rebecca? "Becky, you talk like she's dead."

Her mouth dropped open. She blinked and stared at him like a child whose birthday balloon just popped in her face. "Do I? Hmm...maybe it would just be my worst fears come true. At the time, I was simply thinking it just isn't like Mona not to return my calls. She always has her cell turned on and—"

Brian interrupted her. "Let's begin with the last time you saw her."

She lowered her voice, "At water aerobics at the Reilly Center on Thursday. What are you looking for? What do you want to know?"

There was another silence. He shook his head and asked, "For starters, do you remember Harry Benjamin Keller?"

Rebecca blinked. "God, yes, is he out?"

"No, but did you ever know anyone who knew him? A drinking buddy or, well, any lowlife that might have hooked up with him at any of those bars you have been known to frequent? Like maybe at Irish House or Snug Harbor?"

She bristled, "Watch it, buddy! Am I being interrogated? Are you going to arrest yor' little ole' Beck?"

"No, this is just routine. Hell, Becky, I need to know!"

She reeled back from the steering wheel "Shit, I called you, remember? I wanted to tell you something! Now Mona is the topic of conversation, like she always is! It's just par for the course." She shrugged. "I bet she's made some kind of mistake—something she's holding back or someone is holding over her head. It's not surprising. She's poked around in some pretty crazy places. Writers do that, but she'd have to be dead or unconscious not to be on call for her precious patients. She'd answer her calls as quick as a wink—you know that for a fact."

Brian frowned at her, looking unhappy. He checked his watch with impatience. *Damn it, she didn't answer the question about Keller and associates. I need to pump her about this but I gotta git!* "Rebecca, skip to the chase. What's this meeting for?"

She caught his mood right away and recoiled slightly. "It's just...oh, I just...everything is too much." Tears glistened in her eyes. A breath caught going in. "What I plan to tell you is rather distasteful. Honestly, I wouldn't even bring it up now if Mona was...safe, but we don't know, do we? She's just missing or something, right?" She looked at him inquiringly as if she could get him to confirm what she already knew or suspected. He didn't flinch nor respond in any fashion. She bit her lip again and continued dejectedly, "Brian, this is ancient history, I know. Do you remember the Mardi Gras house party our senior year? The drunken brawl at Mona's? The night the gang got so Gawd-awful blotto and you accompanied me upstairs for a little...uh..." she giggled as if it was a little joke, "massage therapy in that bedroom at the end of the hall?"

He didn't respond to this either, but he remembered very well. Even as his policeman's mind recognized that Rebecca had changed the subject to something personal and painful, she had skillfully avoided answering his questions. Whether the evasion was planned or not, it worked. He felt unstrung by this sudden turn in the conversation. Their nookie party had cost him everything he had held dear. He wouldn't give her the pleasure of knowing he had been thinking with his little head instead of his drunken big head, and that night was the crux of all of his decisions. Rebecca had whispered into the dawn that nothing had happened—they were both too smashed. She swore he had passed out while they were playing nasty. She insisted they didn't do the deed, but it didn't matter. Waking up naked beside Rebecca wasn't something his religious convictions could tolerate. He went to confession and vowed to become a priest—so much for atonement.

The silence between them was deafening. The only sound was the rain lashing about in a renewed frenzy on the windshield. At a loss for words, he cleared his throat and said quietly, "Rebecca, it's been a long time. Now's not the time to dredge up our sordid past."

She put a hand to her breast. Her lips trembled and her eyes filled with tears. It was such a touching expression, Brian wondered if she practiced it in front of a mirror. She enunciated her next words as if to someone with limited intelligence. "Oh no, it isn't *all* in the past. I got knocked-up that night. I would have told you, but you...you bastard! Like you gave a fuck!" She spat out the next words like she'd just stepped in dog shit. "No, you had to go running to Father

Kennedy the very next Sunday. Then you jumped ship and announced your infernal decision to drop all of us—your father's business, the Tigers, Mona, and me! What in hell did you expect me to do? I hadn't had sex in a month of Sundays before or after that night. It sure wasn't an immaculate conception, so it had to be you. I didn't tell anyone you knocked me up, not even my parents. I certainly couldn't confide in my best friend who was busy grieving her heart out over you. Anyway, I couldn't do the abortion thing, not with my Catholic upbringing at Sacred Heart Academy for the pure and pampered girls of the rich and famous!" She snuffled a while and then continued. "Do you remember I took off for a year of school at Queen's College in Galway? Yep, I was in Ireland all right, and so is your kid. I gave it up for adoption. How do you like them little green apples?"

Brian's body stiffened and he stared at her for a moment. Then he stuttered flatly in a hoarse croak, "P—pregnant? My God!"

"Yeah, how 'bout your God? While I was having labor pains you were playing footsie with Mr. Huge God and learning to prattle off prayers. First, you drop Mona like a hot potato...that really knocked her for a loop. Then you've treated me like a flyspeck all these years." Her eyes flashed with pain and anger.

She's as spiteful as they come. It has to be her way to get even. What about Mona? Why tell me now? He bellowed, "Jesus Christ, Rebecca, a baby? Have you lost your mind? Why are you telling me now?"

She laughed in his face then smirked though her tears, "Because I want to. I've got to talk to somebody! I'm about ready to commit emotional suicide over all this shit! Mona has bailed out on me. She's been trying to slough me off like sunburned skin for months now. This disappearance act of hers is the last straw! She needs a little taste of her own reality therapy!"

He thrust his face toward her and hissed, "Becky, Mona's dead! Raped and murdered!"

Rebecca froze. Her eyes grew wide and then she swayed, clamped her hand over her mouth and choked back a scream. "What are you saying? Oh, no, oh Gawd! Don't tell me that! Mona's not dead...she's just playing a little hide and go seek with us. Shit, shit, shit!" She turned toward the window and put her hands to her cheeks. She shouted maliciously, "You're a fuckin' nutless wonder, that's who you are, lying to get even with me about the baby. It is a little boy baby, like you give a fuck! Shame on you! You shouldn't lie like this!"

His shock and grief gave way to the immediate need to calm her down. Despite his unease and his growing suspicions about Rebecca, he studied her reaction carefully. Somewhere in his policeman's mind, he thought, *this is real. Becky can put on quite a performance, but I don't think she's faking this time.* How many women keep their silence? He wondered about Mona. Did women have secrets so painful they couldn't share them with those they love? Looking at Rebecca, he thought it strange that she, too, had sought comfort in the church. He reached a big arm across to hug her. "Shhh, now Becky. Shhh. I'm sorry I told you like that, but you gotta know. *And I had to be sure that you didn't know.* I can't tell you any more, but she's dead, gone for good. She's not coming back. Nothing we can do will save her."

Rebecca's face blanched. She flopped her head back against the seat. "Are you sure it's Mona?"

The pain etched on Brian's face was clear. He insisted quietly, "Yes, it's Mona."

Tears welled. She swallowed, then exhaled, "That's horrible! Who could have done a thing like that? Did that frigin' geek, Julien do it? I know the bastard did it!"

"It wasn't Julien, although I think he may be somehow involved. That's why I asked you about Keller." He recorded a silent observation for future reference. *And you avoided answering the question. I'll get back to that issue later.* At present, he needed to deal with her immediate response. Patting her arm, he said firmly, "Calm down, Becky. Are you going to be sick? I was when I found her."

"Oh, Christ, you had to find her?" She peered up into his face, her quivering whisper barely audible above the shish of the rain against the convertible top and the rumble of thunder. "What was she like? No, don't tell me. I can't bear it." She groaned, clinched her fists in her lap, and broke into a flood of tears. "She was my friend. I couldn't even tell her about us…about why you went off the deep end and hid out in the church. All these years of pretense and now she's dead!"

Brian's cell phone rang. He kept his arm around her, afraid to move it for fear she'd bolt and run out of the car. He eased around and struggled with his jacket pocket to flip it open. He barked, "Herlihy here. Be quick."

Gracie's voice came over the phone. "Brian, we can do better than a commercial flight. There's a Medi-Vac unit waiting for the rain to let up. It's leaving from the helicopter landing pad behind Ochsners Hospital on River Road in half an hour. They're headed for Miami with a liver for a transplant patient. If you hurry, you can hitch a ride there and back tomorrow."

He closed his eyes a moment then took a deep breath and glanced at his watch. He grunted, "Thanks, Gracie, but I may not make it. If I'm not there when they are ready to take off tell them to proceed without me. I'll talk to you later. I'm busy, got a bit of a crisis on my hands right now. Over and out." He clamped the cell phone shut.

Becky dried her tears and looked at him though swollen eyes. "Is Julien in Miami? Go kill the bastard!'

"I don't know if he's there or not and even if I did, I couldn't tell you. Now, I gotta go. You and I have to talk, a lot, but I caution you not to speak of this to anyone—especially not to Darrel Pitts. Someone said that there was no such thing as bad press, but with Darlin' Darrel, I'm not so sure about that. Can you make it home?"

"Yes, I'll make it home to a bottle of scotch!"

"That's the ticket. I could do with a stiff belt myself." He didn't wait for a response, only dragged his raincoat from under his cramped knees, opened the door and fled though the rain.

She watched him sprint across the park, splashing without regard to the puddles. Rebecca's hand shook as she reached for her lighter and the cigarette. She lit it and dragged smoke as deeply into her lungs as she could and blew it out violently, filling the tiny car with the smoke. "Oh, Brian, wait until you hear the rest."

She considered being outraged. He could have been more interested! Instead, she felt hot, sick and worried as she cranked up the car and backed up. The tires screamed her pain as she shot out of the parking lot and spun onto the wet street.

Directly across St. Charles Avenue was the entrance to Audubon Place. She paused briefly to wave in recognition to the man sheltered in the stone guard's post beside the open gates.

Rebecca had a key and knew the security alarm code. She parked under the *porte cochere* of Number 36 Audubon Place and raced across the wet marble stairs. She grabbed a column to keep from slipping down and bent to remove her soaked sandals. Hurling them against the wall, she padded barefooted to the massive Tiffany cut glass doors. Using her key, she entered then paused to tap the security pad and flip on the lights.

Everything was the way it had always been—magnificent. She recalled how many times she and Mona had raced up and down these glowing slabs of honeyed onyx. She recognized how she had longed to live here. She wanted Mona's life. She yearned to steal this life or at least get adopted into it. She would have been satisfied to be Mona's sister. Her family was well-to-do financially, but it was huge. Roman Catholics such as her parents didn't know when to quit. She had six brothers and sisters before they called it a day. Mona was an only child. Yes, she envied her friend. She had even begged God to make her tall, thin and blonde like Mona. She had wanted Brian Herlihy. Not so much because he was a college celebrity, but because Mona had him. She knew in her heart she had deliberately seduced Brian. She had enjoyed her ugly secret for years. It was as if she had put something over on the famous Dr. Mona Wright! Oh God, now Mona was gone, horribly gone forever.

Rebecca stood stock-still with her wet bare feet on the cold floor, then sank to her knees. Bending low, she kissed the cold, paved squares and whimpered, "Now I have it all, Mona dear." Pushing a long lock of hair back from her forehead, she rose to her feet and padded through an archway leading directly into a massive living room. "Now, good doctor, I hate to be a party-pooper, but you were so keen to ferret out all the facts—too keen for your own good. Some secrets are better left alone. Well, you had at least one or two that proved to be lethal, didn't you? Now where did you tell me that you kept your will?"

CHAPTER 7

THE CONCRETE WAS slick with rain reflecting the bright lights of the helicopter as Brian ducked under the rotary blades and swung into the rear seat. In less than a minute, they were lifting into the night sky over the Crescent City and the great curve in the river that gave New Orleans its name. He let his eyes drift out over the Mississippi River and the bridges that spanned its muddy waters—lines of cars moving back and forth, their lights flickering like lightning bugs along a narrow twig. His eyes were dry and grainy, stinging. Even with the sound-damping earphones, the *chunk, chunk, chunk* of the blades overhead was deafening, isolating each passenger in his own cocoon.

Below the vast city spread in all directions snaking along the lazy river. He was still nervy from the meeting with Rebecca—hell, the whole damn day. His chest felt as if an enormous hand was squeezing it. He leaned his head against the glass as New Orleans swept under him. This was his town, alive and corrupt from the poverty-blasted ghettos to the courthouse. The city that was referred to as "the city that care forgot" writhed along on both sides of the bend in the mighty Mississippi River. A great bustling bathtub of humanity, African American, English, French, German, Indian, Hispanic, Asian, Arab, and last but not least, Irish, lived on borrowed time, awaiting the prospect of their bathtub being filled with water from some passing hurricane. The majority of the city was four feet below sea level, a ridiculous fact, the urgency of which the city fathers and mothers didn't like to ponder. Even the graves had to be built in cemeteries standing like haunted mansions on the highest rise of ground between Lake Pontchartrain and the river. A city with a quaint saying: "Don't ask, don't tell." Enjoy Mardi Gras revelry and pretend you are observing Lent—then pass the green beer on St. Patrick's Day. God, he loved this ambiguous old whore of a city with her gaudy, boisterous soul like no other. He heaved a sigh. How could he handle what he had discovered after twenty years? *I have a son. Dear God, I have a son. Am I ready to open old wounds?*

Sometimes he thought his punishment was to be cast out of God's kingdom into some darker place. If so, there was no time to worry about destiny right now. He was functioning on autopilot, tormented by the image of Mona's throat blossoming red. Then he deliberately changed the channel in his brain. He turned to the idea of interviewing Harry Keller and shuddered. Better to just think of the job ahead of him. He'd need to get some rest, however little, in transit. Maybe he could catch a snooze. It wasn't going to make things any better, but all the same, he needed a chance to clear his mind.

He settled back in his seat and snapped the buckle into place. As he closed his eyes, he felt his phone vibrate against his chest. It was ringing, so he barked a hello. Someone on the other end spoke, but he couldn't hear a word. His left hand grabbed the mouthpiece and cupped it as he shouted for the caller to use the pilot's radio. Shutting his eyes again, he hoped whoever the caller was couldn't do that trick. He was wrong. The pilot listened and yelled to him. "Sir, they say the boy's gone missing."

Detective Herlihy felt the hand squeeze him again and thought, *Shit! I should have been a monk!*

OFFICER REME HAD been put in charge of finding William St. Denis. His frantic parents called police headquarters at 7:12 PM. They had ordered a pizza for dinner. Janice had braved the acoustical blasts of guitars to summon her son to come eat. His door was open, but he was nowhere to be found. Robert defied the yellow police tape to search the attic. The family had a home composed of many old apartments strung together out of the original mansion. The boy's father searched all the units from bottom to top. Robert even ventured onto the slate roof. They were used to Billy's frequent disappearing acts so at first they figured their son had simply taken his pain and retired to some nook or cranny. Nothing was discovered anywhere.

The police guards at the side and the front doors swore the boy never set a foot outside, although he had hung around the door talking with them from time to time. One of the uniforms reported that the kid pumped him about Detective Herlihy's part in nabbing Harry Keller. It seems that their maid, Septema Cryer, had been romantically involved with Keller when she was younger. When they questioned him, Billy had gone smug and clamed up. Said that he'd only talk to the Big Un then he made himself scarce. The officers figured that he had fabricated the whole thing.

Gracie put in a call to inform Detective Herlihy of the developments and had been told to handle it. She grabbed her weapon and her purse, dumped her untouched red-beans and rice take-out dinner in the trash and headed for Royal Street. On the way through French Quarter traffic, she contacted the officer standing guard at the side door. She spoke brusquely, trying to sound professional in order to hide how worried she was. "Hi, Colette! I've been thinking about this problem. Ask the St. Denis' where they park their cars. I didn't see any parking facilities attached to the house. I don't suppose there is any underground parking due to the restrictions on that sort of arrangement in the historical district. They gotta' park somewhere close by and maybe the kid slipped out somehow, like across the roof and down some drainpipe or other. I understand he's pretty inventive about avoiding the parental units. Let's not panic his parents anymore than we have to. Redo the search of the interior. Some of these old Southern houses have what they called a priest's hole. It is usually hidden. Check the floors. Sometimes there is a cubbyhole under the stairs. There are lots of stairs in all those vacant units. Get the house plans and the renovation specs from St. Denis and the number for their architect and construction company. Oh yes, get that maid, Septema Cryer's phone and address from him, too. Have Junior check the official files on the Keller case then he's to invite her in for a chat."

She was making little or no headway along a narrow, noisy, fun-filled street lined with T-shirt shops, book sellers, art dealers—the sort of people who sold cheap paintings but pretended to know all about works of art—a street that was more of a concept than a reality. "I'll be there as soon as I can get through this traffic. I may just park it and hike over from Decatur. See ya' Chere!"

When Officer Reme arrived, Janice St. Denis was waving a spatula in her hand. Apparently it wasn't meant as a weapon. She had been unloading the dishwasher when Robert came down with the news that Billy was nowhere to be found. She still grasped the cooking utensil as if she had forgotten that it had become an extension of her left arm. "My boy is gone! The murderer has somehow sneaked in here and kidnapped our boy! Please save his life! We'll pay any amount of ransom money. Will they call? I will never see my Billy again. Oh, why did this all have to happen to us?"

Gracie dodged the spatula. "We'll do what we can, Mrs. St. Denis. Now...why don't you and your husband just sit tight? Mr. St. Denis, will you please take your wife into the bedroom or your beautiful atrium and try to remain calm? I would suggest that you find her a little glass of sherry and one for yourself."

Plans of the house were spread on the kitchen table along with the untouched pizza box. Robert St. Denis obeyed her and took a glass of ice plus a wineglass and headed for the liquor cabinet in the butler's pantry. He opened the cabinet and shouted, "There's a new fifth of vodka missing. I just bought it for the party. We never opened it. It's gone!"

Grace turned from stooping over the blueprints. "Does Billy drink?"

Janice waved her shining spatula and looked horrified. "No, of course our son doesn't drink! He's only fourteen!"

Gracie wanted to laugh, but the situation was too serious. "Well, some kids here in New Orleans get an early start. I have to ask."

Billy's father rubbed his hand across his mouth, "Uh...well, he's been known to sneak a drink from time to time. I wouldn't put it past Billy, especially in the state he's in over all this business." He shook his head. "Now he's invented a conspiracy involving our poor housekeeper, Septema Cryer. He insists that she was the girlfriend of that Heller-Keller at one time." He poured his wife a glass of white wine and himself a healthy slug of Scotch.

His wife wailed, "Forget Septema! Find my son!"

Gracie chose to disregard the woman's outburst and asked for Septema Cryer's address and phone number.

Robert leaned across the table to a bulletin board and snatched an index card from its thumbtack. "Here it is. Just please put it back." He turned to his distraught wife. "Come to the garden, Janice. Let the police handle this." He gently took Janice by her free hand and led her toward the enclosed atrium. He was talking to her in a soothing fashion as Janice continued to wave her silver spatula.

Officer Reme returned to the house plans. Suddenly there came a resounding screech from the patio. Gracie bounded across the room and down the marble hall with her revolver out and at the ready. As she entered the garden, she spotted the parents crouched over a long pair of legs sprawled behind the raised fountain at the far end.

Janice St. Denis was waving her weapon of choice in the air. "He's dead! Billy's dead!"

Her husband was shouting at his wife, "He'd dead alright! Dead drunk!" St. Denis bent to pick up an empty vodka bottle. He kicked a plastic thermos glass across the moss-covered flagstones and into the trees along with two empty Seven-Up cans. "If he dies, it will be from alcohol poisoning."

Janice crouched beside the limp form and rolled him over. "Oh, God! He's covered in vomit! Billy, it's Mother. You speak to me, you hear?"

The boy heaved and groaned.

Janice flew into a rage. She began to flap her spatula against Billy's legs. "You stupid boy! You scared me half to death!" She whopped him again and again.

Robert sat the drinks on the edge of the fountain and grabbed at his wife's flying hand. "Hey, Janice, it's okay. He's just drunk as a tick! Stop that now."

"Enough is enough! You caused this—you and your permissive parenting!" She swatted her husband's legs.

He jumped back a step or two. "Come on now, Honey! He's been through a lot. Ouch! That damn thing hurts! Now, lay off!"

His wife continued to swat and rant. "You better call an ambulance. I will not clean this child up!" She threw the spatula at him and grabbed her wineglass to retreat to her bedroom. The door slammed behind her.

St. Denis shrugged. "I apologize for my family's behavior and all this turmoil we're causing. Will it be okay if I get Billy checked out? It appears he's had considerable to drink."

Officer Reme patted the man on the shoulder. "Sure, I'll call for you. Nobody is used to homicide. This is his way of coping with the shock and anxiety. You leave this to me." She reached over and picked up his scotch. "Here, you deserve it! Where can I find some towels?"

"I'll get 'em! Thank you, ma'am." He seemed grateful to be able to retreat. He shook his head and went to fetch wet towels.

Officer Reme called off the search party explaining through her relieved laughter that Billy-boy had tied one on and she would accompany the kid and his parents to Touro Infirmary.

Officer Colette Couhig shared in the laughter. "Whew! I'll stay here and watch the house. Ask the St. Denis' if we can eat their pizza while they're gone. I'm hungry!"

Gracie laughed, "Will do! Save me a slice. My dinner ended up in file thirteen at the office. This is one for the books, ain't it? The brat will have a doozie of a hangover after this episode, but he deserves one. He glugged almost a whole of a fifth of vodka in less than two hours. I wouldn't want to be him in the morning. Plus he was assaulted with an unusual deadly weapon—a flying spatula. I gotta' call Big Un pronto. He's on his way to Florida.

"Then I'm off to the office to run a check on their maid, Septema Cryer. We'll be rounding her up for questioning. The cocky kid could be making it all up. His parents drew a blank on Keller. Seems Cryer has been with them four years, started out baby-sitting and became their housekeeper. I'll get Junior to check with her family and neighbors to see if she knew Harry Keller or any of his crew at one time or another. She could be involved somehow even though she was not at the Faulkner shindig last night. Still, she may be able to ID our perp."

Brian got a brief rendition of the exploits of William St. Denis from the pilot. He enjoyed the first laugh he had in many hours. He choked up when he realized that he had immediately thought, *Wait til I tell Mona this one*! It was strange still, maybe her murder hadn't sunk in. Oh, but it will! He thought about another boy, somewhere in Ireland. *His son?* That hadn't sunk in either.

CHAPTER 8

MIAMI WAS EVEN sultrier than New Orleans, if that were possible. The heat and humidity had not tapered off and enveloped the city in lethargic summer. Even at night, the air was like steam. It was approaching midnight by the time he reached police headquarters. They assigned him a conference room and gathered everything they could locate concerning Julien Montz and his flaming companion Angela Higginbotham AKA Roxy Rocksoff. Brian shuffled through the faxes and studied the documents—no AIDS treatment, at least under those names, and no sign of the Saturn. It wasn't registered. He wasn't surprised since it was never Angela's car. It had been registered in Louisiana to her dead sister, Ruby Ann. He hoped the crack-head, Angela, might do something as dumb as applying for registration, but whatever else he might be, Montz was no fool. The police had checked on legal car sales, but Montz would never risk selling the car though proper channels even if hard up for cash.

The next bit of information was interesting. The police had traced the phone call to the health club called the Amazon Center, a known front for drug traffic and prostitution. They had searched the premises and found several art objects listed as stolen. Brian recognized the descriptions of one bronze statue and an antique mantel clock fitting the description of articles that Julien lifted from Number 36 Audubon Place. It linked Julien with the club.

As he contemplated the list, his left thumb followed the shape of his bicep beneath his white shirt. He raised his eyebrows, amused to realize Mona had apparently reported them as thefts. Of course, he wasn't sure her insurance company would consider the items stolen, but he had to give her credit for trying. He only hoped the sale of her family's antiques had not paid to have her murdered.

He flipped through the other items she had listed. The computer printout listed her laptop computer, top of the line of course, plus her floppy disks. He had warned her about using portable media—too hard to destroy and too easy to steal. The description of what was on the disks caused him to hurt deeply. She had included the theft of a priceless manuscript for her upcoming novel, *Skiing the Rainbow,* plus references to the dates of proof readings as evidence of the manuscript's authenticity and her editor's name, address and the exact date for the publisher's deadline. He knew Julien had absconded with the valuable laptop, but what in hell did he want with her book? He stared at the insurance claim as if it would tell him something if he looked at it long enough. Christ, Montz was such a prick—he could have taken it just for spite. It's a good thing Mona had sense enough to have a backup. Brian compared the two lists. Julien must still have her laptop because it wasn't listed as recovered from the Amazon.

He realized he was shivering in the over-cooled room. He leaned back and rubbed his head then he left his big hands over his eyes and pressed them hard, feeling the tears behind his eyeballs. *Later...I'll cry later, Mona. I can't afford to indulge my grief until this is over.*

The night desk sergeant entered, bringing with him a welcomed cup of coffee. "Sir, we have a report. A cruiser unit spotted something funny on the beach. It turns out to be a naked woman's body. It is located in a rough part of town—the vicinity of the Amazon Club. We thought it might be the stripper you've been trying to locate. She's pretty banged up. Beaten to a pulp, they say. She's a redhead about five feet six or seven. Her feet had calluses and are lumpy—like she was a dancer of some kind."

"Let's ride down and take a look."

The door swung open on the police car and a friendly voice called to him, "Welcome aboard, Dick Richard at your service. *Comment se va, Cher*? as they say down in de parish."

Brian sagged into the passenger's seat. "You from NOLA?"

"Naw, I'm from La Fourche Parish, but don't hold it against me!"

Brian was not in the mood for small talk, but he mumbled wearily, "Nice to meet ya, Dick. Let's boogie." His head was pounding. He ran his hand over his face. His skin felt raw with tiredness; the bones seemed very near the surface. He lowered his window, inhaling the damp smells of the Southern coast.

The sergeant swung off the Interstate onto a beach road and commented, "This stretch could be called 'the forgotten beach.'"

"How do you mean?'

"There's only one road in and out and it comes to a dead end near the old sewerage plant."

Brian observed, "Hard to imagine any Florida beachfront property could still exist, especially close to the city."

His comment was met with a snort, "Wait till you see it, then you'll know why. There's about a dozen old apartment buildings plus some other crap only crack heads are interested in. Nobody in their right mind would want to live down in this bedraggled chaos."

Parking behind a bewildering warren of sagging, loose-hinged bungalows and roadhouses, they trudged down a slight incline and stepped past the yellow tape to the crime scene. He was met by a half-dozen Miami cops as he picked his way through the litter. His limbs were sluggish as though he was wading through liquid, and he tried not to breathe too deeply. He found it impossible to shrug off the sense of hopelessness that was as palpable as the smells. It was a gloomy sight and completely dark, save for a small island of brilliance provided by the powerful police floodlight from a patrol launch. The lights focused on a collection of professionals and a shapeless bundle lying on the quayside covered by a large white sheet.

When the sheet was lifted, he saw a nude body splayed face down on the hard sand. The red hair was bloody and tangled. Seaweed had been caught in the arches of her arms and behind her shoulders and head. It was obvious she had been there when the tide went out. Whoever was responsible hadn't tried very hard to conceal what they had done; the body would have surfaced somewhere else if it had been dropped from a boat. This close to the beach indicated it had not been dumped at sea and washed ashore. It was a wonder no one had found her before the police did, but the location wasn't an area where any tourists or even hookers or drifters were likely to go. There was no glitter here—only tattoo parlors and body-piercing shops faced the street. On the right was a row of derelict hotdog stands, but the beach was hidden from the general view by oleander bushes and back-washed trash. No, whoever killed her had either dragged her to the beach or killed her here, but the tide had eradicated any signs of a struggle or footprints.

Pulling on latex gloves, Brian squatted beside an assistant medical examiner crouched over the body in the sand. The ME checked the battered back then said grimly, "Alright, bag her hands and roll her over."

When they turned the body over onto a sheet of plastic, her face was a mass of lacerations, hardly recognizable as human; her eyes were rolled back and blank. There was a tattoo of a red rose on her inner thigh plus the name "Roxy." Brian had little doubt who he was seeing. He tilted the woman's arms into the light to expose track marks like Daytona Beach.

He stood up and rubbed the sand from his gloved hands. "It's her, I think. Her real name is Angela Higginbotham. Her stage name is Roxy Rocksoff. The coroner will check for water in her lungs, but I doubt she drowned. I figure he's gonna' find she died of a drug overdose. Her sister met the same fate in Las Vegas." He turned to Richard. "Get back to me as quickly as you can. Check out something else for me. Maybe the Amazon Club folks know something that will help us. My perp may have hung out with a guy I put away some years ago. His name is Benjamin Harry Keller, presently doing life in Angola. Even if it doesn't pan out that this is connected with Keller, I need to find Roxy Higginbotham's traveling companion. His name is Julien Montz, but I doubt he is using that name. Your squad already has a description, but be careful, he may be accompanied by my suspect, one Michael O'Shea, aka 'Irish Mike.' Check with HITS.

"O'Shea is wanted for questioning in a New Orleans homicide. He's medium height and has thinning red hair. It's also possible that O'Shea may have been an associate of Benjamin Harry Keller—and we think our suspect's HIV positive."

TIME WAS RUNNING out. It was approaching dawn in Florida—almost 4:00 am New Orleans time. Brian rubbed his thumb along a sandpaper-rough jaw with a day's stubble. He was exhausted, but exhaustion went hand-in-hand with his line of work. Sleep was essential. Without it, one ran the risk of losing control. He needed to think clearly for this particular case.

He arranged to return to the station with Dick Richard. Relieved to leave the crime scene tainted with its sour smells of rotten fish, vegetable waste and burnt cardboard, they cruised across the city and hashed over the case looking for insights. Talk turned to the possibility that Keller was obsessed with revenge and mostly why Brian's woman friend was in a morgue.

Dick Richard commented, "It sure doesn't make any sense. With the exception of one or two paranoiac examples, most book authors don't need a whole lot of security." He glanced at his passenger and commented, "You okay, man? You look like hell."

Brian could stand it no longer. Running his hands though his hair, he groaned, "Dick, I'm sleepwalking big time—gotta put my head down and then a shower and shave. You got a place close that you'd be willing to rent?"

"Shit, I'm stuck on duty." Richard snorted, "It ain't much, but it's a bed and bath. I'll drop you off, but don't you forget me." He winked. "I'll catch back sometime when I'm in New Orleans for Mardi Gras."

"Will do!" Brian mumbled bitterly, "*Laissez Les Bon Temps Rouler!*" then added, "Thanks for the special attention. Do me a favor and follow up for me. Fax me fingerprints and whatever. I need all the help I can get."

Once alone, Brian stripped off his muddy slacks and shirt. He sat on the bed and pulled off his grubby shoes and socks. Then he collapsed across the bed on his back, staring blankly up at the ceiling. He swiped at his face to clear away the perspiration that beaded on his forehead and upper lip. He wiped his hand on the sheet and turned over, trying to get comfortable enough to sleep while holding his cell phone in his hand.

But sleep wouldn't come. Twisting under the bed sheet, he turned again and lay on his side. He was reluctant to close his eyes...every time he closed them he saw the faces of death. Finally he dozed, and then a fuzzy dream entered his mind, a dream of Mona and their last meeting at Café du Monde. *He had just asked her what would happen if he leaned over and kissed her. She was laughing and saying, "It would stop traffic..." But she didn't pull away when she said it. Her eyes twinkled and her lower lip trembled just enough to give her away but not enough to change anything. She moved her head another inch. He was replying, "pity" and kissed her anyway.*

Then darkness closed in like a pillow over his face threatening to suffocate him.

CHAPTER 9

FOUR HOURS LATER, a buzzing sound cut through the humid darkness and pulled him back to reality. He rolled over to fumble for his cell phone. Gracie's voice blasted him to full wakefulness. "Yo, Brian, what 'cha got? Any sign of Julien or his lady friend?"

Brian cleared his throat and responded. "I located her here. Or rather, we found what is left of her. I'm checking out their pad this morning. Can't say yet who did her in; however, whoever he is, he sees killing women as his life's work and he really loves his job. Roxy Rocksoff was face down on the beach. Didn't find much at the scene. I figure she was killed someplace else. I'm waiting for the autopsy report, but it looks as if she met the same fate as her sister."

She huffed, "Wow, they sure chose the wrong pimp! Do you suspect Julien?"

"Yep, same MO, but the dipstick's not my main concern. I'm still trying to find Montzy or Irish Mike plus any ties to our old buddy, Keller, but nobody in that part of Miami is likely to rat on any of them. Jesus, Gracie, you don't want to sunbathe on the part of the beach I saw last night. I got Miami checking HITS—you guys do the same. I'm gonna shower, eat breakfast and then try and get a search warrant to go over her pad with a fine toothed comb. Maybe there's some connection with our perp—or perps, as the case may be." His heart was pounding as he clapped his cell phone shut.

TWO HOURS LATER, Detective Herlihy, search warrant in hand, was entering 1600 Melrose with several Miami officers. It was a run-down duplex behind the Amazon Center. If the building had ever had air conditioning, it no longer worked. The hall floor was sticky under his feet; the long plaster wall scarred from an endless stream of furniture being moved in and out. The air was thick with trapped heat and the odors of cigarette smoke, greasy food and despair. The door on the right had a grimy plaque that read *Manager*. Herlihy knocked and waited. The door rattled with prolonged fumbling with several dead bolts, accompanied by several curses that crossed all language barriers. Finally, a slice of a woman peered out with one narrowed, suspicious eye. The old landlady was a tiny Cuban who spoke little or no English. Sweat oiled her face as she blinked at the officers uncomprehendingly.

When the officer in charge of the crime scene struggled to explain their presence, the woman started at the word "questions." Even without a translator, Brian had the suspicion that her lack of English might be more a matter of convenience than an actuality. She didn't wait or seem interested in what was going on. She simply nodded and shuffled out to unlock the sagging door to the other apartment. Shrugging her thin shoulders, she retreated to her side of the double, closing the door behind her and engaging all the bolts.

The uniform knocked and announced their presence. When there was no response, Brian stood aside. The Miami officers drew weapons, crouched and opened the door.

Empty.

Entering the one-room studio apartment, Brian pulled off his jacket, unfastened his collar button and reached for his handkerchief to mop his forehead. The sweltering interior was pretty much what he had expected and reeked with the smell of soured damp clothes and pungent body odors. There was no telephone, but that proved very little about who had placed the calls. Mona's cell phone traced the caller to the Amazon Club. Tabloids and soap opera digests were heaped on a coffee table in untidy stacks. Pillows in shades of fuchsia and pink and a few bright colored Mexican throws failed to hide the murky browns of threadbare carpet and sagging couch.

He watched the techs already beginning to dust for prints and stared at the bed, not liking what he saw there—blood again. The rumpled bed was splattered with lots of blood and the lamp on the nightstand was missing. He supposed it had been used as a weapon for battering Angela's nude body. The bottom sheet was intact, covered with dried blood and slime—probably semen, but no top sheet or bedspread. Julien or someone else had probably wrapped her body in them to get her out of the cottage. It was a short walk to the stretch of beachfront where she had been found. The officer who accompanied Brian walked outside and radioed for a team to search the filth-slicked alley and the surrounding area for a Dumpster or someplace where the murderer could have disposed of the lamp base and the covers.

Brian pulled on a pair of rubber gloves and began a careful search of the premises. The bureau and closet contained Roxy's tawdry collection of clothes, including some costumes and make-up.

The bathroom floor was slick with diluted blood; wet towels were flung into the bathtub and the sink was pink. Someone had washed, but not very well. Brian reached into the tub and carefully lifted the wet towels. He shook them gently—out tumbled the hypodermic syringe. Bagging it, he muttered, "Good bye, Roxy. I hope you were so high you didn't feel a thing."

He gave the evidence bag to an officer and knelt beside the bed and swept his hand into the herd of dust bunnies residing there. His gloved hand struck something hard—a cardboard box of some kind. He pulled it toward the edge of the bed and opened it. Narcotics—lots of plastic bags and several more hypos. He scratched his chin with a latex-gloved hand and frowned. If Irish Mike was involved, why did he leave this stash?

From the bottom of the box, he picked up a crumpled Living section of the *New Orleans Times-Picayune* dated two weeks earlier. He squinted at the page, then his eyebrows rose. The lead story featured a paparazzi picture of the elegant Dr. Mona Wright stepping from a limo in front of the radio station. He tried to stifle the prickle of pain that ran up his back. The photo was so painful to look at that his eyes filled until it was as if he were looking at her through frosted glass. It showed a cool, competent woman, but it was her gaze, so proud and direct, that it seemed to challenge the camera. The look telegraphed that this was a woman who was in control of her life because that was all she allowed them to see—a smiling woman with the sunshine in her hair. It had been this way from the beginning, her face—the thing that first knocked the breath out of him. Mona standing beside her father at registration for Newman School that dazzling sunlit morning. He had been captured by a pair of hazel eyes in a perfect oval face. It was a face he had never seen before, and yet one he seemed to have known forever. Many years later, when he came to know her body in more intimate detail, her face never lost its ability to stop him in his tracks. His hand trembled as he thought how wrong impressions could be. How easily pain can be masked by an arresting smile, an upturned titling chin. Someone had circled her face with a red ballpoint pen. He wondered why? *Maybe it was left for us to find.*

There's a snag. It's too pat, too neat and easy—hypo in the tub, woman's body on an open beach, drugs and paraphernalia under the bed—same as Las Vegas. Two scruffy sisters, same suspect, ole' Julien. Bet his fingerprints are all over the place, plus semen—real easy to trace.

Looking at the picture he couldn't help but think that the answer to what happened to Mona was somewhere in her life—or his. Whoever killed her didn't do it spur of the moment. It was staged and the killer had left traces. Could it be that someone was going out of their way to set Montzy up? The evidence had the makings for a simple case of murder over sex and drugs—case closed. There would be no cause for suspecting otherwise. Without this clipping, who would make the connection with the most beautiful, the most courageous woman he had ever known, Dr. Mona Wright? Without this incriminating evidence, the unrelated murder of a known prostitute would never be associated with a murder in New Orleans. So what's a killer to do? *Why the hell would someone implicate Montz if he were trying to even the score with me? Why not me instead?* There was something else going on here and plenty still missing. Maybe those 'up-yours' damn flowers that Mona got were a part of something bigger. Damned if he could figure it out. What did Irish Mike have to do with Julien Montz?

A sharp pain shot though his gut as he whispered to the image in the paper, "Ah, Sweetie, I didn't even get a chance to say good-by. If I had just one day to relive, I would spend it with you—holding you in bed, whispering love between the sheets." Feeling sluggish and stupid with sweat running down the small of his back, he shook his head to clear it and muttered, "Get a grip here, guy."

The sound of his cell phone intruded into his thoughts. It was the preliminary autopsy report. Angela, Roxy, had been popped sometime at least thirty-six hours before. Her system contained enough heroin to kill an elephant. Her lungs were clear, and the beating she sustained had occurred just before or during the overdose. It was hard to tell if she had been sexually assaulted or if she had engaged in consensual sex before death. The saltwater had most likely washed some evidence away. That was pretty much it. Brian thanked the coroner's assistant, urging him to expedite AIDS tests on semen samples from the corpse and the bed in the apartment and report it to CODIS. He requested the reports be sent to him in New Orleans also. He promised to have the mug shot of Harry Keller for Miami police to pass by the landlady, employees of the Amazon Club or anyone else placing him in Miami before his arrest.

The police unit returned with the missing lamp—obviously the murder weapon from the looks of it, plus the bloody sheet and bedspread. Brian lingered at the apartment until there was nothing left to find. The police taped the duplex and the Dumpster then dropped him at the airport where he rejoined the Medi-Vac homeward bound for New Orleans.

Brian had a hunch that Miami wouldn't find anyone's prints except the victim's and Julien's so they wouldn't be able to ID any suspect except Julien Montz. He was puzzled by the late night calls on Mona's cell. Had Julien tried to warn her? If so, why? Angela was working part time at the Amazon Club, but it wouldn't make sense for her to call Mona even if she suspected that both of their lives were in danger. If a paid killer was involved, the newspaper article and the calls would serve to set ole' Julien and his girlfriend up as accomplices or provide them with an alibi. Of course, Julien might have had a change of heart and tried to warn his wife himself. On the other hand, maybe Julien called to set up an appointment to sweet talk Mona. It would be just like the loser to assume that all his transgressions were forgiven. If he expected to get her on the phone, Julien would have rung the house or her office first. Maybe there would be a message. He would check that detail himself. He frowned as his chest tightened at the idea of revisiting Mona's house...*all those memories.*

CHAPTER 10

Rebecca woke up in Mona's bedroom. The sun had come out and everything was bright again. She had endured the horrendous thunderstorm throughout the night, alone in the enormous house. Great lightning bolts flashed and thunder cracked so loudly it shook the windows. Torrents of rain flailed the trees and drenched the tropical foliage covering the back of the house. The gutters became rivulets, forming streams of water gushing down the walks and the circular driveway.

She pushed her hair out of her eyes and twisted around to gaze at the grand opulence of the high ceiling with its ornately carved crown molding. Her eyes swept the Georgian sash windows and the faded elegance of fussy wallpaper with a certain feminine softness. The ancient armoire was enormous. All the furnishings were very old and equally expensive. Mona's room was like the rest of the house—a refuge from modernity, full of old world charm. Sure, the high ceilings had a few cracks, the crown moldings had developed a crazed finish, and the sashes had rattled wildly in the wind, but she was enraptured with the patina of history her house evoked. After all, in New Orleans, an old house needed to be treated like antique furniture or all its allure will be taken away and it would become indistinguishable from a reproduction.

She giggled. Of course she lamented Mona's death, but found it very satisfying to wake up within this house's embrace—it gave her a warm feeling of security. Yes, elegance mixed with a bit of decadence. She leaned back on the pillows and pointed her right toe to the cracks on the ceiling and chuckled aloud. "You belong to me, old cracks. Martha Stewart would pay me a thousand bucks for every posh crack! See how great my leg looks—no cracks here!" Then she leaned to the table beside the bed and lit a cigarette.

Later, she wiggled out of the sheets and stepped into the shower. She grinned as she dried herself with a thick, peach-colored towel monogrammed with a lovely big W. How convenient—Webster and Wright have the same initial.

Wrapped in the towel, she wandered down to the kitchen for some coffee and orange juice. She opened the fridge. There was a carton of half-and-half, a take-out box of pork fried rice, English muffins, butter, and some strawberry jam. Mona rarely stocked food because she ate out for the most part.

Rebecca was in a delightful mood as she made coffee. She had found what she had been looking for the evening before: Mona's handwritten first draft of her last will and testament. The real McCoy would be at her attorney's office of course, but Becky just had to be sure—and now she was sure! Mona left a sizable trust fund to insure her stroke-ridden mother be well taken care of in the event of her daughter's death. That maneuver was probably wise considering ole' Julien's craftiness. He couldn't touch a cent of the trust for her mother. But that wasn't the good part. Mona's scribbling sketched out the heart of her will. Rebecca read a portion aloud. "In order to insure that my mother, Helene Blanche D'Aquin, be provided for in the manner to which she has become accustomed, in the unlikely event of my preceding in death, Mrs. Helene Blanche D'Aquin Wright, my remaining sole relation, shall be the ward of Rebecca Margaret Webster and Brian David Herlihy. Provided that my aforementioned request is met, I hereby bequeath the remainder of the D'Aquin-Wright estate to Brian David Herlihy and Rebecca Margaret Webster." Jesus, what a sentence that one was! Just reading it made her teeth ache. And what a relief that the document was signed and dated. The housekeeper and the yardman had witnessed it. Mona had hinted she was setting it up this way, but one never knows for sure. Now, it was just a matter of time.

Rebecca flung off her towel, rubbed her hands together as she made a little ditty of the sentence then did a mambo around the kitchen on her tippy-toes, clicking her fingers to her own cadence. She swayed and sang, "In order...da-da-dah...that her mommy be taken care of...da-da-dah...in the manner...da-da...to which she had become...da-de-dah...accustomed..."

Her nude performance was cut short by the door chimes. She recognized the voice bellowing though the door. It was Brian.

The deep base voice yelled, "Come on, Rebecca! Let me in! Becky, open this damn door, you hear me?"

"Just a sec, Brian Baby! I gotta' grab some clothes."

"Be quick about it!" he barked. "God in Heaven, Becky, it's eleven o'clock in the morning! What are you doing in there anyway?" He caught a flash of pink skin as she batted past the glass doors and ran up the stairs.

She sang out, "Oh, I've been grieving and exploring. Wait until you hear what I found!"

When she opened the door, she was wearing the same skimpy outfit that she had been wearing in the park. He held out her drenched sandals. "Here, Cinderella, your shoes got wet."

She thought he looked crumpled and weary. She had to admit to herself that it pleased her to see him so—not at all his usual smooth self. She ran her hands through her hair and said cheerfully, "Ha! Thank ya' kindly. Perhaps the days of chivalry aren't dead! Want some coffee? I just made a pot. There's some toast and jelly, too. Want juice?" She turned her back and led him to the kitchen.

He dropped the shoes and followed her, snorting at her all the way. "You have no right to stay here, you know. There are rules about such things...like breaking and entering."

She arched her eyebrows and made her eyes go wide. "Ooo-Kaaay! Now see here, Detective Buck-a-roo! I didn't break and enter. I have a key, so don't go all *policemany* on me. I've been though too much trauma to be scolded by you." She poured him a cup of coffee and slid the sugar and cream toward him. "You gave me the shock of my life last night. I had to come here to be as close as I could be to Mona." This first reference to Mona brought a pause from her for a sharp intake of breath and a suppressed sob. "This house is so full of her memory—it's spooky. Don't you just feel it?"

In the kitchen, four high-back barstools surrounded a marble table in the center of the room. He sat heavily and drank from the cup. "*You've* been through too much trauma? You are such a drama queen! *You* got the shock of your life? How about all the rest of us?"

She bit her upper lip with her lower teeth. She wanted to advise him to do something both unspeakable and physically impossible, but instead, she sobered, took a sip of her coffee and reached out to touch his hand. "Oh, you poor dear, I know how close you once were to her. I didn't mean you hadn't been suffering buckets—"

He grimaced, "Your concern is touching. Cut it out! You don't know the half of it. Don't make out that you do."

Rebecca pulled a face and held up her hands, "I surrender. I'm sorry, Officer, but if you want to talk about making out, then let's just talk about that subject, shall we? You want to arrest me, go ahead, see if I care! Take me in, grill me under a thousand hot lights, don't let me have a pee or have a smoke! Oh, I'll confess, I had an accomplice in the escapade of baby-making! I'll testify to that. How 'bout it, Big Un? You want to take ole' Becky on? Be my guest!"

He gritted his teeth and turned away. "Becky, you are one crazy broad! I don't see how Mona could tolerate your smart mouth all these years. Let's change the conversation. By the way, did you check her answering machine?"

Becky flared, "Puh-leeze, that's Ms. Rebecca Margaret Webster to you, Officer! I allow only my friends to call me Becky! Yes, I listened to two messages from patients—nothing important. They wanted to shift appointment times, but that's impossible now." She grimaced and cocked her head as if trying to remember. "And then there was some breathing—*heavy* breathing—some kook's choice I guess. Sounded lewd. And a hang up, plus a request for a return call from John Warren and Associates. That's her editor and publisher's office. Since all her patients know there won't be any more appointments and there were no calls from close friends or relatives, I wiped 'em out." Her eyes went wide and innocent as she said, "I guess I was pretty whacked." She smiled a smile that was meant to be pathetic. It was her surrender look. "I realize now it was the wrong thing for me to do, okay?"

She paused trying to read his expression—not liking what she saw. "It isn't the end of the world so please, don't scold me. Speaking of closest friends and relations, I have something to tell you, Officer Stuffy!"

He thought, *My God, she erased them? A killer would do that. Was she being deliberately obstructive or is Becky really just plain dumb?* He ignored the dig, looked at his watch and swore under his breath. "You should have told me about the calls last night. I don't think Mona had caller I.D. yet, and if we'd acted immediately we might have been able to trace them. Even if they are on her phone log, I'm worried that the tech-team will ask what you were trying to hide." There was a painful beat of silence. "Rebecca, I don't know what else you have to tell me, but it will have to wait. I have some things to ask you first."

His cell phone interrupted before he could say more. "Excuse me. Hold that thought—Herlihy, here!"

Gracie responded, "Brian, interesting development—it seems that airport security has intercepted Julien Montz in a random security check. We got him detained for questioning. He's wearing one of those baggy suits of his. Plus you'll never guess what Doofus has with him—a briefcase full of cash!"

"Great! I'm detained myself at the moment, but don't bring him in. We don't want Darrel Pitts or any other hotshot reporter getting close to him. Meanwhile, you conduct the interview yourself at the airport. Use any reason you can concoct to keep him under wraps. Get it all on tape. I kinda doubt he knows Mona is dead, unless the calls placed from the Amazon Club were an attempt to make certain the deed had been accomplished or to establish an alibi. If he mentions reading the paper or seeing TV news of Mona's disappearance, just make up something about her still being missing. You know that he is aware of Mona's habit of answering every frigin' call so the fool might have called her knowing that we would eventually trace the call. Those calls would establish an alibi by placing him in Miami at the time of her murder. See if his present residence is 1600 Melrose. Find out if he lives with Angela or knows someone referred to as 'Irish Mike.' You can pump him for information about Las Vegas and make up some stuff about the valuables missing from Mona's house, like this hold-up is an innocent insurance inquiry. While you're at it, see if he sent her those damn roses." He laughed at her response to his list. "Sure thing. I'll leave the rest up to your good judgment. See you in a couple of hours. Have fun!"

Turning back to Rebecca, he offered her an explanation, "We have Julien in custody and I'm on my way to interrogate the fool. Tell me about Julien."

She sniffed, "Good, kill the bastard! What do you mean, tell you about Julien? I hated him."

"Who were his friends? Who did he do business with, drink with, play poker with? What made him tick?"

"You know it was him or one of his friends?"

"Maybe someone in the business."

She made a sour face. "Shit, Brian, Julien is a charmer until you cross him—then he's a turd!"

"Have you crossed him?"

"No comment."

"Why? Am I missing something here?"

"Nothing important, just personal stuff that I regret deeply."

Her voice sounded bitter and Brian suspected the "personal stuff" had been very important. "Anyway, the milksop's sole objective was the realization of his own desires. He set out to become rich and adored and it didn't particularly matter to him how he did it. He's a playboy gambler who lived in that monster house on Esplanade that belonged to his father. He wooed Mona while he still had a broker's license and a partner in an ad agency. More accurately, I should say ex-partner that he left high and dry when it fell apart. Then his father employed him at the bank, but he stole from his own dad's bank and only avoided prison and bankruptcy because his father made good the debt. It wasn't the first time, either. In the eighties, he had some interest in a couple of nightclubs—the old My-O-My and some newer place out at West End Park by the lake. The blockhead drank and gambled himself out of business and picked up some nastier habits. His part in the strip dump turned sour when he screwed somebody's wife."

"God! How old is he?"

"Forty-six, I think. He spends every night in the casinos, has done it for years. Julien is a con artist, pure and simple," she said dryly. "People get taken for a ride all the time because he's good at selling himself while he wines and dines them." She shrugged dramatically, "Gee, the famous psychologist, Doctor Mona Wright, even got taken in."

"So what's he doing now?"

"Dunno. I haven't heard of him since the Millennium Bash at the Country Club, so I haven't the foggiest idea who the fuck head is robbing. I hope he's in hell!"

"Can you give me any person who had a grudge?"

"That's hilarious!" she snorted contemptuously. "Who didn't? He uses the people who fall for him like toilet paper!"

Brian thought, for "people" read "women" and maybe even her own name. Then her message read *"Women like me who fall for Julien…" Damnation! Rebecca seduced another man from her best friend?* However, he decided to simply record the information for future reference. If he wanted Becky to open up, he better not confront personal issues at this juncture. "Okay, enough of Julien for now. Did Mona have any enemies?"

"Maybe a wacko fan or someone who hated her first book although I don't see how. It was all about having fun in your dreams and how to avoid nightmares."

"Tell me about her new book. Did she ever discuss it with you? *The Perilous Ski Lift* or something like that? Last I heard she had sent it off to New York.

Rebecca breathed deeply. "Is it okay if I have a smoke?"

Brian shrugged, "Go ahead, it's your funeral."

Rebecca lit up. "Right," she said blowing out a swathe of smoke like an old time movie star and continued, "Speaking of funerals, should we contact her decrepit next of kin? I think Mama Helene is so far gone, it would probably be better not even to tell her." She shook her head. "Helene no longer lives in the same world as us. Sweet, yes, and still beautiful, but loony as pelican shit! She won't remember, anyway."

Sickened, Brian closed his eyes. "Do what you like about the matter. The office will do it sooner or later. We haven't even announced her death. Mona's body won't be available for burial for some time. You have to wait on events like the postmortem, the inquest and there's plenty still missing. Get to the book and tell me everything you remember. I need all the information I can get before I quiz Julien."

She took a drag, batting smoke away and phufffed, "Interesting. And I was hoping you could tell me what's going on. Her frigin' book...hmm...you weren't privileged to read it?"

Another shrug.

"I'm surprised—sharing is caring, ya' know," she added sarcastically.

Dislike narrowed his eyes, but he was used to her habit of deflecting unwelcome questions by sticking the knife in first. He said quietly, "No, all she said was that she'd spent a lot of time on the research. She wanted me to wait and get a real shock, but she would always say in all capital letters, 'VICTORY IS MINE!' Hells-bells, Becky, I gave up trying to pump anything more out of her and just teased her about exposing the dynamics of a terrorist group."

"Okay, okay—so I'm supposed to feel real special since she talked of nothing else with me. I'll try to remember, provided you stop treating me like a disease!" Rebecca was obviously enjoying center stage. She combed her fingers through her hair and poured him some more coffee. She puckered her lips, looked a little bewildered for a moment, then began. "Last time I heard, its working title was *Skiing the Rainbow*. Mona diddled with the title a lot. She said that she tried *Ski the Last Rainbow* before she settled on the idea of a more active word. She said 'skiing' had movement in it. Mona was really hooked on her book." Tears started to blur her eyes. "I guess I misjudged her for blowing me off. Actually, she discounted everyone and everything when she was writing."

Brian spoke sharper than he intended. "That's a crock! Rebecca, this isn't about you! Why do you always make every thing about you?"

She took another hit off the cigarette and blew smoke in his face. "Because I'm about me! That's why. What's wrong with that? Do you want to hear this or not? If you do then shut your accusatory trap!"

Brian was still stiff with annoyance, but he shrugged his shoulders and said with a deep breath of decision, "Okay, sorry I interrupted you, but I'm pressed for time. Tell it your way. In case you've forgotten, I've still got a murder investigation going on, and the press breathing down my neck. It has me more than a little cross with the whole world."

She calmed down a little and took a deep drag, squinting against the smoke as she looked away seeming reluctant to meet his eyes. "You got a right to be upset. We all do. Now, back to my 'remember-the-book' recitation." She rearranged herself on the stool, leaned back and hooked her bare feet over the rung beneath her. "Let me think...plot's about some radio personality who is also a psychologist—sound familiar? Well, this doctor lady jumps in the sack and has a lot of steamy sex with a Roman Catholic priest." She paused to look at him, all meaningful eye contact, like they were simultaneously reading the mind of poor, dead Mona.

He dropped his eyes and studied his coffee cup, so she jabbed harder. "She stuck in a torrid, forbidden love scene or two—you know, love between the sheets—just for commercial effect." Her eyes twinkled mischievously, "Care to comment on their authenticity?"

Brian opened his mouth and closed it again.

"Anyhow, there is a lot of political blackmail stuff with the IRA that I didn't understand. But the plot revolves around the church fathers taking a dim view of such things. The powers that be have her followed to Aspen, Colorado where she was to meet the priest who was already bumped off somehow. The lovebirds were intending to answer the call of the wild and run off to Ireland together. I thought that part was kinda stupid because everyone knows Ireland ain't especially safe for a renegade Catholic priest and his would-be bride. Anyway, the plot thickens. Someone hires an attractive assassin to take care of business. I always pictured the villain as a James Caan–type, ya know—the actor? I just loved him in *The Godfather*. He can be so smarmy!"

She waited to see if Brian would comment, but he just sat still and eyed her.

"Well, then this ruthless weirdo seduces her into riding up to a very high, black ski slope and shoves her out of the ski lift. Crash!" Becky slammed her palm on the kitchen counter. "The doc plunges to her death—the fall breaks her neck, plus she's impaled on the tip of her splintered ski. The damn thing was just jutting right out of her chest like a bloody sword. Isn't that grotesque but fascinating?" She pursed her lips, pausing, trying to gauge his reaction.

He sat rigid, didn't blink or anything.

Frustrated, she pleaded in a sulky voice. "Ya' gotta understand, I'm leaving out a lot of rigmarole about subplots with a couple of religious twerps from New Orleans and Mona's psychology stuff. She wrote some great scenes about the mountains and a lot of peculiar things like—get this screwy scene: the ski lift was the old fashioned kind, before enclosed gondolas, and the doc was only wearing one ski boot when they recovered her body. It appeared that her killer had convinced his prey that her boots and skis were on the wrong feet! The dumb broad was trying to change them around on the ski lift! That's why she had raised the safety bar over her head and leaned out of the ski seat. Isn't that a funny twist?"

Still no response. A great stillness had settled over Brian's body. As a priest and a cop, he had heard so many confessions that nothing could surprise him, yet he waited with a receptivity that seemed to pull the words from her mouth.

Becky snubbed out her cigarette and reached for another. "God, Mona had such a vivid imagination. For example, the police discovered her bloody right boot was still attached to the remainder of the ski that punctured her.

"Let's see, what comes next?" She looked perplexed for a few seconds as if she was trying to picture the scene. "Oh yeah, this New Orleans couple are newlyweds at the resort. She wrote some hot bedroom scenes about them. Ya know the 'anyone who doesn't like to screw is a ski-ball' stuff. Then they finally crawl out of the sack and go to the ski slope. They are taking pictures of themselves and the landscape with a video camera when this body slams down off the lift!" Becky slammed her palm on the marble counter once more. "Well, it turns out that the couple caught the whole thing on tape—sorta' like the Zapruder film of J.F.K. in Dallas. The husband was sure the woman fell out of the bucket, but his bride insisted that what's her name, the doctor, was shoved out by her companion.

Damned if the lovebirds aren't kidnapped. There's a big search for them and the missing camera and tape. I don't recall if they get killed or not." She paused to drink some coffee.

"So-o-o... the murderer is chased all over the known world, like in a spy movie. He gets caught in Tibet or China somewhere, I think. That part is effing gory. The conclusion gave me the shudders for more than one reason. Oh yeah, I forgot another part, get this—some Irish kid who was in the subplot finally kills the bastard. Seems he is kin to the Catholic priest who got killed at the first of the book. Sound familiar? How's that for rubbin' it in? That part scared the hell out of me, I can tell you!

"Anyway, the book is much better written than a Tom Clancy or Michael Crichton, although they are swell. Mona writes scenes of brutality then—bam! She turns around and gives you the tenderest of love scenes. Jesus, the plot moves so fast it makes your head swim."

He only watched her. She thought that his eyes appeared soft, but there was hardness beneath them, a cruelty even, and it showed. Perhaps it was because he was working on a case and it was a requirement for his line of work.

"But ya know, Mona's books are always more than a whodunit. She brings up lots of ethical questions and psychological stuff all through the thing—makes you think about the state of the world today. I wonder why would a person kill a stranger or acquaintance, or someone they don't even know. Or if they do know the person but aren't related to them, can't inherit money or aren't in love with them." Rebecca leaned across the table and stared at him through half-closed eyes. "Did I do good? Does my recitation deserve first prize, like a good morning kiss, Big-Un?"

He moved back on his stool and stared at her. He thought how much he disliked the pinch marks around her mouth. She wasn't even handsome, just a tight-skinned, spoilt bimbo. He clunked down his cup impatiently. "Jesus, Rebecca, you don't know when to quit! Coming on to me answers your inane question. People like you make a person lash out and want to kill them because you hate what they stand for or you're scared of them and what they know."

"Are you scared?"

"Not scared, goddamn furious!"

She shot him the finger "All business, no pleasure, huh? Now you know how I've felt all these years!" She smiled a private smile. "Well, you're right on target about the motive stuff. The book ends up that the crazy Irish ordered a hit on her and sent this psycho because this woman radio person was real savvy. Well, savvy about everything but how to tell her right ski boot from her left, I guess. And pretty ignorant about Svengalis, plus the danger of messing with a smooth operator like that big, powerful man, her murderer, as it turns out, on the lift. I always figured Mona was writing about us doing the nasty and how she got bamboozled by that smooth operator, Julien Montz! What do you think?" She paused to take a puff.

Nothing from her listener. He just looked at her. His eyes had turned glacier cold.

"I just thought maybe...anyway, the book ends up that this doctor wanted to go to Ireland with the priest because she had discovered some hanky panky going on between the church and the IRA." Rebecca snubbed out her smoke. "Look, Brian, I was mad at Mona at the time so I really didn't care to listen to her yap about the book all the live-long day. I got to where I barely listened." By the time she had finished, she had accordion-pleated her paper napkin into something resembling origami.

Brian nodded but he didn't look at her again. He rubbed his eyes and stood up. "That's okay, Beck, you gave me the gist of the thing—can't say I liked the priest's part much, but that's to be expected. I did dump her. Too bad she won't get to enjoy bumping me off in a bestseller. Now I will be posthumously killed publicly."

Becky made sympathetic little noises, "Ah, Brian, Mona forgave you years ago for pulling away like you did, for hiding in your priestly robes." Silence fell again between them, but it grew too painful for her. "Why *did* you run off to the priest factory?"

Stunned for a moment, he had no breath to reply.

"Oops!" Rebecca smiled up at him—awareness, forgiveness and promise all in a three-cornered smile. Her eyelids lowered and she mumbled with suitable somberness, "I was wrong to say those things. I'm intruding."

He rattled the change in his pants pocket, wanting to say something nasty, but he didn't. He took up his coffee mug and meditated on its contents as if he would find an answer floating on the surface. "No, you deserve an answer. After we pawed each other then jumped in the sack, I took a trip to hell accompanied by scotch or anything else to ease the pain. But I just felt more terrible, so I turned to the church because the feeling was mostly guilt and remorse."

Her voice returned to its normal gossipy pitch as she said sweetly. "Well, Mona came to terms with it. She was never one to hold a grudge."

A glint appeared in his hazel eyes—maybe tears or the edge of rage. "No, *she* wouldn't, but we Irish can hold a grudge for a long time. It can take on a life of its own. I gotta go deal with Julien, and you gotta clear out of this house."

She was irritated that he assumed a badge gave him permission to push her around. He thought he was so superior. But she wanted him to like her again so she replied soothingly, "Brian, Mona would tell you holding a grudge is a major factor in depression. Don't expect too much of yourself. No use fighting things you can't change. Our roll in the hay was a mistake—we both paid for it. Mona wouldn't want your life to change in a bad way over her, but life is bound to change." Suddenly, a 'have-I-got-something-to-tell-you' expression took the place of the expression of philosophical concern. "Please let me tell you what I found. It concerns both of us."

He was at the point where he exaggerated everything and was aggravated. His voice tightened, "Pretty words—sounds just like Mona. Your loyalty and compassion overwhelm me. Next thing you'll be telling me that nobody gets through life without some sorrow and misfortune or some horseshit! Fine words from the most narcissistic female I've ever met."

Hoisting himself off the stool, he started for the door. Then he paused and said over his shoulder, "You can tell me what you got to tell me over dinner. I'll meet you at your condo around seven. Fry me up a steak and have some scotch available." He headed out the door to go to the airport.

Rebecca stuck her tongue at him and snapped irritably at his back, "Really? You think *my* news can wait, wise guy? *You* wait until you hear, then you can preach at me if you dare!"

CHAPTER 11

Brian stood outside the glass partition, preferring to watch the man squirm. Julien Montz was as soft and flabby as ever. Maybe even more so. He appeared to be losing weight—his potbelly didn't hang as far out as Brian had remembered. He was also losing his hair. Brian had to concede Julien Montz had the best looking head of prematurely silver gray hair on the biggest head that he had ever seen. Not big headed as in "swell head" kind of big head, although the description certainly fit him, but as in physically big headed. He had always kept his big head with its pretty hair in perfect condition.

Brian had deliberately let Gracie soften Julien up for three hours. He noticed a stack of tapes sat on the table beside the recorder. She was taping it all. It was strange the pipsqueak didn't holler for a lawyer. Must be some reason. He obviously doesn't know we have him dead to rights on at least one suspicion of murder, illegal narcotics possession, possible stolen car charges, soliciting, leaving the scene of a crime and general obnoxiousness. It was a boon that butthead knew nothing from them about Mona's demise. He probably figured she was still undiscovered in that damned attic.

Brian watched the bumptious social climber con, plead, and beguile while he swiped at his brow with an increasingly damp handkerchief. Then he carefully folded it into a complex bundle and tucked it into its wet grave in the breast pocket of his soiled, baggy Haspel jacket. This debauched Julien was a satisfying contrast to the debonair Julien Montz, the great-great-grandnephew of Bernard-Xavier-Phillppe, founder of the famed French Creole elite along Esplanade Avenue. His lifestyle of old world charm had proved to be an art form. The extraordinary Julien Montz became a penniless bum who, upon his return from flunking out of Duke University in 1988, had swept every woman off her feet with disconcerting perspicacity.

Yes, it was nice to see a seedier, sadder Julien with some battle scars. Still, the detective had work to do. He opened the door and entered.

Julien turned to face him in astonishment, mopping back a strand of his flyaway hair from a sweaty brow as he did so. His brown eyes had crow's-feet at the corners and looked red and watery. The heavy lids made him look sleepy. The scumbag was far from sleepy, though. He was in a state of high anxiety. The once square face sagged and flushed, his mouth drawn in tightly at the corners. Julien held out one moist hand for Brian to shake. Brian ignored the hand, sat in the chair across from him, and began to examine the briefcase that lay open on the table.

Montz screwed his mottled face into a jaunty grin, stuck out his hand nonchalantly and spoke. "Brian, my good buddy, I can explain all this. I can't imagine what the mix up can be. I have every right to carry cash for a cash transaction if I desire. There is nothing illegal in my doing so. I can't believe it! Your partner here, Officer Reme, has detained me for hours. What in the hell is this all about? Am I free to go? I got appointments to keep."

Brian addressed Officer Reme. "You are free to go. I'll speak to Mr. Montz in private."

Gracie picked up the tape recorder and the cassettes. She nodded and left them alone. Brian examined his fingernails for a minute and then he calmly said, "Julien, will you please remove your shoes?"

It was Montz's ears that flushed first, turning a deep scarlet that spread across his jaw and up his cheeks. He looked nonplused. "I beg your pardon? My shoes? What in heaven's name for?"

"We will need to place them in an evidence bag to be examined by forensics, both here and in Miami Beach."

Julien paled, his once properly tailored, track-star confidence chipped away by this dose of reality that his boyhood rival was handing out. He sat and slowly removed his shoes. "You need the socks, too?" he asked in a low voice.

"That would be nice of you, unless you want to wander about in your stocking feet." Brian was amused to see holes in the toes of both socks.

"Look at me, Julien."

Julien looked at him in defiance, but his hands trembled.

Detective Herlihy continued grimly, "Julien, you're in a peck of trouble. Seems you have some unfinished business back in Florida. By the way, whatever happened to your silver Saturn?"

Julien brightened, "Oh, golly, is this about that damn car? Well, ya see, it started actin' up on me, so I sold it. This money is part of the deal. I am bringing the cash to invest in an oil venture I heard about. Do you want in on it?" The sly smile reappeared, but the eyes were dead. "It's gonna be big enough for me to share the wealth. I figured I might ask my wife, Mona, if she wanted to invest, too. We're still crazy about each other, ya know. I tried to call her last evening, but she was out of pocket." He produced a package of cigarettes, put one in his mouth, but didn't light it. "What do you think? Give me my shoes back, we'll phone her now and maybe that redheaded friend of hers will join us at Commander's Palace. My treat, of course. Goddamn it, Brian, I'm hungry!"

Julien tried to call Mona. The thought of this lounge-lizard focusing on Mona, even in the past, much less the present, was disproportionately repugnant. Brian looked at the man with the unlit cigarette dangling between his lips, which were big and sensuous. Julien just missed being an odd looking gent with a head of tarnished silver hair too big for his slim body. Masking his distaste, he merely said, "That's a very generous offer, sir." Then the detective rubbed his chin and pondered the cash before him. "Now, about this pile of dough. Damn it, Julien, you must have sold that Saturn as a Cadillac limousine to a blind man."

Julien laughed too loudly and the cigarette flipped from his lips. "Hell no! Thankfully, there's a perfectly reasonable explanation." His voice straining for lightness, he said, "I sold it outright—drove a hard bargain, too, but I got paid up front in cash." He spread his legs and rested his elbows on his knees. The gaudy tie he was wearing dangled between his legs like a floating exclamation mark as he hunched his shoulders and cast about for the cigarette, but it had rolled to the floor. He straightened up in his chair and waved his hands in the air. "Naw, I just liquefied my assets in all my holdings in the Florida swamps. I had a big chunk in Disney World property sales, ya know! Made a bundle—really cleaned up on that one." Then Montzy smiled.

For the first time, Brian had a flash of what had attracted Mona. When Julien smiled, he had the same devilish quality of Brad Pitt with the same smoothness. The detective leaned back in his chair and placed his big arms behind his head. He was rather enjoying this asshole. *Screw you, wise-ass!* He continued nonchalantly, "Now, Julien, I am to suppose that you have the paperwork on all these transactions? Got taxes to account for, ya know. When will you be able to get the proof of sale on all these deals? And don't forget the Saturn deal. Of course, I hate to tell you this, but I am required by law to detain you until this situation is cleared up. Another thing, it is my duty to advise you of your rights, good buddy. Mr. Montz, you are entitled to have an attorney present when we question you. If you so desire an attorney and can't afford one, one will be provided for you. You have the right to remain silent. Anything you say can and will be used against you in a court of law. Do you understand these rights as I have explained them to you?"

Julien Montz was stunned. "You're kidding, Brian. Aren't you? Am I under arrest?"

Brian stood and closed the briefcase. "You can bet your life on it, Julien. You will need to sign a release for this case of folding money and don't let Officer Reme forget to give you a receipt for it plus your shoes and socks. Tell her to note the holes were there when the socks were confiscated. See you at headquarters. Good night, Mister Montz." He waved through the glass window for Gracie to take over, then he walked out of the room.

As he passed Gracie in the doorway, he winked and whispered, "Play understanding lady—be wowed over his hair or something. Oblige the idiot, volunteer to get him some footwear and food. Say nothing about our suspicions concerning Irish Mike. Find out if he sent those roses to Mona and get me the name of the goddamned bastard he gave that car to and what he sold in order to get that money."

His twenty-four hours were nearly up. Darlin' Darrel, the Pitts, reporter at large, would pop the cork at any time.

BRIAN SWUNG INTO a Burger King on Airline Highway. He ordered a Whopper, fries and a Diet Coke. He requested a handful of ketchup packs and walked to a booth near the back. He ate slowly, relishing every bite, as his big hands fumbled with the small, slick packs of ketchup. He muttered, "Damn things are a nuisance!" Finally, he simply tore the end off with his teeth. He was reminded of how many times Mona had chastised him for doing the same thing in her presence. She complained the packets weren't sanitary. Anyone could have handled those, germs and all. Besides, she hated his fondness for junk foods. She would watch him munching his way through a Whopper and comment with distaste that no donkey would eat the stuff. He'd just wink at her and make some crack like "Well, Doc, all the jackasses I know eat this stuff."

The ketchup packet exploded, squirting across his pile of French fries and splattering onto the white table. A stab of red-hot pain roared though his body. *Blood...all her blood!* He felt his own blood run thick and cold. Nauseated once more, he gave up on eating and headed downtown.

As he drove the interstate, he punched in the office number. "Yo, Paul, any calls from Darrel Pitts? None? Good! We got some time then. Listen, I want you and Gracie to edit the pile of tapes she's bringing in. Make sure you delete any reference to the Florida charges or the phone calls he may have made to Mona's. The dipshit doesn't need to know all that yet. I want our Darrel 'the Pitts' to have the information that we are holding Julien Montz on suspicion of *some* woman's murder. Just see to it that somewhere along the line you retain some vague reference to the murder of *some* woman. Splice it to one tape and run a fresh copy, but keep the rest." He listened to Junior's response. "No, we aren't going to use any of it for evidence. Julien hadn't been Mirandized at that point. It was simply an *inquiry,* nothing more, understand?

"Tell Darlin' Darrel that Mr. Montz was stopped on a random security check at the airport and is in the loving custody of Officer Gracie Reme. She'll be in the office to do the official paperwork in an hour or so. Officer Reme has to take him to Shoe Town to get shoes and socks first then she'll register him in one of our luxury suites. What I'm looking for is just some rattle trap stuff for Pitts to sink his claws into. He loves it when some rich, white, uptown dude gets in hot water. I'm going to do him a special favor and turn that tape over to him later this evening. Have them ready by about six-thirty. Good boy!"

Brian rehearsed his little song and dance he was about to deliver to his good buddy, Darrel, as he punched in the reporter's hot line. "Hi, Darlin'! I'm good at my word. I'm driving in from the airport. I went to Miami to check out a lead and ran smack into—"

"What?" He was interrupted by the brash voice of the reporter.

"Yep, rape and murder. I lit a fire under CODIS. The FBI's national database of DNA profiles. We still gotta get the combined DNA Index System to confirm the semen samples, but let's just keep our fingers crossed. Guess who's implicated—Mona's hubbie, Julien Montz. Sure, you can print it, but...uh...you probably should wait. CODIS is still new, and the genetic profiles of half a million convicted offenders still hasn't been entered in the system. Chances of a 'cold hit' or a match with a known offender are slim. Montz was nabbed at the airport with a briefcase full of—guess what?"

The reported shouted, "Drugs!'

Brian laughed, "No, *Money*! Now, remember he is innocent until proven guilty. There may be a logical explanation. Even if it doesn't make sense, it's no crime to have a bag of folding cash. This ain't Iraq, ya' know! Hell no, Darlin', I have no idea how he managed it. Mona's throat was cut and the woman's body that we located had been beaten. Where? Oh, sorry, we're not at liberty to reveal too much—to sensitive. We don't want to release anything more until he reveals it to us. Get my drift? Don't want him to read it in the paper, ya' know? How did he fool the victim? A disguise, I guess, but don't print that detail. But it is not uncommon for an assailant to return to the scene of his crime. Motive? How the hell do I know? Yes, we arrested him, but pretend I didn't say that. Don't go pointing fingers just yet. My senior officer just brought him in for further questioning. It's circumstantial at this point. Not many facts. But the station seemed to provide a better location for that sort of thing than the airport. No, Blockhead, it has nothing to do with Mona and me! Off the record, I'd speculate it has to do with the money." Conscious of his prevarication, he deliberately dropped his voice to a whisper. "Darrel, he had a shit load of cash on him.

"What? No, you may not interview the St. Denis family. They are still off limits. Ya' see, their kid is real sick. Seems they had to rush him to the hospital in an ambulance. What? Which one? Hell, I don't know. I was in Miami trackin' down Julien, remember? I will keep you up to date after we interrogate. See there! I said you could trust me. Yeah, the ole' ball is in your hands. Go for it, Pittzie baby!"

He deliberately paused as if he had just thought of something. "Listen, I may be way out of bounds here, but do you want a copy of some of our interview? We picked him up at the airport just now so it's not official info. Gracie will smuggle you out a tape so you won't have to use your regular snitch. Yeah, I hear you loud and clear— you don't have one! Like the sun is gonna set in the east tonight, right? Guess you'll just have to improvise this time. Pick up your tape out front at 7:00 pm, okay? Naw, you don't have to thank me. Just go easy on Mona when you write it up and you'll be the first to get the gore later. Gotta scoot."

Brian went to his apartment to shave and change shirts. He had to deal with the mother of his son. It was not a pretty thought.

CHAPTER 12

REBECCA HAD BEEN primping and pondering how to explain the history of her pregnancy to Brian. She had lots of plans for a happy family reunion in the big house. Surely any dream, even a pipe dream, was worth pursuing. She wanted to be gentle but firm. After all, it took two of them to make a baby, and there was always DNA to prove her claim. She'd be damned if she'd let him get away this time, but she figured he'd come around without taking things that far. After all he knew they had screwed. It was inconceivable he wouldn't want to find his son. It seemed to her that all they had to do was wait for events to run their course, then formally take over the management of the estate. Of course, there would have to be a further decent interval before they could come together in a relationship that would be publicly seen to blossom slowly into romance, but she was content to wait. A sly smile crept over her face as she thought. Besides, she had a further enticement—they would have a ready-made heir for the future.

She could hardly wait to tell him about Mona's bequest. It was super. There were lots of properties that had not been in Mona's father's estate. Land in Plaquemines Parish—rich lands ripe for real estate development and just oozing oil and natural gas. These had never been co-mingled during the Wright's marriage. Julien had been livid when he found out he couldn't touch those assets. The land belonged outright to Mona's invalid mother. They were part of the original D'Aquin plantation. Brian could retire from the damned police force and join her in the life of the idle rich!

IT WAS LATE afternoon by the time Brain parked in front of Regency Court. The condominiums were in effect an elongated square with two rows of cream colored buildings facing each other across a central grassy lawn. Between the banana trees and assorted tropical plants was a series of columned porticoes projecting from the terraces to form entrance porches. Each porch provided the apartment number and a door buzzer and intercom.

The sky was darkening and the wind had picked up, like one of those early spring thundershowers guaranteed to pop out of nowhere just as rush hour begins. Brian dashed up the steps from the curb and waited on Rebecca's porch as he watched the western sky turn purple and orange with lavender streaking through the stormy clouds. He thought of Ireland and its soft weather and some young man whom he had yet to meet. *Hi, I'm your dad, Brian Herlihy, and your name is…I wonder what his name is? Maybe Branden? Anything but Padraig, I hate that name*! He scowled and pushed the buzzer.

A glowing Rebecca opened the door. She was sure she looked stunning—hair artfully tousled, makeup discreet, but perfect. Her choice of clothing was a green jumpsuit that fit like a coat of paint then swayed loosely around her legs, managing to cling in all the right places. She twinkled up at the Irish hunk standing on her porch, and twittered, "An' th' top of th' evein', to y'all!"

He rolled his eyes and raised his hands to the heavens. "I'm damp. The shower came suddenly as I locked the car."

"I know, but I'm not complaining." She flirted with her eyes and said, "Nothing looks better on a handsome man in a white shirt than a little rain. Shall we?"

He ran a scathing eye over her skin-tight outfit and realized Rebecca was older than she looked. He grimaced at the idea that she had ever appealed to him, even when drunk. But the thing with Rebecca was that even when you saw her coming, she kept coming. Ran right at you and through you, made you wonder why you tried to ward her off in the first place. The best move in the game was just not to play at all. He decided to keep their conversation casual. "Let's eat, I'm starving! I hope you didn't go get any of that fancy French stuff with all those sauces."

Brushing past her and into the ultra modern living room, he commented, "Swell place you got here. Bet the monthly payments are more than my salary."

"Oh, I doubt it. My father owns the whole complex and I manage it for him in exchange for the rent. Yes, Brian, I know you're a meat and spuds man. Are you on duty, Officer, or are you drinking?"

"I might be coaxed. What have you?"

"Anything—bourbon, gin, vodka and Scotch, and a few other things. I'm not very good at mixing, so if you want something fancy, you'll just have to take your chances."

"Scotch on the rocks is fine."

They had highballs at the bar. Afterwards, eyeing one another like two wary wrestlers coming to the mat, they sat to eat. Their conversation was strained, full of cumbersome pauses. Brian would start to talk, then stop. Rebecca talked in rapid little fits of stops and starts. Both were careful not to upset the other, avoiding any discussion of Mona's murder. After a particularly long lull in the chitchat, Brian told her about Julien's arrest, then he warned Rebecca again about talking to the press. He told her that Darrel would be breaking the news of Mona.

"Oh for fuck's sake! Will it have all the details?" Her skin crinkled in an expression of contempt.

"No, just the general facts, sort of an update to follow up on the story about her disappearance."

She lit a cigarette. "That's good. Are you going to discuss it all with me?"

"No."

"So much for trading information. Seems like I'm the only one giving out any. Oh, Brian, I swear you wrap yourself up in so many defenses your armor clinks when you walk!" She moved into the gray and white living room, taking her wineglass and an ashtray as she went. "Come sit. I have some Crown Royal here someplace. I'll fix us another drink."

He followed her to the chrome bar and sat on a high stool while she poured him a stiff one. He waved his hand and said, "Whoa! Enough. I have to keep my wits about me."

Rebecca poured her drink and moved to an off-white sofa that dominated the living room. She placed the drinks on the glass coffee table in front of her and curled up on the end. Brain would have been startled to know that her mind was preoccupied with calculations as to just how duplicitous he might be and how much allowance she should make for the fact that, as she was now prepared to admit to herself, she found him once again available.

He sat down on the other end of the sofa, pointedly putting distance between himself and her. Maintaining a parody of politeness, he leaned forward and took a sip of the drink. "Now, what is so important it cost you a steak dinner?"

Rebecca picked up her vodka tonic. She took a deep swallow and began. "Well, it worried me that Julien might get everything except Mona's mother's estate if she died without a new will. Then I remembered she had one drawn up after he flew the coop. Soooo, I went over there after you left me in such a hurry last night and found it. Well, actually, I found a handwritten first draft along with a letter from her agent-publisher. That's strange, though. John Warren said in his phone call that Mona's authorship is being challenged. Seems some jerk sent her book in and claims he wrote it. She was plenty upset about how well she was protected because I know that she talked about it with Robert St. Denis and his wife. Janice mentioned it to me in passing when I called the house looking for Mona."

"Thanks for wiping out the phone record—real tidy of you." His voice was edged with annoyance. "Rebecca, I'm not going to beat around the bush. Keep your nose clean and stop plowing though Mona's private stuff. Trespassing is not acceptable to me or to the law. Actually..." Brian paused, discomfort plainly in his eyes. "Look, we're being discreet, so we haven't made a big production out of it yet. There is no tape or warnings at Audubon Place because we are deliberately avoiding sending up any flags by having an official search of her abode. But stay out of that house! You aren't even supposed to know anything."

She leaned toward him and poked him in the chest with a red-tipped index finger. "You're like a stuck record! We're back to that now, are we? I got the damn message, okay?" She swallowed back tears before she spoke with exaggerated patience. "Mona trusted me. If she was away on business, I let her cleaning service into the house and checked her messages. I am...I was...her best friend, damn it! What would you have me do? I was practically a member of the family for the past two hundred years!"

He held up a hand. "Calm down. I know that and you know that, but the law doesn't recognize you as a family member!"

"Well, I am. That's enough." She rolled her eyes and observed loudly, "You are certainly in a vile humor! That is absolutely enough! I can't tell you how frigin' exasperated and disappointed I am that you're copping that attitude. I won't speak to you at all unless we stop dumping all our frustration on each other." Then she softened her tone and sniffed. "Mona wouldn't like it. She wanted us to be together...all three of us or maybe all four of us. Mona had guessed even though she didn't know what she had guessed. Look, before we discuss Junior Birdman, and you get to scold me some more, could you just listen to what I have to say?"

"Shoot."

"Let's see, how can I put this? I knew what Mona had intended to have in her will if anything happened to her, unless you guys decided to tie the knot."

There was something loose and afire in his ice blue eyes as his mind flashed on hugging the porcelain bowl after seeing Mona's body. But he simply took a drink from his glass.

Rebecca watched him for a second, then sighed. "Oh, Brian, I nearly wept. It seems that her will leaves everything including the oil and gas lands she inherits from her mom and the mansion to me...and you, of course. She wanted us to be real well off so we could take care of her mother and keep Julien from horning in. His health is going to be in danger when her revised will is read because I happen to know that the prick planned to sell the place and pay off his debts when it was left to him. Plus he has been using his projected inheritance to guarantee private loans in order to keep blowing dough on roulette. He presumed he'd get everything unless she had a will. Louisiana isn't like the other states. We have some old Napoleonic laws that let a person disinherit their spouse, but not their kids."

He seethed inside as she looked up and their eyes met. His feelings were a clutter of emotions far too complicated for him to hide. His jaw set tight as his mind flashed on a scene of Rebecca screwing her best friend's husband while pumping him about his hopes and dreams about Mona's wealth. He wanted to shake the cold, emotionally stunted, selfish bitch until her pearly white teeth rattled. Then, he realized things were looking worse by the minute. It seemed that she had her own reasons for wanting Mona dead. Rebecca looked uncomfortable and he had to put her at ease, no matter how annoyed he was. Clearing his throat and trying to do the same with his mind, he faked it. He spoke reasonably and carefully, as if discussing something with a child that was beyond the child's grasp. "That explains a lot. Ya' know, Rebecca, I haven't been very nice to you. We sorta fell out after we fell in bed."

She plopped her drink on the table and gave a shaky laugh, "Oh, balls! I didn't give you herpes or anything! Things have changed. Besides, that was twenty years ago when we were young and blotto—drunk as skunks!"

"Did you ever hint to Mona?"

"God sakes, no! I didn't even want to think about it. Did you?"

He shifted on the sofa and tried to wish his way out of the situation. When that didn't work, he looked away and ignored answering her. His voice came out flat and cold. "Do you mind if I ask you a couple of very frank questions? Now, don't have hysterics. They're going to sound like cop questions because they are cop questions. Understand? Just the facts, ma'am."

She bristled, then took hold of her feelings and smoothed out her jump suit. "A couple, as in two?"

"Well three, actually."

"Okay, ask away. But this better not develop into a round of twenty questions because I have one for you. I thought you'd be thrilled and honored that our very dearest friend trusted us to be protectors. Doesn't that just make you feel good all over?"

He clinched his fists. "Don't get carried away on that score," he said dryly. "Question number one: Was there anyone besides Julien who would want Mona dead? Like some scumbag who would do dirty work for someone I was involved with?"

She blew through her lips. "Nope, not unless you want to count spouses of patients who made the decision to split while they were in therapy. That's about a million, I guess, and a couple of goofball radio listeners who wanted to get chummy. One pervert tried to stalk her, but you know about him. He's at a funny farm."

"Number two: You knew where her car was kept. Why were you trying to contact her at that particular time and in that particular place?"

She pulled a pouting look. "Oh, I've told you that I did it by accident. While you're busy dissecting me, need I remind you that if I *hadn't* kept calling, Mona would still be rotting in that attic. I wanted to hitch a ride."

"So you knew her car was probably still at the Royal Orleans. Did you mention the location of her car to anyone you knew or to Officer Reme?"

It took her a moment to register the significance of the question. When she did, he could see she was shaken by the implications. "Did I? No. Should I have? You don't really think—"

"Becky, it's a routine question. We look into all the victim's prior contacts."

But this whole line of questioning wasn't routine and she knew it. She smiled a wily smile and smirked, "Well, it's a black BMW. I wonder if she left it to you."

"Cut that shit!" He noticed that she had again avoided his implication that she might have shared the information with a third party. "I'll get Reme on it. Question number three: What did you think when you got no answer?"

"I told you, not a damn thing! I figured it was turned off."

"No, Becky, that won't wash. They tell you if the unit is not in service."

"Oh yes, they do, don't they?" She frowned before letting comprehension dawn in her expression. "To be honest, I was so pissed that night everything else seemed to go right out of my mind. That's three questions. Are you finished, Inspector?"

"No, just answer me. What was the reason you continued to repeatedly call after that?"

"I don't know. I was worried, I guess." Her eyes roamed the room. The only place they didn't look was at him.

Pretty weak answer—did she know something? "You won't look at me. Are you having a problem?"

"A problem? No." But she kept her eyes on the table in front of her.

"When did she let you in on what was in her will?"

"She told me on the beach in Destin. We went there right after Julien took off with everything he could carry." She phufffed, "Boy! Was she mad!"

"So, you've known for almost three years?"

She took a deep breath, "Give or take a few months. Anyway, why does it matter when she told me or even if she told me?"

"Becky, let me give you some good advice. Keep your mouth shut! Inheriting is tantamount to a motive!"

"What? Really? You don't think..." She looked up at him curiously like an innocent little girl. "Do you?"

"I don't think anything where you're concerned. Let's get this straight. This is a murder investigation. I'm a police detective assigned to the case and you have just told me that you and I are possibly murder suspects!"

Her thin mouth took on an odd expression and she sputtered, "You don't think *anything* when it pertains to me, Big-Un? Well, I got news for you. You're in this just as deeply as I am—maybe more because you were playing footsie with her again. Besides, you know a lot more scum for hire than I do. I'm just the best friend who sinned and fell short of the glory of God and the famous Doctor Mona Wright...and the mother of your baby!"

He croaked, "Brother, I'm in deep shit!"

She grabbed his arm, "Why? You're not going to report all this, are you?"

"Becky, you amaze me! What would you have me do? I'm a detective, not a priest, and this ain't exactly a confessional. You already know the answer. This isn't some sort of privileged information and I'll do what is called for by the situation. You've just informed me that we both have two very strong motives for killing a woman we both loved. And they are biggies." He counted them off on his fingers. "One is money and the other is our secret, illegitimate child. Of course, I'm going to report it."

She scoffed, "Sweet Jesus, what a fool you are!"

"I'm a fool? Maybe you're right! I got a kid somewhere in Ireland and can't prove I didn't know."

"Yeah well, ya never know what's in the bottom of the Cracker Jack's box, do ya, Big-Un? And don't forget how you shocked everyone by ducking the whole thing by going off to become a fucking monk!" She took an unsteady breath. "Looks suspicious to me."

"Cut the crap! Who did you tell? Someone had to help you arrange the adoption.'

"My mother's priest. He arranged it all."

"So it's privileged information. You told a priest that it was me? Does he think I've known all these years?"

She flushed with sudden anger and wagged an index finger in his face. "Ah ha! What if I did? Can't you see this hitting the newspapers? You and Mona have always been such pigs when it comes to publicity!"

He snapped irritably, "Shut your puss when it comes to Mona!"

"Then you shut your puss! I'm telling you in confidence, off the record so to speak, just between us friends."

The hand squeezed at his chest again. Brian rubbed his forehead. "God, this is messy! I gotta' think about this."

"You bet your sweet bippy, you do!" she jeered.

"What does that mean? Who was the priest?"

She paused for effect, lit another cigarette and chuckled slyly, "Your oldest buddy, Father Kennedy at St. Pat's. Life is just packed full of ironies, ain't it? He's known all along about you and me and the kid."

"This is looking worse by the minute. Who adopted the baby? Do you know anything about them? Was there anyone who called himself Irish Mike?"

Wrinkling her nose, Becky snorted, "Irish Mike? Oh clever! Nope, it was some family named McGlynn. After my mother passed away, I found out who they were because I sent boatloads of money through Father Kennedy. He suggested we call it a pledge to Catholic Charities earmarked for the orphanage in Galway, but he saw to it that the Irish couple got it." She dabbed at her eyes, mouth trembling on the brink of a sob. "Don't you understand I wouldn't be telling you any of this if Mona was still alive? She loved secrets and I know that she wants us to be together."

He shook his head and grunted, "Well, it seems she had her secrets and at least one of them was lethal. The question is which one?" Suddenly irked with both women, he raised his voice and bellowed, "I'm not listening to any more of this. You get in touch with Kennedy and find out who else knows. I need the name of the orphanage, the address of the McGlynn's and copies of your canceled checks, front and back." He stood up rigidly and wagged his finger at her. "Becky, not a word about the will or the child to anyone except Father Kennedy. I'm walking a very thin tightrope between statutory compliance to the law and forbidden procedures. Now come on, get me the keys and the security code on 36 Audubon Place. I've got to figure this out."

She went into her bedroom and got the keys plus the security code. As she smacked them in his hand, she cracked tartly, "Remember, Detective, no breaking and entering allowed."

He slammed out of the door.

She wanted to throw her glass at his head, but instead she muttered ruefully, "See the rat run! So much for true love, loyalty, and friendship. Mother always said the more you love each other, the worse the fights. You got it, Boss! My wonderful news did not bring out Detective Herlihy's best features."

CHAPTER 13

THE ANCIENT OAKS along St. Charles Avenue were draped with moss, their limbs ridged with lichen. The well-kept grounds around the enclosed community were abloom with azaleas. After showing his badge to the gatekeeper, Brian swept past the wide-galleried, gabled houses, past other homes with cupolas and fluted columns that loomed large as ships out of the floral gardens surrounding them. He turned his unmarked police car under the portico, swung around behind the house, and doused his headlights. He opened the back door, entering through the servants' entrance. He stepped into the utility area and shut the door behind him. The cool dry air was the product of an efficient cooling system. A tiny red light blinked away on the security panel beside the door. He punched in four numbers and followed them by an asterisk. The light blinked a steady green. Otherwise the house was dark and still, a heavy silence as if the place had been brooding on its owner's fate. Flicking on a small flashlight, he walked through the butler's pantry and the kitchen, then passed through an archway into a large, luxuriously furnished living room with deep sofas and chairs scattered artfully about. His flashlight caught the glow of polished wood and the fine paintings, mostly portraits of ladies and gentlemen of the old south.

He entered Mona's study and paused as his eyes roamed the room. He felt like he had entered another dimension, as if the past had overlapped the present. The room was large but it seemed small because it was painted a dark crimson called New Orleans Blood Red after the by-gone days of mixing cow's blood with whitewash—very popular in the olden days. It was stuffed with mahogany bookshelves up to the exposed cherry beams on the ceiling. The shelves were crammed with leather-bound volumes ranging in size from tall ledgers to thin pocketbooks. There were muted Orientals on the floor, and a sense of aged plumpness in the leather sofa and armchairs. The room looked cozy, but cozy with exquisite taste and a sizable wallet.

Mona's desk occupied the west corner and was piled high with journals and texts. Tape cassettes formed a semicircle around a tape recorder. The fax lay on the desk along with Mona's brief response to John Warren. It stated that her laptop and floppy disks containing her finished manuscript had been stolen and she had proof of same due to an insurance claim filed on November 6, 1999. There was no mention of Julien's part in the matter. She informed the publisher that she was flying to New York to discuss the problem after she consulted her attorney. There was no indication of when she would arrive, but an airline ticket on the desk was dated for the day after the Faulkner reception. Whoever the murderer was, he hadn't wasted any time.

Brian turned these ideas over in his head and felt they had a certain thematic consistency. If so, what had they to do with the murder of Mona? How could anyone get involved with her book in the first place?

The phone did have a caller ID box. He used a pencil to activate the memory button. Most of the numbers were unfamiliar to him except for Rebecca's. The phone number of the last caller on the digital readout was one of the patient's numbers listed for the day after the party. Those could be followed up on later.

He checked the answering machine. A recent call from John Warren's office inquiring as to her arrival time and a couple of hang-ups which were probably Rebecca's calls from that evening. They'd be on caller ID along with the times the calls came in. Rebecca had done an efficient job of deleting all the earlier calls. He seethed. Shit! So much for evidence. Maybe the Miami police can trace any calls from The Amazon Center. He carefully retained the new incoming calls and wiped the machine. No use in alerting his force to either Rebecca's presence in the house or his own for that matter.

Her Rolodex was missing, if there had been one. Mona had a new palm pilot so maybe she had disposed of the old file. But Rebecca could have taken it also.

He discovered the reports of a private investigator. Mona had hired an old high school teammate of his, Grayson "Bulldog" Trotter. He turned on her copy machine and made a set of every item. While the machine warmed up, he scanned Trotter's reports. It looked as if the P. I. couldn't find Julien at first, but finally traced the Saturn to Nevada. He had included several colored photos of Ruby

Ann, Angela, and Julien. In the back of one of the shots, there was a head facing in the opposite direction. It looked as if it might have red hair, but the man was seated in the silver Saturn. The shot was taken at noontime; the glare caught the windshield at the wrong angle to get a good look at the occupant. Bulldog mentioned some bookie named McClintoch that Julien was hanging with in Vegas. That could be the Irishman who called himself Irish Mike O'Shea. The report didn't put the man in the car together with McClintoch, but there was a good chance Trotter couldn't get a good look at him either.

Grayson noted the murder, or rather the death, of Ruby Ann under suspicious circumstances had been deemed drug related. The result was the release of Julien and Angela. There was a brief reference to a female visitor, but no subsequent information. Brian made a mental note to notify Vegas authorities in case they had a description of the bookie or the woman visitor. The flatfoot concluded with the suggestion that Mona forward him some more funds in order for him to trace the couple after they left Las Vegas. Apparently, Mona had given up the search. It was probably for the best—Trotter was known to bilk clients as long as they would pay up. He wondered if Bulldog had information not in his reports. The PI had the scruples of a lizard, and if he knew about the forthcoming book or her publisher, John Warren, he could have made some deal to sell the information. But Brain couldn't see Bulldog aspiring to become an author.

After the copies were completed, he folded and tucked them into his jacket pocket, wiped down the machine and turned it off. Then he gazed around the room filled with her memory. He could feel the ache of her sitting alone at 3 a.m., parents gone, abandoned by her lover, tapes, files, and reference books spread before her. But all that had been changed. Now all he could do was try to accommodate events outside of his control and over which he might not have had control in the first place. He realized that he must not let his grief and anger blind him, not now.

The flashlight pooled on her crowded desk. Her appointment book was open to the date of the Faulkner bash. Other pages were clearly marked with many patient appointments and a seminar or two. He used his handkerchief to nudge the pages backward until he had checked all the mundane little details that make up life. *Brian—dinner, concert and ? Staff meeting—Memorial Hospital. Beck's b-day. Visit Mom (talk to her doc). Church. Dry cleaners.* He thought of the woman who had written these words, printed neatly in black ink. He closed the book and was so overwhelmed by sadness that for a moment he couldn't move.

He looked at a white pitcher with blue flowers and a framed photo of him in police uniform. Tears sprung to his eyes. Rubbing his face hard, he backed into her seat behind her desk and fell on his out stretched arms. Great sobs racked his body as the dam broke inside of him. The violent rain smashed against the windows and shot down the gutters, but the storm outside was nothing in comparison to the storm raging inside of Brian David Herlihy. His head came up with a jerk as he vented his pain against the world in general, but mostly himself, with an agonized roar, the wordless cry of an animal wounded beyond recovery. He howled, "Mona, I'm so sorry I fucked up! I loved you more than anything—more than God Himself! I can't make it up to you, but I swear I'll get that bastard."

LATER, HE SLOWLY got to his feet and wandered through the empty house, looking at this memento and then another, remembering happier times. She had kept a trivial brass sailboat he had bought her one summer at a junk shop on the Gulf Coast. There were pictures of her family. Her father in a tuxedo wearing a red sash holding a champagne glass for the Krewe of Rex at some Mardi Gras ball. Seeing the photo reminded him of how much he had loved her dad, Berkley Wright, a retiring English gentleman of the old school who went by the nickname Berkie. They had shared a love of sports events, good food and beer. Another one was a Christmas picture of a mammoth Christmas tree with glowing lights and a star on top. It featured a much younger Mona, Rebecca, and Helene. He had tolerated the overly demanding Helene with all of her pointless social scruples simply because she was Mona's mother. Helene and Mona stood gazing happily down at Rebecca sitting beneath the tree opening a gift.

Then there was Rebecca. Shit, why had he done it? Why in bloody hell he didn't Mona divorce that bumptious social climbing, fancy-pants jerk? I'd have married her in a New York minute!

He resisted going upstairs. He figured he had suffered enough pain, hate and regret without ferreting out some more. Up those stairs were too many painful memories. He couldn't afford to get caught up in another emotional nightmare, and there was nothing he could do about the anguish of the past. *A son in Ireland! Mona, I have a son in*

Ireland. He sighed and headed for his car as he mumbled to himself, "Not our son, Mona Baby, but I can pretend, can't I?"

As he swung the car onto St. Charles, he called the office and left instructions for the next morning. They were to conduct a thorough search of 36 Audubon Place and tape it. He specifically underlined the necessity of restraining any visitors—especially one Rebecca Webster. He left orders for Officer Reme to confiscate the computer and its records, in particular the disks containing any transactions concerning her editor and her book deal. He instructed her, "Listen, I think I may have stumbled onto something in Miami that may have bearing on the case. It's a newspaper clipping and photo of Mona in New Orleans. Jules sure as hell wouldn't have needed it to identify her, but someone else would have. Get Miami to send a copy along with fingerprints and such—you know the drill. Send Sergeant Dick Richard copies of Keller's mug shots and trace any calls made from that health club in Miami.

"Get me a hard copy of her manuscript along with John Warren's phone number and schedule a telephone interview with the publisher for around two p.m. today—New Orleans time." He added, "Tell Warren the nature of the call and stress it's urgent I speak with him." He then requested his partner to begin an in-depth inquiry concerning the bookie, McClintock, last known whereabouts in Las Vegas." *Less said the better about how he knew about Grayson's reports.* He'd have to risk it with Gracie to not ask. He'd explain later that Mona had apparently hired Grayson Trotter to track Julien. He hurried on, "Bulldog mentioned the stranger who visited them, and I'm particularly interested in McClintock's activities in relation to Julien and the sisters. Get a description and run the sister's pap smears past CODIS. He may have left a calling card—stress looking for HIV positive." He added, "And Gracie, while you're at it, find out if he is a redhead or has ever been a redhead—check his history and where he was when Mona was killed. Also fire off all of this info to Miami. Have them put out an APB on the Saturn and McClintock. Tell them Irish Mike O'Shea may be AKA Padraig or Pedar McClintock, and you guys do the same. Set up a heart to heart chat with our favorite maniac, Harry Keller, ASAP." As an afterthought, he informed Gracie he would be detained in the morning.

"I'm going to visit Reverend Father Kennedy on some—" he paused, searching for the right words, then cleared his throat and said, "uh, personal business."

The weather didn't help his mood. Relentless rain continued splashing down as the streetcar rumbled past at the crossing in front of him. Brian watched as the windshield wipers thumped and groaned in rhythm with the passing streetcar. The wiper-blades flashed across the glass and clicked in and out of sight, leaving a brief clarity behind—first allowing a clear view of the azaleas and the camellias then obscuring the view with the rain. It took on a surreal effect. *Like love*, he thought, *first you see it and then you don't*.

CHAPTER 14

AT SEVEN-THIRTY THE next morning, Brian opened his eyes to glance at the clock next to his bed and then starred at the ceiling. As usual, the sheets were coiled around him, twisted and knotted like a rope. Something was even more twisted in his heart as he remembered the times they had lain together in the bed, their bodies cleaving to each other, arms entangled, breath against breath.

"Why God?" He asked softly, his chest heaving. "What did she ever do to deserve to die like that?" Then he struggled to stop thinking about it.

He shifted slowly to extricate himself from both his thoughts and the sheet. Swinging his legs over the edge of the bed, he sat up and stared at the floor beneath his bare feet. Then he got up and headed for the shower with the idea of clearing his head, but stayed only long enough to sluice the sweat off. He dressed more carefully than usual. He combed his unruly hair and cleaned his fingernails. Dressing for church was very old ritual—getting all spruced up for confession and Mass. He had ignored his religious duties for three years. There was too much shame and confusion on his part to continue after he bolted from the priesthood. Mona encouraged him to return and finish the business, calling him a Catholic diehard. *And it was you, my sweet therapist, who died hard!* As he prepared to interrogate the priest of his childhood, he pondered what to say, where to begin. *How does an ex-priest-type, Irish NOPD detective ask his previously ignored Father Confessor about the adoption of said ex-priest, Irish NOPD detective-type's long lost son?*

He frowned at the image in the mirror. His blonde hair was thinning and creeping up his scalp. Smiling a face-splitting grin, relentless and pitiless, he smirked, "Are we having fun yet? Oh, Yo! Faddah' Kennedy, how's y'all's momma an' 'nem? Say, Cher? Have y'all heard from mah sonny lately? Jest' thought Ah'd drop by ta' let y'all know Ah'm shor' interested afta' twenty years. Say hello ta' the Big Fellow Upstairs while y'all are at it. He hain't heard from me lately, but Ah been busy procreating with mah girlfriend's buddy and findin' the woman I loved slaughtered!" He bounced the hairbrush off the mirror, grabbed his weapon, coat and cell phone, and left his apartment.

BRIAN HAD CHOSEN to live in the area between Magazine Street and the Mississippi River known as the Irish Channel. His family had always lived there, but when they died, they got to move to higher ground. He had buried his hard-drinking bruiser of an Irish pop in their family crypt high in a walled city of tombs known as The Cemeteries. The location was about as far from the Irish Channel as the family could afford. The expensive final resting place didn't make any sense, but the elevated stuccoed brick vault was a practical response to the city's swampy site. When Brian's mum died, his da' had leased a wall vault known as an "oven" with the help of his mutual aid society. The bereaved Irish plumber didn't want any of his family to float around in the gumbo mud for eternity.

The St. Thomas Housing Project now sprawled where his family's house—if you could call the shotgun shack a house—had once stood. There was an ongoing archeological dig to study the life of the Irish. *What life?* Immigrants' shacks that hung on the edges of muddy ditches fallaciously called streets with such lyrical names as Annunciation, Felicity, Terpsicore, and Constance. For God's sake! Archeologists were interested in the contents of their old privies! Society had romanticized the grimly depressed Irish to the point of insisting there should be some Celtic riddle imbedded in the filth, something besides disease.

Brian had heard the stories of his great grandparents, tragic members of the first wave of emigrants after the potato famine struck Ireland. The Irish flocked to the New World of hope and promise. What folly! They should have stuck to black potatoes! The racial oppression was replaced with Irish immigrant oppression. The great flood of Irish was greeted with signs in windows, "Help Wanted—Irish need not apply." His ancestors dug ditches and picked cotton, abysmal tasks considered too dangerous or too poor in pay for the former slaves, now elevated to the status of free men of color.

He eyed the wooden street barriers encompassing recent excavations surrounding the housing projects and the old church. He hoped the digs would reveal the thousands of skeletons of the lowly

Sons of Ireland dead from Yellow Fever or Black Plague epidemics. Funny how those diseases have common names based on the discoloration of the victim's skin. Maybe they should call alcoholism by some name such as Ruddy-Jowl Fever or Bloodshot-Eyes Syndrome. Plenty of grim Irishmen embalmed their shattered hopes and dreams then went home to beat their wives and children. Maybe an Irish kid's disease could be named Black and Blue Fever. God, but he was depressed!

He parked and entered the haven of most Irish women-folk, including his mother, Breeta Byrne Herlihy. What a woman his mum had been. She had led him to believe the myth that God, the Blessed Mother, and the Son could solve every problem given enough prayer, good works, and time. Well, her magic solution had eventually worked for Breeta. Her problems were solved during her last pregnancy. Father Kennedy had been the young priest who told Breeta's first born son, age of eleven, that God had taken his mum to her reward. Now she was with God. *Say hello to my mum for me, Mona. Hey, Mum, this is Mona Wright. Mona, this is my mum.*

The sanctuary smelled exactly the way it always smelled—musty and sweet with flowers, candles and furniture polish. It had always caused a dull ache in Brian's gut, like the funeral of his mother. No amount of praying and good works had ever made that smell or its accompanying gut wrench any less difficult to bear. After his one night of debauchery with Rebecca, he had figured he was such a sinner that he deserved pain for the rest of his life. He stopped near the entrance and gazed up at the statue of St. Lucy. She stood serenely, holding a palm branch in one stone hand. Her other arm extended toward him; on her outstretched hand she held a plate upon which her eyeballs rested. He knew the legend. Even though she was tortured and raped, she had chosen to dig her eyes out rather than forsake her religion. *Hello, Saint Lucy. Let me introduce you women-folk. This is my mum and this is my true love, Mona Wright. Say hi, girls.*

A hand touched him on the shoulder. He turned to face Father Kennedy. The two men stood and looked at each other for a moment. Father Kennedy's face was full of sympathy. He had obviously read this morning's paper. The short, baldheaded priest had a brogue thicker than Brian's mother's had been and when he spoke—"will" came out "wail," "there" as "thur," and so on. It was the thick Irish spoken in the north, in the gray coal towns where the mills stand and the soot hovers like a cloud. At present, Father Kennedy spoke softly, "*Thur*, Brian, my son. I've been praying for you. Mona was a unique woman. But you *will* realize after the horror wears away, that she is—"

Brian stiffened and finished the sentence himself, "Gone to her Heavenly reward. I know the drill, Faddah'. Her bloody raped body with a slit throat is at home with God, right?"

The priest registered some shock, but after thirty-five years in the Irish Channel, he was prepared for anything and remained calm. "You are deeply distressed, Brian. But we can talk and pray about your personal disaster. Come with me." He gestured toward a confessional.

"No way, Boss! You pray later." His voice was tinged with sarcasm. "I want to go to your office. This is official police business plus some unofficial Brian David Herlihy business tossed in for good measure. If it makes you uncomfortable just give me the word and we'll adjourn to my office downtown." Brian was aware he was being brusquer than was needed, but he felt it was some kind of emotional defense mechanism. Mona's voice echoed in his brain, *"You're doing that official policeman act again, Brian. Come off it!"*

He followed the black shirt down the center aisle. The interior was dark and cool. Varnished wooden pews lined the way to the altar surmounted by a golden replica of the church and a magnificent crucifix. The skin on his chest jumped as if a string were pulling it. Brian stopped to make a fumbling gesture. His hand trembled as he touched his forehead, chest and shoulders. He refused to duck and kneel at the knees. His back was suddenly very stiff, his waist riveted in place. He did manage to tilt his head a little. *Sainted Mum Breeta must be having one of her cat fits.*

Father Kennedy entered his office and shut the door. "You look drained. Anything I can get you? A soda? Do you care for some coffee? I got some Bushmills to sharpen the taste. You look like you could use some Irish fortification."

Brian was sorely tempted, but he shook his head. "Naw, Faddah', some other time perhaps. I'm on duty. I'll take the java if it's the real stuff with dark roast and chicory."

Father Kennedy poured the thick, aromatic brew into a Styrofoam cup. "Cream? Sugar?"

"Naw, this is fine, thanks." He put the cup to his lips and blew across the steaming surface then took a cautious sip—not so hot it would scald. He drank half a cup to ease the dryness in his throat. "Let's get this over with. I need your help in two matters. I don't think they are related in any fashion, but they've come up now because of Mona's...death. Now, one may involve you breaking a confidence, but I have it straight from the ho—horse's—er—lady's mouth that I can delve into the matter. You can call her if you doubt my word."

"Brian, Brian, my son, I don't doubt your word. I never have and never will." The priest lifted a concerned hand as if to absolve him.

"Look, Eamon Kennedy! I've known you all my life. We did the priest thing for a while together, but it makes me shiver for you to call me 'my son.' Do you mind knocking off that crap?"

"My word...testy, aren't we?" Kennedy had a deep, mellow voice, strange for one so thin and small. The priest relaxed and poured a cup of coffee for himself, then added a slug of Bushmills. He held his cup up and slipped into his very best pure-porridge Northern Irish accent and said solemnly, "Fer Lord's sakes, Brain, yah got a fearsome burr up yer bum. I think I need this, if you don't mind. After all, you have stated you are on duty, but if you are going to defrock me, I'll stand here in me long johns and have a wee nip. I reckon I'm NOT on duty, so to speak."

Both men laughed. The tensions eased a bit. Brian leaned back; his spine didn't seem quite so fused. "Hell, Eamon! I always thought you looked fetching in your undies. Thanks for bringing me back to earth. You know this church has a way of giving me a case of the willies. That's in the best of times and this is the worst of times. So overlook my knee-jerk reaction. I met with Rebecca Webster last night. She seems freed up enough since Mona's...passing...to reveal a drunken misdemeanor of ours. Well, strictly speaking, more than a misdemeanor—a real blockbuster sin. She tells me that we have a kid somewhere in Ireland. Is she telling the truth?"

Eamon Kennedy tilted his head, studied his cup for a minute. He reached for the whisky then changed his mind. "I don't know if your involvement is true. Rebecca tells me it's true, but if you have reason to assume it is your child, and I do recall your confessions at about the...uh...time the child was conceived. I suppose those will suffice, at least for our present discussion of the delicate matter." He tugged at his thick, wire-rimmed glasses, only making them droop over his nose in an even more angular fashion. He looked thoughtful and shook his head. "Brian, you understand, I am not at liberty to reveal anything Rebecca may have told me in confidence, even to you." He crooked his index finger at Brian and waggled it around. "I will not speak of Rebecca or her part in the matter to you as an interested party or to you as an officer of the law. Are we perfectly clear?"

"Set any boundary you need, Eamon. I'm not interested in Rebecca's confessions...." He hesitated and thought *that statement is an out and out lie. I want to ask if Rebecca confessed to humping a dissolute gambler who was married to her best friend.* Instead, he added wearily, "...or any of the details concerning her part in our past folly. I just need to trace the kid. There are more reasons than I can explain to you at this point. It's complicated as hell. What happened to the kid?"

Kennedy relaxed. "Well, in that case, since you are the presumed faddah', I suppose there is a basis for your inquiry. I helped the young woman to enroll in a year's program in Galway College. She boarded with my da and stepmum until after the baby was delivered by a midwife. She pressured me to find the child a home. I never officially enlisted the help of Catholic Charities, although I must confess I did allow the young woman to believe I went through proper channels. However, due to the high profile of her family's position in New Orleans society, I deemed it prudent to select the help of my stepmother to secure a suitable family. The couple has told the child, a young man now, that his mother was an American college student. They have been very open and above board with the boy."

Eamon frowned and jerked off his specks. He cleaned them industriously against his cotton shirt and wiggled them back into place on his face. "I'm not certain if they even knew her name or where she was from, but we made every effort to eliminate the need for secrecy. My stepmum and her son, Sean, made the arrangements. The young woman in question has continued to be most generous where finances are concerned. She has insisted on shouldering a goodly part of the boy's expenses by herself. I assure you, this was not an easy burden. Her parents never indicated to me that they knew about the pregnancy or the matter of the funding. I imagine her folks simply assumed it was all a part of their generous clothing allowance. So you see, it wasn't mysterious. Most things have rather mundane explanations, no matter how strange they seem at first. At any rate, the family has proved to be a satisfactory placement." He paused to cough. "Under the circumstances, I would send the young woman's checks to my stepbrother, Sean. In order to protect her identity, he would cash the checks and see to it that the monies were placed in the family's hands. He handled it personally until the young man reached the age of eighteen. That was about a year ago, I believe."

"I know the name of the family. Rebecca told me last night. It is McGlynn, right?"

"Well, that certainly proves the young woman in question has taken you into her confidence, doesn't it? Yes, their names are Fionnuala and Malachy McGlynn." He held up his hand, "Now don't laugh, this isn't fiction you know. Those are perfectly presentable old Irish names. They live somewhere out on Dingle Bay. Sean has all that information, but I haven't been able to get in contact with him. He and the boy, presumably your son, left soon after the child's eighteenth birthday. They were headed for Belfast, last I heard from my stepmother. Sean has some ties with a foundry up North. I believe he was looking for jobs for the both of them. I had encouraged the youngster to go to college, but you know impulsive young Irish boys, and I had very little to say in the matter. He has to get it all out of his system."

Brian nodded but he was perplexed. Something about Northern Ireland and 'the troubles' rang a bell. *Something? The IRA and the Church—a priest...shit, he lost it.* He asked, "What was he supposed to get out of his system?"

"Oh, boys change a lot during their teens. Besides, I never was in their inner circle. I venture to guess the guys are sowing a few wild oats or finding out what the Resistance was all about. The old Orange and Green thing bubbles under the surface for all the Irish—Republic or whatever. The Irish gotta' have their heroes."

Brian finished his coffee and stared at his hands then crumpled the cup in his fist. "Well, I hope my son isn't one of them!"

"Don't you sound paternal now? Brian, you mentioned something else you needed for me to attend to. What is the other matter?"

Brian sat up. "Oh, yeah. Trouble is this information has injected an even more personal note into this case. I guess I'm taking this father thing too seriously. Rebecca hit me right between the eyes with it. What's my kid's name?"

The priest laughed, "You guess!"

Brian looked as if he smelled something bad. "Don't tell me that they named him Padraig! I will not call my son and heir, Paddy!"

"Oh, Goodness no! He's named after the biggest Irish hero of them all. He is Branden Michael McGlynn. Can't you just smell the green, white and orange in that?"

"Hey, Priestie, don't you go making fun of my kid, ya' hear?"

"Brian, I love yah' tough ole' hide! What else is on our agenda for today?" Father Kennedy fumbled in his breast pocket and pulled out his pipe. He opened a worn leather pouch and tamped some tobacco into the pipe, then lit it with a single match.

Brian noticed his companion's uncharacteristically trembling hands. "You ever had any dealings with a bookie named McClintock? He may have been at the Faulkner Society party in the French Quarter. We have a couple of witness reports stating that he's a slightly balding redhead, tall and skinny, and he has big hands. A witness held a conversation with a guy calling himself Irish Mike O'Shea. Our witness is working on a sketch of the suspect."

The clergyman was genuinely shocked. He turned white, ran his finger around his collar and reached for the whiskey bottle. The hand shook slightly as he missed his cup and splashed booze on the desktop. He took out his handkerchief and wiped it up very carefully. "Damn cups! I hate these things—can't hit 'em in a month of Sundays." He put the handkerchief to his nose and breathed in for a moment. "Ah, I can't tell if I like the smell or the taste better." The priest rubbed his hand across what was left of his frizzy gray hair and adjusted his thick gold-rimmed spectacles. "Now, let's see...what did you ask me?" He puffed deeply on his pipe and spoke slowly. "Yes, a redheaded Irish Mike or someone named McClintock? Well, I don't recall any red hair but, Brian, my stepmum's first husband was named Padraig McClintock. His son is my stepbrother, Sean, but it's got to be a coincidence. I assure you Sean doesn't have red hair. He's tall and thin...or was the last time I saw him. But he had blonde hair—as blonde as yours, but a lot longer. Of course, he may have bleached it for some part he was playing. As a matter of fact, my da' made fun of Sean's flowing curls. He'd snort around calling his stepson Goldilocks. Sean is the artistic type. I recall him doing a bit part—nothing special, just a walk-on as a sword carrier in an Abbey Theater production while he was living in Dublin. My da's favorite wisecrack was that the Abbey must be at doing a modern version of Spencer's *The Faerie Queen*. My stepmum commented he ought to be proud since he loved the English classics so much."

The older man stared into his coffee cup, laughing at his memories. "No, I assure you, Sean was skinny as a zipper, looked like a young Joseph Cotton in drag. He smoked a long cigarette in a ridiculous cigarette holder and pranced about like the ballet dancer in *Der Rosenkavalier!* Oh my no, my friend, Sean was a character, but he couldn't be your man—not capable of murder. Especially not a murder of a woman that included a sexual assault."

"Why in hell not?"

The priest fidgeted and took a drink from his cup. "Because he was a little...conflicted. Is that the word? At any rate, Sean was...uh...not inclined toward women. I tried to get him interested in a religious life while I was home. We were having a heart to heart chat, but it evolved in to something similar to a confession. I am a priest, and Sean confessed he was already a member of a community of sorts. Listen, I'm telling you this in utmost privacy. It's bordering on...well, you know how I feel about such confidential matters, plus it being a family matter ta' boot. At first, it didn't make sense. I fancied he was referring to the artistic community—actors, musicians, painters, writers, that sort. But I got a surprise. He was speaking of the gay community. He never actually came right out and said the words, but I got his meaning." The priest puffed anxiously on his pipe and blew a long stream of smoke across the desk. "No, Brian. I don't mean to slight your work or abilities, but Sean Padraig McClintock was definitely not interested in women. He is as meek as a little lamb."

Brian frowned, remembering the coroner's report. *Perp was HIV positive.* He countered with a scoff, "If he is as meek as a little lamb how come he was looking for foundry work?"

His companion looked miffed. "You're right. I had forgotten that detail. Well, he was always a risk-taker but certainly no laborer. Maybe he was looking for advertising work. I don't know what his situation was, but he can be very charismatic when he wants to be. You'd probably like him if you met him. Everyone though the sun shone outta' his arse—including me. Sean could sell the Pope a condom. Yes," he laughed a nervous little laugh, "my stepbrother was something of a con artist, you might say. I suppose he looked for a job in some sort of sales, but your son, Branden, would be suitable for heavy work. He was quite the jock. Played rugby at his school and was outstanding. Built like a brick outhouse, just like his da'! I had hopes the youngster would be eligible for a sports scholarship of some sort and follow in your footsteps. My stepmum says the McGlynn's encouraged him toward the clergy, but he's a rounder just like you—not religiously inclined, I fear."

"Neither is his da'. Not these days when I got a murderer to catch."

Kennedy shook his head and frowned. "You shouldn't have given up on yourself so quickly. You were always—"

Brian cut him off. He didn't want to be reminded of that dark period in his life. He had made his bed and now he had to lie in it.

"Listen, Eamon, I can't hang around to find out where this is headed, but I'll send my partner, Grace Reme, to get names and addresses. Could you round up any information you can think of? We'll keep it hush-hush. I'll need any family photos that include Sean and the phone numbers. Better yet, how's about you giving your folks a call to see if you can track them down? Maybe they or the McGlynns have had word from the guys. We need a little diplomacy for the time being. No need to give Officer Reme the poop on Branden Michael." *The name slipped easily across his tongue.* The men shared an understanding look. "That's a matter best kept between us guys of the cloth, okay?"

The priest jerked himself up from the chair. "No, I haven't any pictures. Sean was always too vain to allow any candid shots. He used the stage name of Pedar. The Abbey Theater might have some of him in make-up and such."

Brian was surprised at the anxiety in Kennedy's face. *Too quick an answer.* He nodded and said, "Too bad. But no problem. I'll have Grace Reme bring a police artist to get a sketch of Sean. Be sure and allot enough time to get it right."

He rose to say goodbye then added, "You haven't ever discussed Mona's novels with a PI named Grayson Trotter, have you?"

"No, don't know the man."

"You ever run into Robert St. Denis' housekeeper? Her name is Septema Cryer."

The priest thought for a moment then shook his head. "Hum, no parishioner by that name that I recall. Why?"

Brian shrugged, "She was associated with Harry Keller at one time."

"The villain you put behind bars?"

"Just a shot in the dark. You ever have any dealings with anyone that knew Harry Benjamin Keller?"

Father Kennedy's eyebrows shot up. "He involved in Mona's murder?"

"Don't know yet. Just answer my question, Eamon."

"Brian, if this is a revenge killing, I am on your side. But if you are asking me to reveal subject matter involving the confessional, I'm on the side of the Mother Church. The Keller family lives in the Irish Channel. Sorry, this is real bloody business, but I'm not at liberty to say more."

Brian shook his head. "It's God's business I'm about, and God knows there is also a real bloody law concerning withholding evidence in a homicide called obstruction of justice. Up until now, you have been forthcoming in your responses with exception of this last one. Thanks for your time."

"Well, Brian, that the way we Irish are. We hide our feelings—inscrutable." The priest tilted his head as if he meant it as a joke, but he remained stiffly upright, his features expressionless. Only his fingers, clenching and unclenching the pipe between his lips, gave any clue to his internal state.

"Bullocks! We will need a statement later. It's possible you are involved without knowing it, so I suggest that you give us all you can." He strode from the office.

THE STREET IN front of the church was slick with rain, but all that remained of the shower was something between a drizzle and a mist. The air was marked by a humid breeze that sank into the trees like soap in a sink, but it felt fresh after the closeness of the church and the good Father's pipe. *Something else rattled the old bird*. The sun was out, shining bravely through the passing clouds. He stood on the steps of Saint Patrick's Church and glanced up to see a rainbow. *Skiing the Rainbow!* His eyes lit up. He waved at the sky and felt the release of knowing he was right. "God bless you, Angel-face!"

He retrieved his cell phone and punched in his office number while he descended the steps to the pavement. "Hi, Gracie. Get over to St. Pat's with a sketch artist. I interviewed Father Kennedy and he may have some leads for us. Use some of your French charm. The old man is being fairly cooperative, but something is not right. Have Junior check with Immigration. See if he can flush out a couple of Northern Irish fellows fitting the description of any recent immigrants from the Belfast or Galway areas. It may be that some Sinn Fein creeps were unhappy with Mona's book. Get on the names, Sean Padraig or Pedar McClintoch, or our perp, Michael O'Shea, and a kid last reported traveling with McClintock. The boy is about eighteen, blonde, blue eyed, big and well built. He's called Branden Michael McGlynn." He thought, *my son*.

"While you're at it, cross-check with Immigration for Visas from Canada or Scotland. Lots of Scots-Irish Macs and Mc's in the clans there. The duo left Galway headed for Belfast sometime in the past year, give or take a few months. Have Junior print out a hard copy of Mona's new book from her computer files. I'll need it ASAP for the interview with her publisher, John Warren, at 2:00. He glanced up at the sky and added, "Mona's book is named *Skiing the Rainbow*.

Gracie, look out the window if you can. A miracle is happening. There's a rainbow over the city."

He was about to sign off when Gracie mentioned Julien had revealed that the buyer of the silver Saturn was a woman named Rise Stevens.

Brian did a double take. "Rise Stephens? Shit! That's the name of an old redheaded opera star! She a mezzo-soprano famous in the late 50's for belting out arias from *Carmen*...no, hell's bells, Gracie, not Carmen Miranda, Goofus! The other *Carmen*, the Spanish Flaming Mame, written by Bizet! Mona loved her damn old recordings when we were young. She'd fling herself around the room and mimic the diva to a tee!" *The scene flashed across his mind.* His voice trailed off in a choked sound. "Sorry, I'm just a damn bit choked up—been to church, ya' know."

Gracie retorted testily, "Pa-leese! If you been to church, then watch the profanity!"

"Hey, I'm damaged and vulnerable to harsh criticisms, Mommie Dearest! Jeeze, don't take it personally. I got 'cha, God and Gracie don't like dirty talk. I'm headed for Rebecca Webster's house. I think she knows more than she's told me. That reminds me—I need for you to contact Grayson Trotter, the private eye. I don't want him arrested or anything, but the buzzard's got some explaining to do. I need to pump him concerning some work he did tailing Julien in Vegas. He may have a make on a bookie named McClintock or may be using the name Pedar. There's something about a woman visitor. Get Junior to check on any vacations the St. Denis' housekeeper, Septema Cryer may have taken to Vegas. Have him track down any of Keller's family in the Channel and check out any association between Cryer and Harry. Eamon Kennedy is kissing the Pope's ring and determined to keep his trap shut about them. Get Trotter to the office before I am scheduled to talk with John Warren. And, Gracie, be nice to the man! I know scumbags are not your type, but we need for this one to be cooperative." He laughed as he listened. "What reminded me of our favorite lurker? Well, Trotter has the foulest mouth in Louisiana—worse than your Cajun plumber dad. Of course I remember, who could forget?"

CHAPTER 15

Rebecca was lounging on a folding chair in the backyard of her condo. The newspaper lay across her lap. There were wads of Kleenex on the flagstones beside her chair. On a glass-topped table nearby stood a glass that looked as if it held tomato juice and probably vodka. She appeared to have a head start on the day and had not answered the doorbell. So Brian had walked around the side, opened the wrought iron gate and walked onto the patio.

She didn't move or look up. "Can't a gal have a little privacy?"

He bent down and removed the paper. He couldn't help but notice the lead story. Darlin' Darrel Pitts hadn't wasted any time making it to the front page. **DR. MONA WRIGHT FOUND BEATEN AND MURDERED!**

Brian's heart screamed.

She removed her sunglasses to reveal slits of swollen, red eyes. "Don't you dare read it. It's full of crap God wouldn't like. I could wring Darrel's darling neck for exploiting everything he could about our poor dear. He calls Julien the *estranged* husband. After the bastard goes on and on about Mona's wealth and social position like it's a sin, he suggests Julien is suspected of some altercation over finances resulting in the death of his spouse. Is the man nuts?"

"No, Pitts is just a little misleading with his facts, that's all. You really can't blame him. He had to write something." He smiled grimly as he screwed the paper into a tight ball and dropped it onto the stones.

Rebecca opened her fist to reveal a sodden tissue, which she pressed against her eyes. She then reached out with an unsteady hand and pulled another tissue from the box. Her throat was congested and she cleared it. "Well, he was rarin' ta go at it! You just talk to the prick and get him to straighten this all out!" She snorted into the tissue.

"Oh, yes, I'm sure I'll get to straighten him out," he grunted. "He'll make damn sure of that. Rebecca, tell me something. Did Mona ever mention any guy named Sean Pedar McClintock? Did you ever run in to him while you were in Ireland? He's the artsy-fartsy type—did some plays at the Abbey Theater in Dublin using the stage name Pedar. Kinda looks like a young Joseph Cotton."

Rebecca's eyes roamed around the garden for a minute. Scowling, she responded in a sarcastic tone, "Oh God, nope, but Mona had some PI tracing ole' Julien, her *estranged* husband, as in *real-strange* husband. Maybe he found him playing house with the guy. Julien wasn't too particular in that regard. Any old hole would do for Julien. He liked actors, dancers, painters, musicians, authors..." her voice broke. "Authors like our Mona and..." She buried her head in her hands.

Brian reflected on what he knew. "She told you about Julien's affairs and the investigator?"

"Of course she did." A muffled sob. "She feared some sort of creep would get pictures or a videotape of Julien while he was fuckin' a freak and threaten to expose him on the internet like some fool guy did with Dr. Laura. Mona had a lot to lose either way." She paused, reached for her drink and took a swig. "If she divorced Julien, he'd get what he always wanted—half of her family's estate, and do considerable damage to her spotless image at the same time. Jesus H. Christ, she was terrified of what the pervert might do. She figured he might even star on the tapes himself just to get even with her. The other rock in the hard place was if she didn't cut him loose, some other bag of slime could blackmail the hell out of her. For the longest time, she couldn't find the S.O.B. It was like waiting for the other shoe to drop." She drained her glass.

"Did she still have feelings for Julien? Is that why she never told me all this crap?"

Rebecca's expression hardened. She retorted contemptuously, "Oh, don't make me laugh! Yeah, she had feelings for Julien all right—feelings of hate and repulsion. And loads of regrets. She didn't tell you because you are a policeman, damn it! She was terrified of what *you* might do. Plus she was ashamed of being so gullible." Her face fell into a pout, then she hiccupped. "And because Mona loved you, you diehard Catholic fool!"

He nodded curtly and snapped, "Thanks, Beckie, like I needed that. I figured she was a little conflicted. I figured it was either because she didn't believe in divorce or because she still had feelings for him. I never could bring myself to discuss it with her because I wasn't sure where my heart was on the subject. It's nice to know she was protecting this diehard Catholic fool and not in love with that little shit. But it's just like her to handle all of it by herself. I guess you women have to have your secrets." He threw her a meaningful look, "Like your messing around with Julien and—"

A flush spread up her neck. Then she winked and flashed him an amused glance. "I'm sure I deserved that. But it is hardly living dangerously, is it? How does a gal know what she's capable of if she never tests herself?" Then her demeanor shifted and she sputtered, "Detective Herlihy, that's really calling the kettle black, ain't it?"

It was his turn to blush. He decided not to press her. And he was reluctant to stray into any area that might raise more questions than it answered. He snorted, "Okay, let it go for now, but how about babies and trips to Ireland. Tell me, when Mona went to Ireland, was she interested in the troubles? How about the IRA?"

Rebecca sulked as she picked up her lighter and a cigarette. "Mona loved Ireland. Partly because of you. But she was digging up all sorts of crud for her new book. She took pride in doing things well—liked to get everything authentically correct. That was the way she was. She'd get an idea in her head and just do it. My God, she was consumed with the Roman Catholic and Protestant shenanigans! She rehashed the plot for hours. It was like my best friend was rehearsing a CNN special. I didn't want to talk about Ireland for my own reasons, so I quit listening."

She fumbled around and finally lit the cigarette, but dropped the lighter on the stones with a clatter. She shrugged and slurred her words, "Ah crap, forget th' damn thing! Julien was busy robbing her blind, going to Harrah's, welshing on gambling debts, screwing everything that moved. And you, my friend? You weren't around to listen—no chance! You were up in the clouds somewhere playing martyr, listening to God or somebody." She began to fidget with the empty glass even though her speech was already slurred from alcohol. "Shit, I'm out of fuel. Lessss see. She made a couple of trips—one to the north and one to the south. Sounds like Dorothy and Toto in the Land of Oz. I don' think she called on the Wicked Witch of the West, but she might have met up with a couple of hags on a heath somewhere." She waved her empty glass above her head and lifted her bronze hair off of her neck with the other hand, making her nipples poke against her halter-top. She winked and said, "Yo, defective detective, ya' want a drink for auld lang syne?" Jiggling her boobs, she lunged forward and fumbled with her empty glass. "I'm ready for another one."

He recognized it wasn't lunchtime yet and Becky-poo was snockered. He declined the drink. "Becky, you need some food inside you. How's about a Shoney's special? My treat."

Leaning out of her lounge chair, she snatched up the crumpled newspaper. Hurling it at him, she shouted roundly, "Shoney's? I wouldn't get caught dead at Shoney's! You bring that slop in here and feed it to me and I'll thick my fingers down my throat. Besides, I don't want to eat!" She squeezed her eyes shut, trying to keep the tears from slipping out. "I want to drink and cry!" Then she grunted, "Grub gets in the way of the booze...but not in the way of sex, does it, Big-Un? Leave me the hell alone or I'll call the police!" She struggled to hoist her rear off the chair.

Brian grabbed the glass and helped her up. "You could navigate better if those shorts weren't cutting off your circulation from the waist down. Becky, you do *not* need another drink! I want the name of Mona's attorney."

She flopped against his chest. "Mind your own damn business, Officer. I like my manner of undress." She made an attempt to pull down the shorts and pull up her brief halter at the same time. "Oops, nearly got my man-you-ver upside down, didn't I?" She giggled up at him. "Get it? It's a play on words...*m-a-n*-e-u-v-e-r—maneuver? Okay so don't laugh, you ole' sourpuss!" Pushing her hips against his crotch, she glared up at him defiantly. "You know her lawyer. Obviously it's Robert St. Denis! Ole' Robber-the-Hood St. Denis—the owner of the highrise attic of ho-o-r-rors!"

Brian led her into the house and dumped her on the sofa. He got a tuna fish salad out of a take-home carton and some French bread. He put them on the table in front of her, went to the bathroom and wet a towel that he placed across her forehead.

Becky didn't move at first. Then she took both of his hands, pushing them down hard on the towel and groaned, "Um, that feels good. I knew a man like you once. Y'all got anything else you want to push against me, Big-Un?"

At that moment, her features went skeletal and her beauty vanished. Repulsed, he jerked back his hands.

Rebecca's fists clinched around the wet towel and she threw it at him. Her eyes focused briefly, full of resentment. Glowering at him, she hissed vengefully, "Just go fuck yourself! Don't you dare try to call me!"

"Not to worry, Beck. I'll call you if I need to talk. Probably the next time you and I see each other will be in the interrogation room at headquarters when we both become principals in a conspiracy to commit murder investigation."

He turned and walked out of the front door. *God forgive me but I hate that bitch!*

The hot sticky air wrapped around him like a wool blanket. He phoned Gracie. "Hi again! I'm on my way downtown. You want me to pick up some carry-out? Okay, a Shoney's Special it is. Listen, Gracie, I want to thank you from the bottom of my heart for being there. I'm about crazy right now. Take up the slack for me will you? That's a good girl. By the way, you used to look great with that bunch of French braids pulling your eyes up high until you looked Japanese. Yeah, I also remember what kind of snowballs you used to like! Anyway, you want mustard, catsup, or mayonnaise? All three? No kidding? Look, get Robert St. Denis on the tube. Tell him I need a peek at Mona's will."

He listened a minute. "Yeah, I know it's messy. Well, do what ya can. Tell him that I'll get a court order if necessary. I'm outta here."

CHAPTER 16

THERE WERE THREE TV camera crews and about ten relentless, pitiless news hounds waiting in front of Police Headquarters. Brian parked in his assigned spot and was stopped a half a dozen times between his parking space and the door. Everyone in the French Quarter knew him and the reporters were out in force. He brushed the crowd aside with the standard generalities containing as little information as possible. "No comment at this time. I'll get back to you as soon as there are any new developments. Yes, the murdered woman was Dr. Mona Wright. No, she was not nude. No, it was not suicide. Yes, we think there was some evidence of an attempted sexual assault and that Dr. Wright was killed intentionally. Yes, we do have a suspect under surveillance. No, there was no confession or admission of any guilt whatsoever. Yes, there are other suspects. No, I am not at liberty to give names or other information for fear of jeopardizing the investigation in progress..."

He ignored all questions relating to his relationship to the victim. *Yada-yada-yada! The press sucks*! "Yes, I realize you're just doing your jobs, but that will have to suffice for now. You'll appreciate that there are matters we can't discuss. Sorry, guys and gals, but I gotta' do my job, too." He conjured up a semi-smile and waved from inside the glass doors.

Entering his office, he said gruffly, "Thank the Lord for small favors, Darrel Pitts wasn't at the front door! Here's your grub. I got you a chocolate shake. We can share the French fries—half the calories that way. What 'cha got for me?"

Gracie grabbed the bags, "Ugh, Injun Girl Friday, eat first—talk later. Umm, smell them onions!"

They ate in silence until Gracie noticed his milk shake was strawberry. "Who decided that you get the strawberry one? Why didn't I get a choice?"

"Oh, hell, Gracie, take mine. What's the difference?"

"The difference is that you got to choose and I didn't! Let's share. You can swig on mine with your straw and I can swig on yours with my straw."

Brian shrugged and shook his head. "Same ole' Gracie!"

Officer Paul Simmons entered and swiped a French fry. Brian waved him off. "Get your own grub, Junior! I don't run no catering service here!"

"It's a good thing, Big Un. You'd go broke the first week." Brian thought he saw pity in the officer's eyes, but Simmons continued hastily, "I got a lawyer named Nicholas Mouton. He's Julien Montz' cousin and counsel. Shall I take him back?"

"Yep, but stay with them until you are told to leave. Get what you can, Junior. Any news on Grayson Trotter, Septema Cryer or Mona's attorney, St. Denis?"

"Uh-huh, got in touch with all of them. Septema is a real piece of work—so stiff she makes the Church Lady look like Whoopee Goldberg. She knows the entire Keller clan and says that she lived with Harry after they both gave up educating themselves in the New Orleans schools. It's all in our interrogations before and after you collared Keller. She reported him for roughing her up a couple of times. Put her in the hospital more than once. She hasn't any priors and seems to have kept her nose clean. Septema thinks God intervened in human form, namely you, and that she was lucky not to be the last woman he lived with seein's that one got stabbed to death. Her brother vows he'll kill Keller if he sees him, but she swears that she hasn't had any contact—no prison visits on record. No phone calls or letters. Her family has no idea who his friends were or are."

Brian seemed distant and slightly melancholy when he asked, "You believe her?"

Junior shook his head up and down, "You bet!" Then he hesitated before adding, "Well, as far as it goes. But something's missing. Them's angry folks! They hate the bastard. Also, she offered a weak alibi for time of the murder—claims she was at Mercy Hospital with a sick relative. So far, it doesn't check out."

Brian grunted, "Who was the sick relative?"

"She wouldn't say. Claimed she didn't want to involve anyone. Want me to keep at it?"

"Don't keep at it. I'll send Gracie. Sometimes girls like to talk to a woman. So on to other matters."

"St. Denis is willing to cooperate due to the situation. He proposes that he read Doctor Wright's will and will answer any official police inquiries which he deems pertinent to the case. Says that's as far as he can go legally at this time. If you want a copy or anything other than that, he will require a court order. Otherwise you will have to wait until the official reading of the will. Trotter is on his way down here as we speak."

Brian wiped his mouth. "Good enough. Encourage St. Denis to stall on that official stuff. Inform the chief and get a judge versed on what we need. I'll fill in the blanks if I need it in a hurry. When can I interview Harry Keller?"

Simmons tossed a slight salute-like gesture, "I'm on it now. Looks good for a quick trip upstate tomorrow morning about 10 a.m. Better pack thumbscrews. He's a tough customer."

Brian didn't smile. "Our lead time with the press is over. Too bad I couldn't see the bastard this evening. But the timing gives Gracie and me a legitimate reason to be out of touch. Hate to be a party pooper. Notify the brass that I think that you can have the pleasure of handling the herd."

Junior mumbled, "Whee, thanks! Talk about screws!" and disappeared. As soon as he had shut the door, he reemerged. "Trotter's here."

"Swell, send him in."

Gracie removed the food parcels and stood by the door. They heard a wheezing cough as Grayson Trotter lugged his two hundred and ninety pounds of sweaty flesh encased in a shiny blue suit through the door. He winked at Gracie and bantered, "*Bon jour*, Frenchie! Boy, oh boy, *ma che'rie*, you look like a million bucks in uniform. Wow-wee, want ta' rumble?"

Gracie caught the scent of stale tobacco and sweat, rolled her eyes toward heaven and replied, "Now, Grayson, you constitute an entire gang war all by yourself. Sit!"

Grayson continued to ogle her and guffawed, "Ya' are some great lookin' gal! Ya want ta' go to work for me? You'd be swell company on a stakeout. And I pay better than NOPD." He wiggled his eyes, winking broadly. "Not to mention the perks!" He unbuttoned his jacket as he squeezed his bottom into the chair in front of the desk then grunted, "Damn sorry 'bout your loss, Big 'Un. What's shakin'? Did you bring me in to ask about when I nicked Al Pacino's Mercedes in a parking lot?"

Brian grimaced at Grayson's slicked black hair and his wide nose that showed signs of several violent collisions with blunt objects. The man's flattened features had earned him the name "Bulldog." At present, his beady eyes were squinted with suspicion. He chose not to respond to the stupid question. "I was hoping you could tell me. Let's get down to business. Your former client, Mona Wright, is deceased. You have no legal problems with revealing the content of her case."

Gracie shot Brian a puzzled look as he opened a gray folder and placed the copies of Trotter's notes on the desk.

Brian's lips pursed in an unreadable expression and gestured to the PI. "These reports were confiscated at Dr. Wright's residence by a police officer. Please examine them and tell me if they are correct. I need some further information—anything you can add will be appreciated."

Bulldog blinked in surprise and thumbed through the notes. "Yep, these are pretty much it. Can't add much to what's here, but where's the—" He stopped himself mid-sentence and looked perplexed. Then he shrugged as he ran hands the size of oven mitts through his greasy black hair and flopped the file back across the desk. "What 'cha want to know?"

"Where and when did Julien Montz meet his bookie, McClintock?"

Trotter was looking more and more uncomfortable. "Hell, I don't know when. Probably right after he and Ruby Ann hit Vegas. I started tailin' them a couple of days before the big Millennium bashes. I picked up their trail by watching Ruby's sister's place. It was an apartment-hotel sorta place for transients where no questions is asked or forwarding addresses given.

"The sister was Angela somebody, but called herself, Roxy Rocksoff—one helluva body that gal had! Phew!" The PI waved his fat, black-spotted hands in the air and smiled with his mouth, but his eyes stayed stupid and cold. "Roxy's sister, that's Ruby Ann, was callin' herself The Silver Saturn. Julien hung out at the casino where the sisters worked in a bar act. Shit! What an act! They played sisters, which they were of course, and came out all dressed like nuns. Then they commenced ta kiss 'en feel each other up under their habits. Then the sex kittens ditched the nun stuff and had on skimpy little Catholic schoolgirl outfits—sweet bows in their hair and everything. The thing got hotter and hotter until Roxy 'en the Saturn was both just about naked. Then ole' Roxy went to rubbing the ole' Silver

Saturn down with a bunch of Rocksoff! They commenced rubbing their legs together along with—"

Brian interrupted, "Cut the crap! Answer my questions!"

The PI mopped his flush brow then swiped the dirty handkerchief around his thick neck. "Oops, sorry, ladies present…" He wiggled his eyebrows and gave Gracie a wolfish grin. "No time ta' git a hard-on! Well, sir, I watched Julien with this flaming redhead. He or she—I don't rightly know which it was—did some book makin' for Julien. The bartender told me the fella was named Pedar 'er something like that and that the pair had one helluva name callin' fight one night. This Paddy was shoutin' at the dude—that's Julien, of course—that he'd better pay up 'en quick or he'd end up with his throat cut 'en buried on the desert some place. Now I didn't put all this in the doctor's report. It was just grubby hearsay, so I thought I'd spare her. Anyways, Pedar 'en Montz must have patched it up somehow because they got real buddy-buddy."

Bulldog Trotter fumbled with the file, pausing long enough to focus on the photographs. He removed the pictures and pushed them across the desk. "Here they are. Not too clear, though. Only candid shots of a Saturn." The PI's thick finger came down on a section of the Polaroid. "Yeah, I suspect that 'un with his head turned is Paddy McBookie. Listen, no doubt in my mind them gals was ass-deep in drug trafficking and turning tricks. I saw plenty go down, I can tell y'all!"

"In these reports, you mentioned a female visitor. Be more specific if you can."

"Sorry, not much to tell. At the time it was none of my concern. Maybe some kind of cleaning lady. But shit-ass tall and not much to look at. Wore clumpy shoes and a sorta cape with a hood. I recall thinking it was too much clothes for the weather, if ya' know what I mean."

"How long was she there?"

"Don't rightly know."

"Why? Donuts calling?"

Bulldog's jowls bounced back and forth as he sputtered, "Nature calling—loud and clear, okay?"

Brian leaned back in his chair and steepled his fingers. "Did you notify the proper authority concerning your suspicions of prostitution and drug peddling?"

The man paused to look down and began to pick at a thread in a loose button on the jacket of his ill-fitting suit. Then he carefully brushed off the front of his pants legs and shrugged. "Naw, I was on a job for the good doc. Lookin' fer somethin' more important for her." He glanced up at Brian. "Ya know what I mean?"

Gracie noticed an odd look pass between the two men—something shared but unspoken.

After getting no response, Trotter shifted uneasily in his chair. "I couldn't blow my cover. Besides, what proof did I have the scumbag was peddlin' drugs and flesh? The next night, Angela got randy with Julien and started practicing her bumps and grinds on top of him. Next thing I know they're both under suspicion of murder when Ruby Ann gets whacked! After they were cleared seems Julien backed up his new squeeze. They both swore it was Ruby who was hopped on drugs and sweet Angela had just been protecting herself. It was ruled accidental. Accidental, my ass! Then they skipped town in that silver Saturn of Ruby Ann's. I notified Doc, but she never replied, so I came back to New Orleans to follow up on—" He stopped himself again. "That's pretty much it."

"Didn't you run a check on the bookie? Where did he live, work, that sort of thing?'"

Bulldog waved the matter aside with a chubby hand. "Tried to, but the creep was always movin' around. He swung his tail at a gay bar from time to time, but I think it was just cover up. The sleaze joint was called The Rise and Shine Club or was it Rise Up and Sing?" He shook his head. "Uh, I ferget. Anyways, the *Up Something's* gimmick was the gents got dolled up like famous women opera stars and the dykes dressed as male opera stars." The PI jiggled and waved his hands in the air. "Everyone got into the act...like all the hard cocks and hot cunts become bullfighters or some such nonsense. I never cared for opera, so I didn't go inside. Don't care much for all that lip sinkin' hooey by homos either! You can check it out. The management may have some stuff on Pedar. Say, I do recall something funny—the Pedar fella was bald as a billiard ball. The barkeeper told me Julien had pulled the guy's red wig off during their set-to!"

Gracie added, "Mr. Trotter, have you ever run into anything concerning a woman named Septema Cryer?'

"So, the woman speaks." Trotter ogled Gracie again. "My, my will wonders never cease! Nope, can't say that I have, but wait—hey! Wasn't she the broad who was hangin' with Heller-Keller a few years back? She involved with Dr. Wright's killin'?"

Brian calmly dismissed the ball of fat. "Thank you for your time, Grayson, but let's not drag this out. Right now, I owe you one." *You incompetent asshole!* "You've been helpful, but stick around. If you think of anything else funny come tell us, ya' heah?"

Trotter asked slyly from the doorway, "Sure. Glad to clear my name. May I inquire what 'cha want with him? You got Julien?"

"You may not ask. What did you know about Dr. Wright's new book? Did she say anything to you about her manuscript or sending it to John Warren? We can have your computer confiscated and your phone taped if you lie to me."

The PI stared balefully at the other man. "Me, lie? Hell, ya' know I don't read books. Who is Warren?"

"Okay, that's all I need to know. Good-bye, Grayson. Stay in town and stay in touch!"

Trotter hesitated at the door then turned to face them. "Look, if Frenchie here will indulge my renowned affinity for tall, dark-haired gals and consent to have lunch with me someday, I'll put another bug in your ear."

Gracie looked like a storm about to happen.

Brian coughed, "Officer Reme, retain your sense of humor. No deals, Bulldog, or I'll make you a deal you'll remember forever. At the present time, you're our prime suspect."

"*Shee-yit*! What for?"

"For starters, you were privy to Dr. Wright's most intimate secrets and could have tried to sweat her. Maybe she refused to pay up and things got out of hand. Extortion has a nasty ring to it. If you whisper a word of *anything* pertaining to the victim around town or withhold evidence, police justice will be swift and sure! I'll arrest yer arse! So, what are you talking about?"

Trotter laughed nervously and sauntered back into the room. "Oh, hell's bells, I'm just kiddin' y'all." Greasy sweat showed on his face but his eyes narrowed as he added slyly, "You showed me only a part of my reports. 'Course, it's none of my concern, but I figured you knew that weren't all, didn't ya? I came back to New Orleans to check on another person for the doc. When you said that line about if I thought of anything else that seemed funny, well, this is pretty peculiar, I'd say. Doc had me run a check on her sorority sister, an LSU Golden Girl named Rebecca Webster."

Brian sat up in his chair. "What did you find out*?*" *Either Mona or Rebecca read and destroyed the reports, why?*

"Oh, nothin' much. Webster's folks are clean, never so much as a parking violation. Her dad manages downtown real estate—owns a bunch too. Mostly parking garages and some condominiums on St. Charles. The family is big and spread all over Louisiana and Texas. Her brothers and sisters are spotless as far as I can tell. Several brothers went to Nam. Ms *La-te-da* Webster manages her dad's real estate on the avenue. She fiddle-farts around with various gentlemen friends, mostly sports has-beens, her tennis coach at the country club, and used ta' hang with Doc's hubbie at some watering holes 'round the lakefront. 'Course that was before Montzy took off with the stripper." He winked. "Doin' some undercover work in her own way fer' the doc, don't cha' reckon? She's been engaged four times but never managed to make it down the aisle. She drinks pretty heavy, but this is New Orleans, right? She's a posh looker on the prowl, I'd say." He rolled his eyes and winked even more broadly at Brian.

"The Wrights got a place on the beach at Sandestin. She and the deceased doctor go—or went—there frequently, I should say. The only blotch on Rebecca I could find was she went to Ireland, enrolled in a college in Galway, and got knocked up about twenty years ago. There is a birth record of a healthy male baby born to her while she was there. I had a hell-uf-a time tracing his adoption, but the kid was farmed out to a family on Dingle Bay. The kid jumped ship recently and when last I looked, he was on the list of IRA suspects wanted for some hijackin' mischief. A buddy of his took off for Cuba but let the kid take the heat. I'm told the IRA got lots of training camps and illicit drug deals in Castro Heaven where we kain't git at 'em. I gather the rascal is coolin' his butt in some Irish or English cell by now. Shor' weird that Doc didn't retain those reports." His eyes narrowed and he winked slyly at Brian. "You wonder why—them dern thangs cost her a chunk of change, I can tell you."

Brian's face froze. "Thank you, Grayson. I don't think it's is relevant to this case, but thanks for sharing it just the same. Keep all that personal stuff under your hat and bring all pertinent information directly to me. You can't risk a law suit for malicious slander or anything more serious like a shake down—if you know what I mean."

The oily-haired, foul smelling PI swaggered out of the office with a wave of his hand. "Ya' kain't scare me, Big-Un, that whole thing is jes' a crock! Shor' thang! How often do y'all git somethin' fer nothin'? Nothin' that is, unless Frenchie wants to even the score!"

Gracie would have flipped Trotter the bird, but Brian bellowed. "That's it, Gracie. That's how Irish Michael O'Shea alias Sean Pedar got to Miami Beach! He left Vegas after Ruby Ann was murdered, probably went to Cuba and slipped back into the country on a drug boat. He must have arranged to meet Julien and Angela, provided they beat the Vegas murder rap. They drove the silver Saturn down to meet him. That's when the guys had to eliminate the only witness to any of their deals and why Julien was carrying a load of cash. He planned to launder it through Mona's land holdings. That's the damn big oil deal that Peabrain was bragging on at the airport!"

Gracie asked, "What does that have to do with Mona's murder? I don't get it. Julien needed her alive if he was going to pull this scam off!"

Brian stood and paced the office. "Shit! Maybe Irish Mike had other plans and set Julien up. Hell's bells, I don't know…"

Gracie tapped her foot on the floor, the way she did when something made her feel unsettled. It was obvious that he had copies of Bulldog's reports from somewhere he had no legal right to be and was leaving something unspoken again. "You seriously think Grayson had his fingers in the till?"

He folded his arms across his chest. "Could be. Trotter is a bottom feeder and ain't above blackmail. We've established that the perp was someone Mona knew. The woman visitor in Vegas is a mystery—could be some kind of contact with Keller, but we may never find her. If Septema Cryer didn't go to Vegas, we can count her out. Then ask Junior to check flights around the date Grayson reported seeing her. He better check with Vegas. If someone else was involved, they may have an unidentified body. But Bulldog sure as hell didn't kill Mona. He's so fat he couldn't get his ass up those attic stairs if his life depended on it."

He caught her disapproving look that telegraphed her suspicion that he was being evasive. "I just rattled his cage a bit to see if anything would fall out. Look, desperate times call for devious methods, okay?" He fingered the picture of the figure in the Saturn. "On the other hand, maybe Mona knew too much after her research on the book. It could reveal connections with IRA and Sinn Fein's illicit drugs or weapons. Where is that copy of her manuscript?"

Gracie headed for the door. "Sorry, no time for leisure reading. It's nearly 2:00. Remember your call to John Warren. You want me to stall him?"

"No way, I'll just wing it. Gracie, this case is breaking, I can feel it!" Brian stopped pacing and looked at his watch. "Ten minutes!"

Paul Simmons knocked perfunctorily and stuck his head around the door facing. "Detective Herlihy, Sir, Julien Montz and his attorney, Nick Mouton, wish to speak with you. Mouton says it's concerning his client's shoes and a release. He's demanding to see the evidence against his client."

Brian looked at Gracie, "Now them, you can stall!"

Gracie laughed, "Right on! Montz is probably gonna accuse me of using undue force to get him to buy sneakers at Shoe Town! I'll deal with them. You get on with your call and good luck!"

CHAPTER 17

MY SON IS in jail! The son I didn't even know existed is in jail in Ireland! I should have been a monk! I should have been a monk for sure! Mona, I'm so lonely and sorry it happened! He should have been our son! He recognized Rebecca had handled the thing all wrong. He remembered the Sunday when he had confessed about the drunken huggie-huggie, kissie-kissie, but he had deliberately withheld the girl's name. His Father Confessor hadn't questioned his decision to abandon football. It had seemed peculiar at the time that Kennedy had done nothing to stop him. Brian David Herlihy put his head on his desk. *Shit, nobody tried to stop him.*

The phone rang.

"Herlihy here. Yes, put him through after you inform him that I'm going to tape our conversation. Inquire if Mr. Warren has any objections. Tell him it is procedure in order for us to keep the facts straight and as a courtesy to keep him from having to repeat it all in a deposition. We'll send him a complimentary copy if he so desires. Okay, I'll wait."

He cleared his throat and reached over to press the record button on the tele-recorder attached to his phone. "Hello, Mr. Warren. This is Detective Brian Herlihy of the New Orleans Police." A pause. "Yes, we are being taped as we speak. Is that satisfactory? Thank you for speaking to me on such short notice...no, if we need any further information or have questions of a legal nature, we will advise you of that event." After another pause, Brian proceeded, "Yes, I know your time is valuable, so I won't waste it. You can wave client privilege since, as you have read, Mona Wright is dead. This tape will not be used in a court of law. Any testimony on your part would be done in a deposition."

There was a lengthy pause. Brian could hear muffled voices on the other end of the phone along with that scratchy sound that people made when they were trying to cover the microphone. John Warren discussed this matter with some other person. Brian assumed it was his legal counsel. Then Warren resumed their conversation with a discussion of Mona's upcoming novel and the problems of authorship. Brian already knew that Mona had been sending portions of the work to John Warren for several months. Warren had been as surprised as she with the arrival of identical manuscript, and with the addition of her recently added dedication and acknowledgements to her sources in Ireland. Brian asked that those portions be faxed to him.

The plot of the book was similar to Becky's rendition. Lots of intrigue and political issues and a great deal of her philosophy and worldview. Brian realized he was going to have to read the manuscript to find out if the book revealed anything that could get her killed.

The only connection Brain could see was Septema Cryer. The family was very devout Catholic and any earth shattering information Rebecca revealed to Father Eamon Kennedy about Mona's novel could have been passed on to them. Rebecca wasn't noted for keeping her mouth shut, especially these days since she took up drinking like the proverbial fish. It had been known to happen with other writers. Look at Salman Rushdie! But John Warren drew a blank at all the names, Grayson Trotter, Septema Cryer, Rebecca Webster, Julien Montz or Father Eamon Kennedy. The publisher seemed at a loss to explain what it could be. Warren explained that of course, he was not Catholic and Dr. Wright had altered names in the manuscript plus he deemed the contents of the novel to be just that—a worthy work of the author's imagination.

Their discussion seemed to be winding down and had been pretty disappointing as far as evidence was concerned. Brian looked at his scribbled notes. "Well, that's about it. I do want a copy of the other author's final manuscript by overnight mail. No, there will be no legal ramifications. Consult your attorney and get back to me."

There was a pause while a muffled conference took place.

"A release on the royalties? Sure, I'll fax you a copy and send you a true copy ASAP." This time he didn't wait for a response, he just plowed ahead. "Now, one more question. Who is this fellow anyway? Say that name again? 'Peddler,' as in 'dope peddler'?"

The single word caused Brian's fingers to tighten on the receiver. "My God, what kind of name is that?" He listened to the response, unwilling to believe his ears. He mumbled, "A pen name? Is that legal? Doesn't he give his real name? Are you certain that he didn't use the Irish name, *Pedar or Padraig*? No? Well, you can't sign a legal contract with a fictitious person, can you?" The response came quickly. "Oh, I see. You wouldn't consider it if the author proved he owned the material. When would you do that?" His blue eyes widened and then narrowed. "Listen, do us a giant favor. Please contact said Peddler, try to find out if his real name is McClintock or Sean anything—*Padraig* or *Pedar*. Those are kinda close to Peddler. Get him to assume there is a fine chance that you will decide in his favor since Doctor Mona Wright's heirs have no interest in exploiting her death through further legal actions. Tell him that they have requested you remove Doctor Wright's claim. Sweeten the deal as much as you can with promises of a considerable advance and that you have the authority to proceed with publication with him as the author."

Brian could hear an animated discussion that seemed to lead to some interesting conclusions. After considerable time, Warren resumed their conversation by exploring the legal issues of Mona's heirs concerning the book.

Brian spoke in a hushed tone. "Well, it's difficult to explain over the phone. They are in deep grief, but I know for a fact that Dr. Wright's heirs feel exactly that way at this point. I am in constant contact with her heirs and have their word on the aspect of royalties and such matters." *Remember the tape is running.*

"What I want you to do is assist me in flushing out a possible suspect in her murder. Do you have a contact number, e-mail, phone or address? You have to have someway to reach him." He listened and frowned. "Good point, I suppose it could be a woman. Well, okay, I know the legal risks you are taking so let's keep it confidential, but arrange a meeting in your office. I want you to dangle the biggest literary carrot you can manage. Put nothing in writing if possible, but tape record any conversations or have your attorney listen in. A couple of witnesses to any conversation would be even better. Sir, remind your lawyer that this is a homicide investigation. I assure you that I am your witness. It is never meant to be a legitimate book deal." Another lengthy wait. "I can't stress how much we need your cooperation. Thank you. Let me hear from you the minute he takes the bait. This person may be a freak. Someone damaged beyond fear into a species that is unpredictable and therefore dangerous. I need to caution you, never arrange to meet with this individual without police protection, even if it is a sweet old woman named Septema Cryer, a fat Private Detective named Grayson Trotter or a redheaded Southern Belle named Rebecca Webster. Since we don't want any unwelcome surprises, I will fly up the minute you can arrange the meeting."

"What?" He brightened. "Oh sure, you can still publish the novel when we get finished. That was precisely what I was thinking. There should be a great market for it by then. Consider helping us as doing your civic duty plus a great investment in the future of a bestseller full of assassin's revenge. Say, think of this as a terrific advertising campaign. What a gimmick for the press releases, right?" He continued enthusiastically, "You can probably go on *Oprah*, *The Tonight Show*, the *Good Morning Show*, the BBC, even *Larry King Live*! And who knows, you may even get another book out of it. Something like *There's No Such Thing as an Agent—Only Cops Disguised As Literary Agents*." There followed a long series of "ums," and "ahas," then silence. He laughed, "You like the idea? Great! I'll help you pull it together after we nab this bogus author. Thank you again. I assure you, Dr. Mona Wright thanks you, too." He hung up and double-checked to be sure he had turned off the tape recorder.

Gracie stood at the door and shook her head in consternation. She cracked, "Boy, that was stagy, you must be going for an Academy Award. Got a little carried away, didn't you? That's rotten police work to be crossing lines between the truth and the untruth. We don't know the heirs, and we can't give this literary agent any letter of conformation."

He settled back in his chair and put his feet on his desk. "You're like a mother hen. Relax. I know what I'm doing. I know the heirs—quite well, in fact."

She looked surprised. "Who?"

He fixed her with an enigmatic gleam in his eye. "Gracie, my buddy, this is the city with the motto, "Don't Ask, Don't Tell! How's our inmate, Shoeless Joe Montz?"

"I stalled Nick Mouton, the lawyer. He'll contact you in the morning when he brings Julien some clothes and suitable footwear. I'll be checking those shoes to be sure they don't have hollow heels full of coke or something. By the way, we can hold Julien indefinitely, but Miami is requesting extradition on the grounds of homicide. They got more than enough to indict. Bed sheet is full of fresh rooster tracks presumed to be his or Irish Mike's. Or both. And his shoes are splattered with Angela Higginbotham, alias Roxy Rocksoff's, blood. His fingerprints are all over the place including the lamp base and the hypos. Julien must have been high as a kite when he killed her. He doesn't have some other dame to corroborate his alibi this time around. The stash box had no fingerprints inside or out but we got him dead to rights on her murder. All they need is a DNA work up on the...uh...sticky stuff. They said to 'tell that big guy thanks.'"

"Good, tell them I was happy to help. Any news on the Saturn or the entertainer, Rise Stephens, Sean Padraig McClintock or Irish Mike O'Shea?"

"None as yet. You want to get the Irish terrorist kid up in Belfast or wherever?"

My son! Branden Michael McGlynn! Brian shrugged. "Naw, he's okay were he is for the time being. Let's not muddy the waters. We can get to it eventually. I'll keep it in mind, but there's usually some profit in taking a route that's not been sign-posted so avidly for us. Let's dig around for double connections and who stands to gain what. The kid is probably just as annoyed at Sean Padraig—or *Pedar,* as the case may be—McClintock AKA Irish Mike leaving him to hold the bag as Julien Montz is."

Gracie's eyes flashed darkly as if she was trying to read his thoughts. Then she shook her head and gave him a quizzical look. "I'm sorry, but I don't follow. Am I missing something here? This boy could be the son or maybe a nephew of Septema Cryer? We don't know if he's still in Ireland. What if the freak is our perp? Waiting isn't standard op. You are usually all over any lead like gravy on rice. How come not this time?"

"Learn to pick your battles, Gracie." He leaned forward and added curtly, "Help me out! We need to focus on what we got here at home. For the time being, we're going to track the leads we have." He watched closely for her reaction. When her face showed none, he added firmly, "The last thing I need right now is to tangle with the government of Northern Ireland. I said when the time comes!" His voice lost the ring of conviction as he reached for his collar and suddenly realized he had already unbuttoned it. He sucked for air and softened his voice. "And because I have enough personal emotion invested to want to finish this job and do it right—*and* because I'm tired and need a drink, a meal, a shower and a bed in that order. And because I got to hike upstate in the morning to talk to a real freak! Want to join me—in the drink and the meal at least?"

She felt her heart stop beating for a moment and then resume on automatic. Gracie sensed there was something going on. "Okay, I'd like that but it's only 2:30. What do I do until then? Go get a manicure and a massage?"

Brian scoffed, "Whatever trips your trigger and blows your skirt up, Frenchie!" He laughed then tapped his fingers on the top of the desk emphatically. "Just get me that manuscript and check the APB on the Saturn before you leave. You can get Junior to try his hand at finding out if Rebecca Webster or Septema Cryer or any member of their respective families have ever been cozy with the IRA. Then, if you aren't too busy, fill out all the paperwork crap on Julien. Dot every I and cross every T. I don't want any holes for any of those rats to crawl out through. Fire off a copy of our tape to John Warren. That ought to show good faith and keep his lawyers rich and busy. Last but not least on your list of to-dos is a visit with Septema Cryer. She may need a woman to talk to. Work your magic and find out what she is hiding. I gotta call Robert St. Denis about Mona's will and somehow get a permission or two.

"After that, I'm dropping by Rebecca Webster's house. She deserves to know about the reports Grayson made on her. I got to get her to sign some papers."

Gracie looked confused. "What papers? Is there something I forgot?"

Brian grinned and shook his head. "You can't forget what you don't know. It's a personal matter, okay? Keep your nose out of it or I'll pick up Bulldog Trotter and you can sacrifice yourself to his lechery if you're ready to debauch a bit. Meet you at Mandina's. If you get there first, make a mark and if I get there first I'll rub it out! Get a table and order me a beer. I'll try to make it by 6:00 before they get so crowded that we're drunk before we get a table instead of being drunk afterwards."

She finally got to shoot someone the finger that she had intended to give Trotter, even if it was to his backside and shouted, "Up yours! I'll see you at Mandy's at six-ish unless I get a better offer!" Then she muttered to herself, "I don't know whether to laugh or cry…"

ROBERT ST. DENIS was very cooperative. He answered the questions. It was exactly as Rebecca said it was. St. Denis was cautioned about pushing for a reading until the case was solved. He promised to keep everything confidential.

That matter accomplished, Brian picked up the bulky manuscript and called Becky as he headed out of the door. A groggy voice muttered something about being in bed with a hangover. He didn't give her time to think up an excuse not to see him. He instructed her to have a beer ready for him, but nothing for her to drink except an Alka-Seltzer on the rocks.

CHAPTER 18

Later, Rebecca, drink in hand, met him at her condo's front door and leaned her face so close to him that the alcohol made him catch his breath. She quipped, "Still checking up on me, Big-Un? I guess that's a good sign, huh? You look awful." She held up her glass and drained it. "Join me? Oops, I forgot—you're on duty. Well, can I get you—like a glass of water or something?"

He followed her into the kitchen. "Nope, just need to tell you a couple of things." He was pleased that Rebecca was being so cooperative. She seemed subdued, but it was obvious she had been drinking all day. Perhaps her so called hangover prevented hysterics when he told her about Trotter's reports. It didn't seem to phase her in the least.

She refilled her glass and laughed the information off with a dry comment. "Really? Mona was having me tailed? So that's why scuzbucket Trotter was poking around here. Came to the door looking like Ignatius J. Reilly from John Kennedy Toole's book, *A Confederacy of Dunces*. The Neanderthal said he was a census taker then he asked a lot of dumb questions—even propositioned me! What a wretch he is! I ain't that bad off—yet."

She waved her hands in the air and suddenly clicked her fingers together as she said, "Say, maybe he was the heavy breather on her phone. Or maybe ole' Ignatius sent Mona those dumb roses at the radio station. It would be just like that dickhead to try to make time with her. That's a laugh! Do you think Mona knew about the baby in Ireland all along? That's another laugh. But it's just like her to keep it to herself. She went to see Father Kennedy a lot when she was researching that damn book of hers. Oh, don't look so surprised! He and Sean were her connections with the IRA. She probably knew their secret handshakes and had a decoder ring. Your precious priest is involved in the Irish struggles up to his eyeballs. Yeah! There was all sort of togetherness you never knew about! He arranged all of our warrior queen's trips for her and knew about her book. God have mercy, there are organizations a gal shouldn't mess around with and the IRA is one of them. I didn't admit to you that I knew the stepbrother but all that terrorist stuff drives me bonkers."

"Pretty grim business. I'm glad you're catching on that it's wise to tell me now."

Glaring sideways at him with a glassy look, she snapped, "Don't go blamin' me! Mona's research scared me to death! But no matter what I said, she kept sticking her nose where it didn't belong. It was no coincidence she stayed with Kennedy's folks. But I can't imagine Eamon telling her about us. Especially since I sent gobs of money to take care of the kid. That money wasn't easy to come by, either, but I sent it out of the goodness of my heart, you understand?"

Brian stayed quiet. He was learning more by letting her rattle than he expected. Maybe this was the right approach. But the signals she was sending out were so jumbled, he couldn't figure out what she was hiding. Besides, if he believed anything Rebecca said he was an idiot. She'd tell him anything as long as the vodka was flowing. Still, he wondered about the money. Rebecca wasn't especially famous for doing anything out of the goodness of her heart—particularly if it entailed bleeding green backs.

She searched for a cigarette. "Damn it, Brian, say something! This silence is killing me. And stop looking at me like," she stuttered, "l-ike a damn cop. I need a friend to tell me that I had nothing to do with Mona's murder. Tell me my money went to our son, not to the frigin' IRA."

Her wide-set eyes seemed to shift in and out of focus. Her nostrils dilated and the skin of her face drew back against the high cheekbones. "Maybe Father Kennedy sent her those dumb roses to warn her or something. What 'cha wanna bet he was helping the IRA with my money! I know Eamon's stepmother found out her first husband, Padraig McClintock, was never killed. He was involved up to his ass with the resistance up north. His son, Sean, was a sick prick and just as evil. They were pumping drug money into the IRA along with every thing they could extort from people like me.

She stared at him, full of emotions he could only guess at. "This is hard for me, too. I knew something was wrong, very wrong, when Mona received those damn flowers with no name. I thought it was strange that she had the Pillsbury Doughboy tracing Julien after all this time. But she didn't even tell me he was checking up on me!

Then it was stranger still when she had the flowers traced to the florist who delivered them to WGSO, but never mentioned a word to me." Becky's voice became sarcastic. "What if Ole' Saint Humbug sent those roses? It may have worked in some way because I sensed she was on to something. She stopped having anything to do with Father Kennedy or me until the last week before she was killed." Becky tried to snub out her cigarette and missed the ashtray. She made an elaborate effort to sweep the ashes off the counter into the container then she clunked the ashtray on the counter. "Murdered!"

He cleared his throat, "Becky, did you or Mona ever talk about Septema Cryer?"

"Who is Septema Cryer? Nice name, though. Sounds like a Cajun name or one of Mona's fictional characters. Nothing unimaginative about Mona's portrayals, no sir! I can see a broad with a deceptively innocent face who is obsessed with revenge as she slashes and cuts her victims in an orgy of violent self-expression."

"You ever tell Father Kennedy about the contents of Mona's book?"

"Oh, I might have mentioned it in passing. All of us having spent time in Ireland and him being so gung-ho about Irish freedom and all that."

"Do you ever mess around with the various bizarre folks that hang out in Irish pubs and talk about the book?"

"Hell, no! I was pissed at her about the damn thing. If I'd had my way, we'd of had a book burning before the crap got published. Anyway, after she spooked me about talking with Father Kennedy, I thought things got real weird. Mona called me on the Thursday evening before the Faulkner party. Maybe to warn me, I don't know. But something was a little *off*." She shook her head then rubbed the back of her neck. "It scared me shitless to think he might have told her about our baby. I kept going, 'Mona, what are you thinking'? But she wouldn't listen to me."

He looked into her hollow eyes. She looked twice her age and he thought he could see her as a made-up Barbie doll with petulant mouth and empty eyes in a nursing home forty years from now. Alone, spending her days lost in the bitter smoke of her memories. He asked, "What do you mean, 'off'?"

"Dunno, just not normal. Like she knew something she wasn't telling me. She swore to publish her book, come hell or high water. I didn't understand at the time. Then she told me she had talked to Kennedy that morning. I changed the subject, of course, stupid me!

Mona knew I was evading—she always spotted my evasions. She actually liked saving me from the truth. Trouble is it wasn't always good for me and certainly not good for her. I thought it was about...well, you know...what I thought it was about. She rang off and didn't even say goodbye. Here I thought we were best friends, so I was pissed."

Brian didn't know whether to believe this confession or not. Becky had lied to him about Mardi Gras night, and she always had been a spinner of yarns. She'd say anything that suited her fancy. Had Mona destroyed the evidence of the flowers deliberately? He'd have to check at her house. No mention had been made by Trotter—neither in his reports nor his conversation. Maybe Bulldog didn't think it was relevant, or maybe Mona had told him not to mention it. Was she thinking that she was protecting him because of the baby? At no point had he had time to step back and take stock. First the devastation of Mona's murder then a weeping Becky on his hands with her desperate explanations—all the while telling him about the results of their one night stand. She never said that she was sorry or that she hadn't meant for things to turn out like they did. Then there was Miami. Damn—he had to read that book of hers. There was a moment of heavy silence, then he mumbled harshly, "That's okay, Beck. Let's drop it. Hindsight is twenty-twenty. Give me some space to sort it out."

She reached out and patted his hand. "Do you think she knew about the baby?"

Brian felt a stab of familiar pain but simply moved his hand. He shook his head and shrugged, "I don't know, Beck. Will you just stop harping on it? Maybe she guessed. She was around us...drunk and sober."

Rebecca tittered, "Yeah, I know. I kinda like it when you talk like that. Officer Herlihy, I plead guilty to drunkenness, your Honor, but innocent to all the rest, which is a pack of lies." Then she sobered, "I won't have to testify to all this, will I?"

He nodded vigorously. "I'm afraid so and soon. Just sit tight, avoid any more of your nostalgic side trips to Audubon Place and try to stay sober. I have to speak with Eamon Kennedy first."

Rebecca's voice filled with anguish. "Will they arrest me on some charge? They can't arrest me over a...past indiscretion, can they?"

He shook his head. "But, Beck, I can be..." he struggled with the word... "implicated and so can you." He intended to leave no doubt in her mind about the seriousness of their position. "Remember Mona's last will and testament?"

She rose and moved around the bar as if to get another drink for herself. She stopped behind him and began to slide her hands up and down his arms. When she spoke, her voice was devoid of humor. "Oh shit, I had forgotten all about her will. We're screwed."

He shook her hands away and stood.

Rebecca, eyes alight with impish malice, puckered her lips at him and said in a velvet slur, "All business! Brian David Herlihy, give me a kiss for old times' sake."

He shook his head. "Cut that stuff out!" He turned toward the door.

"Where are you going?" she whined.

"There's work to do. I have to find out if Padraig McClintock's murdering son is alive or dead." Brian felt an odd sort of relief he always felt when unconnected things troubling him clicked together. He wished the bastard was dead, but he needed for him to be alive. Maybe the law can kill him later. *Padriag. Now I know why I have always hated that crappy name!* He shuddered.

Becky gave an elaborate shrug and in a flat voice sighed, "Do whatever you want, Big Un. I don't care anymore." She shook her head, lips tight and pale. "I'm feeling woozy. Think I'll stumble to the couch or go back to bed with my favorite medication." She was still on the sofa when he let himself out.

CHAPTER 19

Rebecca staggered off the sofa when the doorbell rang. Rolling her eyes, she grumbled, "Shit, what does the fella' want this time?" She shouted, "You're really pissing me off here. I'm not in the mood for lovin', Brian Baby, so stick it in your ear!" Thick-headed, unsure of where she was, she paused and grabbed the back of a chair. The room was swaying or she was swaying, she couldn't tell which.

The bell rang again. "Okay, just hold your horses!"

She wobbled though the entryway on quaking legs and peered through the side panel. A brunette woman stood on her porch. Becky didn't recognize her, but the person seemed at ease—very tall and voluptuous yet dignified in an aqua business suit that looked expensive. She had a bunch of roses—probably a neighbor expressing her condolences or better yet, a reporter. A niggling thought inserted itself into her brain like a pencil point being pushed into Silly Putty. Even though Brian had said to be cautious and to keep quiet, Becky longed to be in the spotlight with all this murder stuff. Flowers were such a nice touch. She mumbled groggily, "Oh, horse feathers. Brian's being an old stick in the mud about everything and I'll speak to a reporter if I have a mind to, Doctor-Hog-It-All Wright. This is my fifteen minutes of fame. The press can know me, too. You and ole' Beck have been seen together at all sorts of social functions."

Rebecca twitched her shoulders, glanced at herself in the hall mirror and raised a hand to flick a strand of bronze hair from her forehead. It promptly flopped forward again. "Forget it!" Fluffing up her hair, she muttered, "Jesus, I'm a mess! I hope she doesn't want pictures." She shouted through the door, "Just a minute, sweetie."

The woman on the stoop waved the roses at the door. "Take your time, *Senora* Webster." The voice was strangely guttural with a slightly theatrical Spanish accent.

Rebecca found her a bit strange, but she called out, "Hey, just give me a second, I need a little fixin' up before I meet my public." She moistened her lips. "Lipstick, oh lipstick, where art thou?" Then she adjusted a drooping fake eyelash and spat on her index fingers to slick down her eyebrows.

The voice sounded slightly urgent and the accent was heavier. "No *problem-o*. Let me enter *pronto*, then we shall fix you very special."

Becky stared into the mirror and tried on a smile. Her reflection looked like death warmed over. "Oh, what the hell, I can always say the damage is caused from grieving so much."

She opened the door and craned her neck in both directions up and down the deserted street. "Where's your car? It is the rainy season, you know. There's a security officer around here somewhere. Did you run into him? He'll give you a ticket for parking on St. Charles."

The tall woman brushed past her and tittered in a high, raspy voice, "No, Senora, I didn't see hem. I parked around the corner in my own space."

"I run this joint. You don't live here do you?"

"No, oh no—just visiting an amigo and doing a leetle beziness."

Rebecca noticed the woman's eyes were pitch-black with a crazy glint as if the light were reflecting off of something fractured behind them. "Phooey! I thought you were from the newspaper. Is this some sort of a sick joke? I'm not buying anything! I just lost my best friend and don't have time for sales pitches. Besides, there is a no house-to-house solicitation ordinance in these condos. I think you'd better go."

Irritated, Becky reached for the doorknob to usher the woman outside. Suddenly a strong, gloved hand grabbed her arm and spun her around into the hallway. The roses scattered across the floor as the woman jammed a flat palm against the door behind her. The door slammed shut. The woman then threw the deadbolt.

Rebecca lost her footing and slammed onto the tile. Her visitor grabbed her by the hair and jerked her prone body into the living room. The stranger stood over Rebecca's quaking form and spat out words with sudden clarity, "Now, Miss Bitch, you're dead if you scream. Get yourself up and onto that chair. We got some talkin' ta' do. Be bloody quick or you'll end up like your friend!"

Rebecca gasped, unable to right herself. She struggled to her knees and began to drag herself into the chair. A foot caught her in the thigh as if to help her on her way. "Move your butt! I haven't got all day." The Spanish accent had disappeared, as well as any trace of a feminine pitch. This was a man's voice, low and feral, the growl of a wolf, as lethal sounding as death itself.

Rebecca sank onto the chair and looked up at her assailant. The face had gone from looking engaging to damp and enraged. His black eyes were pitiless with hate and fury. Rebecca's voice sounded like someone else's—little and broken and far away. "I don't know you. Why are you doing this?"

His gloved hand reached up to his head and pulled at the hair there. He shoved the wig in Rebecca's face and cackled with the sound of breaking glass, "Yes, you do know me, you cunt! You're the rich American bitch who dropped a baby on my parents. Oh, now you remember your glorious stay in Galway, don't cha' now?" He hissed, "I'm the blighter who took your money when you fobbed off your crappy kid."

Becky scrambled back into the chair like a wild thing, eyes wide with panic and dismay, her mouth open wide. As recognition seeped into her eyes, she put her hands over her mouth to muffle a scream. "You're Sean McClintock, Father Kennedy's brother!"

The hand slapped her hands away. "Yeah, only it's *stepbrother*. Sean." White spit collected at the corners of the garish red mouth. "Now let's get down to business. You told anyone about our deal or me?"

Becky slumped backwards, her heart thumping, perspiration cold on her lips, paralyzed by not knowing what to do. She tried to think straight. "No, only Father Kennedy knows. My parents don't even know. You're only—"

He interrupted her as the hand flicked out and slapped her hard. "You lie, you rich bitch!" He grunted, "Bosh! Your parents been payin' through the nose." His wine-colored lips drew back in a ghoulish grin. "Too bad you never told 'em what really happened. You Yanks are good at ignoring things you can't be bothered with..." he laughed a humorless laugh, "...until your sins bite you in the buns. Your deception worked fine fer Ireland, the good padre and me!" His smile vanished. "The frigin' IRA is to blame," he said angrily, forcing the words between heavy rasping breaths.

Rebecca was seeing double from his blow and feeling close to being sick. She sobbed, "Money—I've got money—"

He grabbed her face, turning her toward him. "Forget your dough, you fucking little slut! The frigin' IRA forgot me—hung me out to dry. So fucking proud of their pandering—so righteous—so fucking proud of themselves and the damned church playing God! Bugger 'em all!" Sean's eyes glared relentlessly down at her. "That goddamned psychologist knew! She twigged to the racket, got it right all right. The buggers fobbed me off after years of me doing their business. They turned on me after usin' me as their pet assassin. Me, killin' blokes fer them along the way, 'en gettin' nothing good from it all. Chucked me fer sellin' their damn drugs, they did! How am I ta pay for my disease? But now *her* book is *my* book!"

"What?" she sobbed, but could see he was not really speaking to her. His fake eyelashes fluttered as though he was going into some kind of trance.

His tone became matter-of-fact—no pride, no regret. "But the good doctor was quite keen to ferret out all the facts. Too keen for her own good, eh? But she didn't forget ole' Sean. No way!" His bald head bobbed up and down in a macabre rhythm as he grinned and said, "Oh, she just kills me. Kills me! Kills me! Wrote me into her book, she did. The arrogant, medlin' fool did a great job, too. Shame she's cold and stiff. Alas, I'll just have to dedicate the book to her. Too bad she didn't make the connections she should have made with the troubles, but I'm gonna straighten things right out. It's gonna sure get up their arse!"

He seemed to be considering something as he nodded his shaved head. "The world is gonna' remember Sean Pedar McClintock as the main character in that fuckin' novel." His distorted face looked annoyed through the heavy make-up. "Only problem is, she calls my character, Padraig McPherson." Again the cackle, "Hell, what does it matter? Fame is fame, right?"

Something was rising, something terrible. Whatever it was had passed, he had settled it. Blinking his fake eyelashes very rapidly, he looked at her with an amused expression. Suddenly his eyes narrowed like a snake's as he barked in derision. "Oh yes, you know me."

Rebecca gasped—under the aqua skirt bulged an erection.

"You can make me famous, can't you? The best part is that nobody will ever know and yet the whole world will know who I am! You agree with that, don't you, Duckie?" Two fingers of the gloved hand reached out and pinched her cheek. Then he grabbed her chin, leaned down and presses his mouth to hers.

She wrenched her head back, cringing in terror and pleading shakily, "I didn't tell Mona anything. She must have found out in Ireland. She hired a private investigator—he's to blame! Go talk to him! Just take the money—please let me go. I'm *sorry, sorry, sorry.* I won't tell anyone."

Sean smiled cruelly through smeared magenta lipstick. He reached out and put his right hand behind her rigid neck, patted her red hair with the other glove and whined in mock anguish, "Pretty, very pretty. I used to have a fine head of red hair like yours, but I sacrificed it for the cause of Ireland. I wish I had it back." His hand swept up a handful of hair and closed hard. "Ummm...red hair makes me hard. May I have yours?"

Rebecca had no time to answer before he jerked her out of the chair and twisted her body backwards until she was on her knees before him. His penis smashed against her nose. She couldn't help but scream. It was almost a pretty scream—high and sweet, but of short duration. As the scream left her throat, he kicked off the heels and planted his feet firmly as he stood astraddle her head. Sweeping his strong right arm around her shoulders, he twisted her hair in his other hand, smashed her small head back against his crotch, and twisted. His black eyes half closed at the satisfying crunch of the small cervical bones as they snapped in her neck—a slight popping like cracking peanut shells. Experience had taught him that the bones tended to snap loudly when he crossed the line, just like a saltine, with no warning. Rebecca went limp, a final scream locked in her throat forever.

He whispered in her ear, "*Hasta la vista, Chiquita.*" And eased her body face up onto the chair in which she had been sitting. He cackled joyfully, "Creamed in me panties, I did!" The moisture oozed down his thigh beneath his skirt. He shuddered, "My, my, but isn't life one big gigantic joke? Nothing but banana peels and pratfalls! A fart in a cathedral! If this is my fault, then it was a *snap*! Quick and with very little clean-up!"

He spread his legs in front of Rebecca's unseeing eyes, took a lace hankie from his pocket and daintily wiped his crotch.

CHAPTER 20

BRIAN ASSESSED HIS encounter with Rebecca as he cut across town at peak traffic time toward Mandina's on Canal Street. He braked for a red light and sat staring at the gridlocked intersection. He even considered pulling out his little red beanie light to signify the police, but thought better of it. He needed some think time, and the traffic provided it. *Did you know about us, Mona? I got a kid in an Irish jail. Crap, gotta get her out of my head.* He shoved back those thoughts in favor of focusing on what he had in the way of facts—or speculations. The evidence in the attic proved Julien Montz did not kill his estranged wife. But if the perp worked for Julien Montz—and Brian thought he had—what could be the motive? Neither of them would profit in any obvious fashion as a result of crime. If Montz bought a hit on Mona to inherit the family farm, then his partner may have double-crossed him by setting Julien up to be brought down for Ruby's murder and then traced back to New Orleans. What in the hell was Julien doing with that wad of cash? What did he have to sell?

Then there's Harry Benjamin Keller. The killer could be either a professional or low-life that Keller had called in. But he left hairs and DNA at the scene of a botched rape. Keller seemed to be too smart to make such mistakes unless he didn't care. Either something rattled him or it was deliberate. *Revenge on me rather than Julien?* It was plausible that the bastard wanted someone to know for certain that Mona's assailant wasn't her cocaine drenched ex. But who the hell was it and what would he gain from killing her? If it was Keller, he had already set Montz up to take the fall for Angela and probably Ruby, so why so careless?

Then there was Rebecca's constant obsession with the baby, and her spitefulness about having trusted Julien—probably with her money as well as her body. Not to mention her deleting the messages from Mona's machine and her fears about what that damn book could reveal. She insisted they would own the rights to the new book. Christ, that fact alone could bury them. The book presented a nest of personal problems. It disturbed him to think of making a buck off that book. Even if he and Becky were exonerated, maybe they shouldn't profit in any fashion for *their* past crime either. But that would have to be decided later—much later.

There was something else odd. Something had jarred him when Rebecca made a crack in passing to Ignatius J. Reilly—Toole's king of the Lucky Dog salesmen. He hung out at some New Orleans bar on Canal Street, a transvestite's place with a parrot act. Something about the circumstance rang a bell, but it teased him by hanging just outside of his mind's reach. He frowned as he tried to remember.

CHAPTER 21

BY FIVE, GRACE had accomplished what she could of the endless list of tasks Brian had given her and then delegated the rest. She grabbed her purse and side arm and headed for the address of Septema Cryer in the Irish Channel district of the city. She parked in an auto-booting zone and plunked her police parking card on the inside of the windshield. No officer in their right mind would leave it under the wiper. It wouldn't be there when they returned and they could be on foot if the car wore an elaborate orange boot.

Cryer lived in one side of a camel-back double. The weathered porch sagged and the second story, set back off the street, looked as if it were ready to collapse. Camel-backs were ingenious inventions to save money. Houses of that era were sold and taxed by the number of feet that ran along the street. By shoving the second story back a room or so, the price of the house dropped considerably.

A string of Christmas lights was looped haphazardly from one porch support to another. Gracie ducked some decaying Mardi Gras beads dangling from the broken central light fixture and knocked. At first, she thought that there was no one home. But after several loud knocks, she heard someone limping down the long hall to the door. A curtain in the door's glass window was gently pulled aside. An eye stared bleakly through the smudged window. Smiling, Gracie held up her badge and said, "Hello, I am Officer Grace Reme of the NOPD. Septema Cryer?"

The door opened slowly. A dwarf of a woman stood in the hallway. Her skin was a soft yellow even though her features showed clearly that she was of African-American extraction. Her head was wrapped in a faded red bandana, and large golden loops swung from her earlobes almost touching her shoulders. Her dress was faded blue and stopped mid-calf revealing brown orthopedic shoes laced above the ankles. One shoe bore an elevated sole and a metal leg brace.

Gracie displayed her badge again.

The woman eyed the badge with a look that was not quite scorn but had anger in it. When she spoke, her speech was the typical Cotton-eyed Joe talk used to give the impression of a slightly dimwitted but trustworthy servant. Gracie recognized it as a familiar ploy to disguise the intelligence of many Southern blacks. "What cha' wantin'? Ah be Septema Cryer 'en Ah want to be lef' alone. Y'all done sent a boy-cop to talk to me. What cha'll need now? That doctor's killin' ain't none of mah con-cern, ya heah?"

Gracie had been on the force long enough to know better than to confront the woman. She spoke firmly but with a smile to soften her request. "Yes, sorry to bother you again, but I just want to check out a few things. May I come in?"

"No, Ah'll step to de porch. Yo kin' sit a spell on the stoop if yo's a mind to."

Gracie obliged and they sat down on the steps.

Gracie was glad to stay outside where she could keep an eye on her car. It was prudent to do so in this neighborhood. She sat forward on the step, her hands held out, palms open toward Septema. "Ms. Cryer, we can't confirm you were at the hospital unless you have someone we can check it out with. This is just routine, you understand, but I have to tie up all the loose ends. Then we'll leave you alone."

"You'll leave me alone no-how, Baby Girl! Shor' Ah done tolt' a lie to dat fella 'cause he wuz jes't a fresh-faced youngen' 'en. Don't have no business hearing mah story. But between jes't us gals, Ah has a notion to fill in the gaps." She patted Gracie on the arm like a mother sending a child off to grade school. "It kin' be tolt to you."

Gracie wondered if Septema had deliberately given Junior the run-around to stall for time, and if so, why? "Why didn't you give the information to Officer Simmons?"

Septema wrinkled her brow in thought then gave a little nod. "Oh, it were stupid of me, now Ah sees thet, but at the time I wuz busy sortin' thaings up a bit in mah mind."

"Why did you change your mind?"

"They's knowed thet big guy done all of us'n a favor puttin' Harry away. Ah owes him a lot fer fixin' it so's Ah kin sleep at night. Yo reckon yo kin' stand ta hear mah reasons?"

Feeling awkward, Gracie responded, "Ms. Cryer, if you can stand to tell me, I can stand to hear it."

Jane Stennett

"That man ain't human. Harry Keller is a devil-demon. Ah wuz seventeen. Ya' think Ah look right ole'? Well, I ain't old. Ah be torn up inside. He beat the life out of me...broke mah hip 'en punctured mah womb what wuz carryin' his chile. When mah fambly took me to the Mercy Hospital, they took my dead baby 'en tolt me Ah kain't never have no more babies. No matter that beast been locked up fer' killin' my chile, he done give me the syphilis. Now, Ah'm only half-a woman. No man gonna' marry half a woman."

Gracie thought it was strange that any woman named Cryer could relate all this horror and never cry. She tried to say something comforting, but the words caught in her throat.

Septema heard the other woman's sharp intake of breath. For a moment, neither of them spoke. Then she sighed, "Ah wuz at the church-house on the evenin' that lady doctor wuz kilt. Father Kennedy gives me a job cleanin'."

Grace concentrated on not overreacting, but she was even more convinced that the woman had something up her sleeve that required more time than she had been given. Perhaps someone didn't expect Mona's body to be found so quickly. She kept her suspicions to herself and inquired softly, "Septema, why didn't you simply tell the officer where you were that evening? If it isn't relevant, why lie?"

Septema sighed, "Ah wuz protectin' myself. St. Denis fambly wanted me at their swanky affair, but too many white folks kin' give me the jitters. Ah don't like their pity and their stares—like they's gonna' put me in one of their books 'er somthin'. Besides, Ah always clean on thet day, no-how. Couldn't risk losin' neither job, Missy." She hesitated, then continued in a whisper, "En, keep this between us women-folks. Ah wuz shieldin' the priest, too."

"How so? And why the change of heart now, Ms Cryer?"

"Missy, Ah wuz low in spirits 'bout tellin' dat spiteful lie to da' putry boy-copper. But Ah didn't knowed what to do, so's Ah ast' mah fambly. They say thet Ah gotta' tell y'all."

"Go on then, tell us what?" Gracie demanded irritably. She thought Septema was overdoing the affected black speech a bit.

A smile came to the speaker's face, though it didn't reach the eyes. "Father Eamon treated me with kindness 'en he done found work fer me with the St. Denis fambly afta' they moved here. So, Baby Girl, ya' kin see how hard it is gonna be to tell on him?" She rolled her eyes comically and huffed a time of two for effect, "Ah might as well be out with it—the good Father Eamon Kennedy has got a woman-friend. Ah wuz finishin' thet evenin' when up come a tall Spanish-lookin' lady in mighty fancy dress. This woman went into his private rooms—y'all know what Ah mean? They had some kinda' spat 'bout sending' roses to some other lady. A sort of horror done come over me, but Ah kain't keep silent no longer. Father Eamon bein' a priest 'en all, it didn't seem fittin' fer me to say. He's been good to me."

When Gracie said nothing, Septema continued off-handedly, "A 'course, Ah wuz sorry Ah seen it, but Ah swear it done happen by chance. Must have been the Good Lord's will 'cause Ah wuz strayin' from mah duties and wuz drawn to dustin' de windowsills in the hall what leads to Father Eamon's apartment. But Ah seen them embracin' 'en thet' bitch tried to kiss him, shor' 'nuff."

Gracie bit her lip in thought then asked, "You can describe this woman?"

Septema said, "Oh yeah. A hussy ain't easy to fergit! Mah folks is beholden ta' thet' Big-Un fer puttin' Harry in the slammer. Thet' devil woulda' sure come afta' me fer revenge." Her affected cover slipped off as she said very clearly, "Officer Reme, tell Detective Herlihy that he shouldn't complicate things. We'll work it all out ourselves."

"How?" Gracie asked, her eyes still fixed on the woman's shiny face. A chill came over her, but she managed to not let her feelings show.

The woman shrugged, "Vermin is vermin," she said. "Ya gotta' control 'em somehow." Suddenly the vaguely confused expression left Septema's face and the phony speech was gone. She was talking deliberately, holding Gracie with her eyes. "You want me to be frank? Harry Benjamin Keller will never forget a copper either—'specially the one that put him away in the first place. That upright gentleman could never begin to understand a heart so hot for revenge."

"Revenge?" Gracie looked incredulous. "Is there some threat? Explain it to me. Is there something I don't know? I know Detective Herlihy can take care of himself."

"If ya' think that, then you don't know very much. Now, will you please give him my message?"

"Of course, I will, but—"

Septema rolled her eyes then closed both of them. She made the sign of the cross, and with her lips pursed firmly, she whispered, "Oh, I suppose I've said enough for one day."

It had been a fluent piece of speech, and Gracie wondered how uneducated Septema really was. But it was painfully obvious that

Septema had terminated the interview and would reveal nothing more. Exasperated, Gracie got to her feet to leave. She dusted off the back of her skirt, and said, "Thanks, Ms. Cryer. Never mind, I trust that we'll explore the subject of revenge later. I'll be sure to warn Detective Herlihy. Can I get back to you with a police artist?"

"Fine, anything I can do to help. I hear that your artist is extraordinary."

Gracie turned back to wave goodbye to Septema, still seated on the sagging steps. She was surprised to see the tiny woman watching her. Her face seemed to have slipped and changed. Now, Septema was open and smiling, her eyes squinting in the sun as though they had done nothing at all save exchange jokes and talked about gardens. The cover slipped back in place as the black woman drawled, "Ah does look forward ta' passin' time with ya. Maybe us gals kin have an R.C. Cola 'en a Moon Pie next time, Missy—that is if ya'll is a'mind ta' brang 'em.'

Septema Cryer was not what she seemed. Nothing was as it seemed. Gracie thought. She held up a hand in Septema's direction, partly a wave and partly a warning and said sharply, "Ms Cryer, you are far too sensible to continue to insult my intelligence."

Septema Cryer clapped her hands like a child and cackled, "Sho 'nuff, Missy! 'Nuf said!"

CHAPTER 22

BRIAN SWUNG INTO Mandina's parking lot. He was very hungry. As he entered the favorite neighborhood hangout, he was assailed by the aroma of seafood. There were men and women standing along the crowded bar. Some were watching a basketball game. The Final Four. They drank old fashions, beers and assorted drinks for which the place was famous. The business suits belonged to legal eagles hanging out here after work and talking sports, women and shop. The cigars puffed as some of the city's biggest business deals were made here at Mandy's bar.

Huge trays of steaming bowls of turtle soup, plates of French bread dripping with butter, and platters heaped with French fried onion rings and the best seafood in the world swung over waiter's heads—waiters who had been here since they inherited the job from their fathers. The cafe had a worn, faded look with pictures of old streetcars that used to trundle up and down Canal Street and ships at the docks.

Brian nudged his way through the crowd toward Gracie's table. He waved and shouted over the commotion around him, "I've changed my drink order. I'll have a Scotch on the rocks—twice as much Scotch as rocks!"

She shouted, "I already told K.J. He's got it ready. I ordered for you, too. How does turtle soup followed by French fried onion rings and trout *meuniere* sound? I can cancel it if it's wrong. How did everything go, okay?"

He returned her grin and sat. "Order is swell! Sure, the heirs have signed the book's release." He patted his breast pocket.

"Let me see it."

"Nope. Wait and be surprised like the rest of the world. But you can stop worrying, Mother Hen!"

Grace shushed him. "Listen to this. It's strange that Septema opened up like a swinging door to me after all that stalling around with Junior. Seems her family got her to come clean. She claims that she was too embarrassed and fearful of losing her job with the St. Denis family to tell Junior the whole story. It was like she had been stalling for time. The woman is quite an actress—got the sarcastic Uncle Tom's Toddy thing down to a science. Junior's pretty sharp to pick up on her omissions. Seems she cleaned for Father Kennedy on the evening they wanted her at the party. She is a mini-person, no bigger than a minute. She is definitely not the visitor in Vegas. She was mutilated by Keller. He *murdered* her unborn baby and he busted up her hip something awful. Then he gave her venereal disease in the bargain. Anyway, after a womanly chat and before she could wow me with her rendition of 'Ole Black Joe,' she told me that she overheard a squabble about roses between Kennedy and some fancy-dressed woman. She called the dame 'Father Eamon's woman.' Apparently they were lovey-dovey or something in his apartment." She felt as if she had been blathering non-stop, but all their conversations had been like this lately—strained, full of pauses. She stopped talking as the waiter served their drinks.

Brian lifted his drink with an unconcerned glance in her direction and took a long sip. Then, closing his eyes, he sighed, "Great, mighty great!"

Gracie eyed him suspiciously and quipped, "You aren't surprised about Cryer at all are you?"

"I sent you to do a job. You did it."

"And I bet you already knew she was a mini-person, didn't you? Well, maybe this will set you back on your heels. Septema sends you a warning about her old beau, Harry Keller. Told you to keep hands off. Her family is involved in something, but she clamed up. I had Junior check them out. It might interest you to know that her cousin, Rufus, is employed at Angola as a guard."

Seemingly unperturbed by the information, Brian drank deeply again and commented, "My, my, fancy that. Seems Septema invented a witness protection program of her own. He'll keep an eye on Harry Keller for us. By the way, where's your date, ole' Ignatius J. Reilly?" Then a thought hit him like a bolt of lightning. "A woman? Eamon Kennedy has a woman? Oh, I don't think so! I think it is our tall stranger from Vegas—and may not be a woman at all. Gracie, we've been looking in the wrong city for that Saturn!"

He grabbed Gracie by the hand across the table. "Shit, Toole had Ignatius Reilly in a bar here in New Orleans! Someplace like the old My-Oh-My Club full of transvestites and female impersonators. Damn it! The killer returned. He's an entertainer and was working in a club in Miami when he met Julien and Roxy doing their Bonnie-and-Clyde thing. Call Vehicular to locate the Saturn in New Orleans. Our perp took the car to drive here after he helped Julien dump Roxy. He was planning to meet Julien with the cash then finish Julien off. He deliberately left that news clipping to set Julien up for Mona's death, but we nabbed Montz before the two could reconnect here. The killer hasn't left because we got Julien and the cash! So, he's gotta move and he's gotta move fast. Whatever he's planning, it's either about to happen or it's already in motion."

Gracie straightened up and grabbed her cell, cupping her hand around the instrument to block out the noise. "Get me Officer Paul Simmons." She listened then gasped, "What? *Who*?" She glanced at Brian. "When? Where? We'll get right on it!"

She turned to Brian. "Boss, we got a real problem. That priest of yours has turned up missing. He was in a confessional with some tall, Spanish woman this evening. The janitor, Innis Moyer went to fetch him when the police sketch artist was leaving the church about 5:30. Innis says that he and Septema Cryer watched Father Kennedy and the woman take off in a silver auto—Innis and Septema both remember it because they argued about the make of the car. He thinks it was either a Lexus or a Saturn. Septema said to tell you it is the whore she told Missy about this afternoon."

"Oh, Christ!" Brian didn't wait. He dropped a couple of twenties on the table and jumped up, hurrying between the tables. He dodged through the crowd at the bar. He jostled past a teenage girl and in turn was staggered himself by a hefty woman whose shoulder grazed him as he shoved past to the doorway.

Gracie followed him outside. "Hold up! There's more! We have to get to City Park. They've located the car, but there's trouble! It was called in by two joggers who saw a brunette woman jump from the passenger's side and flee the scene. The couple thought it might be car trouble or a medical emergency so they went over to see if they could offer assistance. When they got to the car, it wasn't empty—it has a body in it. They called 911."

CHAPTER 23

The bayou at City Park was a scene of organized chaos. Lights from patrol cars, police personnel taping off the area, and the two joggers were standing at one side, eyes covered, shoulders shaking. The ever-present Darrel Pitts, a moose of a man with burly shoulders, the typical athlete gone to pasture mostly behind a desk, was trying to interview them. Officer Paul Simmons was shoving the reporter outside the tape and saying sternly, "Stand back please, and let the officers pass."

Brian looked like a grizzly about to attack. He ignored Pitts. "Fill us in, Officer Simmons. What happened here?"

Junior shook his head. His voice cracked as he spoke, "Boss, those joggers said a woman ran from the car. They were curious and jogged back by. They came over to take a peek, and got the shock of their lives. We've identified the body. It's Father Eamon Kennedy, sir. He's dead. His throat has been cut, severed really. Almost decapitated with some instrument like a machete."

Brian looked at the Saturn parked beneath the trees, its silver body catching the gleam of the headlights deep within the gloom. He squared his shoulders and strode rapidly to the hood of the car, stood shakily, and then with a deep breath of decision, pushed himself away from the front fender to walk to the passenger's side. His mouth was dry with dread as he put one hand on the top of the car and leaned inside. The rich, warm, coppery smells of bloody death wafted to his face. His jaw dropped and his vision blackened around the edges. He felt as if he had just been sucker-punched. A body baptized in its own blood, the smell of acid-sweet death melding with the scent of pungent pipe tobacco.

Atop the back of the bloody seat, the man's head stared blindly at the ceiling, mouth lolling open, chest not moving. Father Kennedy had let go the ghost. The old man's hand seemed to be reaching for his wire-framed glasses as if to put them back in place on his severed head. The ashes of his beloved pipe had burned a hole in his pants before being extinguished by his own blood. Brian resisted the urge to brush them off. Instead he involuntarily crossed himself and murmured, "Rest in peace, Eamon Kennedy."

Gracie shuddered as she joined him from the driver's side. She was no plebe. As a rookie, Officer Reme had worked traffic detail and seen mangled bodies before. As a homicide detective she had seen the perverted things humans can intentionally do to others: gunshot wounds, car crashes, beatings, drugs, drowning, but nothing to compare with what she had witnessed this past week. First Mona and now this—her priest, butchered. It was something out of a nightmare. "I'm sorry," she said softly.

The initial shock ebbed. Brian recovered and groaned as he gently retrieved a crumpled paper from the dead priest's fingers. It was a list of check numbers from the account of Rebecca Webster. Anger flamed through his chest. *Who would be next?*

Turning with a scowl, he said, "Gracie, get Simmons and some uniforms over to the St. Denis house. Also, just as a precaution put some protection on Rebecca Webster's place. Make sure they warn her that Mona's killer has struck again. This looks as if our perp is finishing off witnesses."

"I'm on it. You gonna stay here?"

He waved a dismissive hand. "Oh, no indeed not, I've seen all I need to see. The coroner will fill me in later. You stick around here. I'm taking the car and going club hopping alone. I got an odd sort a' hunch but nothing definite. And patience isn't one of my virtues. No sense in tipping the scum off by having cops beating the bushes. If I find anything, I'll call you for back up."

Gracie put a hand on his arm. "Brian, don't let him in your head!"

"Too late, Gracie," he said.

Her throat was dry. She knew she should say something more, but for the life of her, she couldn't think what. So she shook her head and watched him leave. He needed to do what he was doing alone. Standard operating procedures be damned. She shouted after him, "Is this where I'm supposed to say, 'Just be careful'?"

He didn't answer her; he simply left in the car.

Darrel Pitts looked puzzled for a few seconds. Then the reporter's predatory smile appeared, and he disappeared through the crowd of gawkers. Backing out of the park, he swung his auto in behind Brian's unmarked vehicle.

The detective headed out West End Boulevard toward the lakefront. The shaded picnic benches of West End Park were empty—the only thing left was the breeze off Lake Pontchartrain. Weeds ran knee-high around the old fashioned New Orleans lampposts surrounding the perimeter, but the lights were mostly nonfunctional. Trudging through the weeds, there was a grassy levee-hill whose purpose, whether functional or recreational, could not be divined. At the east end of the park, there was a swampy lagoon filled with modern memorabilia—trash and rusty grocery carts. The mosquito-infested pond's crowning glory was a multicolored modern sculpture with most of its pieces broken off. The park used to be a place where families could catch a street car for a day's getaway, but now it was mainly a place for university students and the under-aged to get their drinks on and their rocks off in pot-clouded Camaros. Many an illegitimate child had been reputedly sired here. West End's most defining characteristic was its lack of one.

There was plenty of graffiti, dirt, and hopelessness, plus several derelict watermelon stands and crab joints huddled around the semi-circular parking area. They looked like houses of cards waiting for the wind or waves to wash them into piles of corrugated aluminum and flotsam during the next big storm. West End Park was not always a tempest-tossed ghost town. Brian could recall a beach, an amusement park and seafood restaurants that had endured wind, fire and water as well as the tides of history. Here and there waves lapped at tangles of wrecked wharves and forlorn pilings in testimony to losing the battle to the elements and changing times.

Nightclubs came and went as well. The parking lot in front of the famous Fitzgerald's Seafood Restaurant from years past was scattered with rusty gas-guzzlers, chopped-down motorcycles, vans and a couple of gleaming convertibles. Ramshackle Fitzgerald's had been recently occupied by a dive called The Satellite Dish. A garish neon sign designed to resemble a projectile of some sort, a space rocket or phallic symbol, one or the other or both, proclaimed *THE MOST EXPLOSIVE SHOW IN TOWN!*

Brian pulled around in a tight circle and parked in front. He sprinted up the stairs onto the outer decking. His heart was racing as he paused to straighten his coat, patting his shoulder holster as he did so. On the lighted marquee, he looked at a shadowy photo of a tall, willowy brunette with big eyes and loads of glitter-sprinkled eyelashes. The sign announced, *WHAT A BLAST! SEE OUR*

NEWEST ACT: THE CUBAN MISSILE CRISIS EXPLODES INTO OUTER SPACE!

DARREL PITTS WATCHED Brian's taillights turn off onto the curving parking lot. He quickly turned off his headlights, parked and waited. Lake Pontchartrain was on the right, invisible beyond the garish lights bordering the seawall and the boathouses. Behind him, the city lights lit up the low clouds shrouding the great buildings. No hurry. He didn't want to scare off his prey. He was in his element. His heart pounded with the familiar lurches he always felt when he knew there was something big going down. Pleased, he leaned back and closed his eyes. Oh, yeah man, he could smell a story, a big story, right around the corner. He could wait. His cell phone rang.

He answered, "Pitts here. Shoot."

As he listened to the incoming message, his eyes narrowed only to pop open. "Shit! Who? Dead? How? Any witnesses?" He listened then responded. "I can't go right now. Get Angola on the line, pronto."

CHAPTER 24

THE DIVE SMELLED like old sweaty gym socks, and the noise was deafening. Faces rippled with neon, the eyes of the men were lighted like they had come to score whatever and whomever they could—booze, reefer, meth, or a hump.

Brian located the owner-manager, Walter Henton, standing at the back of the dimly lit room. Walt had previously managed the My-Oh-My on the lakefront where he was well known by the NOPD for producing the most smut in town. He had finally scraped up enough cash and nerve to buy the old restaurant and set up a smut shop for himself and other perverts.

Walt was a man of average height with slicked brown hair that he combed forward to hide a receding hairline. He had a small thin-lipped mouth, with the ruddy, mottled complexion of a heavy drinker. He smoked a cigarette as he leaned against the bar, his potbelly preceding him by half a foot, and beamed as he watched the crowd. It was crowded for a weeknight. His strippers were flitting their bare tails, flopping their bare boobs, and selling drinks like mad. Walt was a happy camper until he was nudged on the shoulder by Detective Brian Herlihy, badge in hand. This wasn't in the happy camper's game plan. He straightened his posture, stood to attention and shouted through the crowd noise, "Well, if it isn't our scoutmaster, good ole' Detective Herlihy. What can I do for y'all?"

"Tell me about your new act—the drag queen calling herself The Cuban Missile Crisis."

The owner threw back his head and laughed, "My oh my, Officer, she ain't yer' type, but she's a very talented young lady. She showed up last week. Wait until she does her act—comes up next. You'll see I have taken a liking to the classics. She does impersonations of famous opera stars—and I ain't talking the Grand Ole' Opry, neither.

But shit! Ya kain't have everthing. Great legs and a million kilowatt smile. What ya asking for?"

Brian answered the leering face with a shrug. "Oh, just checking on a car registration."

"They so hard up downtown that they are sending a detective to check on autos? Guess y'all better raise our taxes! Wait, here she comes!"

The stage darkened for a minute. When the spotlight came up, a large round cylinder with a molded flesh-colored canvas head stood in the middle of the stage. After a series of squeals and static, the antiquated sound system churned out a rock and roll version of a samba.

Suddenly a tape recording blasted through the room as a male voice crackled, "It's show-time at the Satellite Dish! Attention. This is your flight commander, Buzzy Bee Aldren, announcing the blast off of The Cuban Missile Crisis! Uncross your legs and get ready for the biggest blast-off you have ever experienced! Count down begins: Ten, nine, eight, seven, six, five, four, three, two, one. We have IGNITION!"

The cylinder rose with a puff of smoke. As the smoke cleared, the crowd roared its approval. Under the capsule stood a writhing figure of a woman, an almost naked woman, a sleek almond-colored creature of wondrous height and beauty. She had long smooth legs and gentle curves leading to full hips, and firm and rounded breasts. The harsh light hit her face and made her skin look bronze and shiny. She had a crimson smile right out of a bad horror movie. But it was her large dark eyes full of mystery and hunger that held his attention. They were rigid, black and dead, the eyes of a predator. Brian felt nauseated. He leaned on the bar and ordered a club soda from the mesmerized bartender.

Walt patted him on the shoulder. "Yes, sir, she really makes your mouth dry, don't she?" He smiled sarcastically. The smile made his flabby, too-white face into a clown mask. "Your drink is on the house, Detective Herlihy. You be good now!"

When the act, if you could call it an act, was over, Brian stood in the shadows until the whistles, clapping and pounding of drunken feet subsided. Walt led him to the stage door where he was expected to wait. Instead, Brian pushed past the owner and entered the hallway.

He approached the sweaty figure. He noticed she was wiping most of her Spanish-ness onto a towel. Walt rushed behind Brian and shouted over his shoulder. "I'm sorry, Ms Rodriguez. This is Detective Brian Herlihy of the NOPD. He has a few questions to ask you."

The dame, if you could call her that, moved across the floor in a stylized, slightly unreal fashion, like the movements of an old motion picture. She extended a red clawed hand with an expression of welcome. A high-pitched voice with a heavy Spanish accent chirped, *"Buenos Noches, Senor* Detective, I'm Alma Rodriguez. You are so sweet to greet me in your fine city."

Brian ignored the comments but stuck out his hand. The dancer had a grip that could crush stone. The stripper held his gaze. Her eyes were unnaturally black, like someone had colored them with crayons. He said coldly, "I have some questions to ask you. Let's go where it is less noisy and more private."

The dancer raised painted-on eyebrows, "Oooh, I've always had a thing for *bieg hombres*! I'm delighted you have many questions." She gestured to the crowd of small doors just behind the stage and twittered, "I'm thrilled you seek discretion. *Venga conmingo, pronto!* Come with me, I lead the way to my private salon!"

Brian eyed his suspect warily, the deeply bronzed face with the mop of hair hanging loose to the shoulders like a shawl of black petroleum. The Cuban Missile Crisis had no concealed weapon—the G-sting wasn't enough costume to hide even a razor blade. A police officer walking into the backstage hallway hadn't shaken the dancer in the least. She glanced back at him, looking more distracted than alarmed. *Strange—no protest.*

Ms. Rodriguez languidly swung her pink and tan streaked butt in a pattern of theatrical movements as she went through the narrow doorway. The small room smelled of mold, cold cream, and a mélange of old cologne, booze and sweat. The nearly nude apparition sat at a makeshift dressing table and fingered a silver cigarette holder. Brian found himself looking into his reflection in black eyes.

She arched her neck and swept back a strand of jet-black hair that hung like inked Spanish moss. She stroked it for a minute, making the red fingernails perform graceful lilting gestures, and stared at him, cold calculation flickering behind eyes that glistened like oil. Then she leaned over and let the cascade of hair tumble across her face. *This crapper is trying to seduce me!*

Their eyes locked in the mirror as he leaned over and plucked at her head. "Oh, wait, you have something caught in your hair."

Brian jerked off the stripper's wig. *Bald as a billiard ball*! He snarled, "I think we better continue this discussion downtown."

The creature's painted face fell into a cunning pout and she tittered sweetly, "Oh, dear me, what's a girl to wear? Are you going to do that thing you do? You know, read me my rights and handcuff me? May I put on some clothes, Officer? A little wrapper or something?"

Brian spoke sharply, "Oh yes! I am going to do all those things policemen do. Get a wrap—haul ass!" He couldn't figure out how she had kept her composure as the charade continued.

The stripper babbled away as she rose from the stool before the dressing table. "I hope everything is satisfactory with my papers. I'm in the country legally even though I'm rather nomadic, you see. Honestly, I must confess to a little illicit drug possession. That's the only blotch on my otherwise spotless record. But, honey, where I come from, drugs are a simply a lifestyle! Oh, what to wear to a police station..."

Brian watched the performance with interest. The strange creature's black eyes grew round and innocent, then flicked away.

You have to admire this perp—never saw anything so cool.

Brian sat on the stool that the ludicrous parody had vacated. He looked in the mirror and said firmly, "You are under arrest for the murder of Dr. Mona Wright and your stepbrother, Eamon Kennedy, you Irish bastard. Now put some clothes on!"

The stripper calmly fingered a robe hanging on the back of the door. Brian watched her long, red nails slide behind the apparel. Suddenly a long sharp blade shimmered in the mirror. Brian saw it coming—glittering death arched past the side of his head. He ducked as the blade smashed through the air, cleaving the flimsy dressing table in half. He twisted and caught the hand. The muscles of his forearm bulged like corded iron.

Relieved at surviving the close call, Brian was a second too late in dodging the foot in the stiletto heel that caught his chin. The stripper had sprung with the speed of a cat.

Spitting blood, he reared away from the stool, tucked his body and spun around. *Fourth down and inches*! He planted his treelike legs and made bodily contact. He bore directly into her chest and hit flush-on like a tugboat ramming the body into the wall.

The stripper's slim figure slammed against the door and doubled up across Brian's broad shoulder. Ten long nails gouged holes in Brian's shirt. He felt pain and heard the shirt tear. Then he heard the fake nails snapping away, leaving bleeding nubs that became fists. The stripper's body twisted and turned like a seal. He felt a jab to his jaw and a sudden splintering pain as he bit his tongue. *Damn—no mouthpiece!* Then he hugged, a great rib crushing bear hug. *Fifteen yards for roughing the passer! Sometimes it's worth the penalty.* He heard a sound he had always yearned to hear. The sound of bones snapping—deep bones, not little bones. A sound he both loved and feared.

The figure screamed in pain.

Take that, you bloody bugger! Brian released his hold and the stripper slumped to the floor. *Player down on the field! Call an ambulance!*

The door burst open, slamming into the motionless figure on the floor. A low moan escaped from the prone stripper. Darrel Pitts craned his neck around the door.

"Hi, Darlin'! We're about to win this game. Will you do me the favor of calling headquarters? Or are you just gonna stand there and enjoy the view?" Ribbons of blood slid down his jaw and soaked his shirt collar. The muscles in his shoulders quivered with fatigue, but it was a good fatigue—the exhaustion of victory.

"Shit fire and save matches, Brian! Is it dead?"

"Naw, just a little the worse for wear, I'd say. Broken ribs and maybe a smashed disk or three. All in all, a very satisfying hit. Not clean, not nice, but absolutely brilliantly satisfying."

Blood followed words. He rubbed his split lip on his shirtsleeve. "Darrel Pitts, meet Irish Mike O'Shea, alias Sean Pedar McClintock, alias The Cuban Missile Crisis, alias Alma...oh, what the hell, alias some Spanish name! You're my witness. This perp attempted to assault me with a very deadly weapon. It's over there hacking up the dressing table."

He spat blood onto the front of his shirt and took out his handkerchief. "This attack occurred when I was in the line of duty arresting said bastard! I'd call trying to slice my head off resisting arrest, wouldn't you?"

Pitts was irked at missing the big fight. He knelt beside the body and rubbed at the grease-painted face. He snapped irritably. "Too bad he had shitty aim! I've already called Gracie and my office for a photographer. They should be here any minute. I was curious as to what would cause you to haul ass from a murder scene in such a hurry, so I tailed you. Got some news that will interest you while I waited in the car. Your old buddy, Harry 'Heller-Keller' will never beat up any other woman because he is permanently out of commission. Four guys went into the showers, three came out. Keller caught a shiv. Deader than a doornail with no witnesses. He had bled out by the time the guards found him. Seems several inmates discovered the body. Get this coincidence, his ex-gal-friend, Septema Cryer's cousin, Rufus, was the guard on duty and reported it."

"Couldn't happen to a nicer fella!"

"I figured you'd take that position. But I better get this damn story because I didn't hop on that one."

"Choices, choices!" Brian mumbled.

"So anyway, I got fed up with sweating in the car. Finally, I stopped cooling my heels and came inside this dump. Gracie musta sensed something was wrong. She's on her way, you jerk."

Mona, we win! The game is over! He wiped at the blood gushing from his chin. "Gee, Pittzy, you're a real intuitive fella. What can I say? I'm keeping my word that I'd give you a first in on the story. Sorry you're missing the fun at Angola, but this news saves me a trip. It's a good thing you followed me. Your mother will be proud of her eager beaver. You were always there after I made the tackle. Tell the medics to take off the bastard's damn contact lenses before they do anything else."

Brian's jaw was pounding and the tendons at the back of his head had solidified into steel pipes. He groaned as he worked a kink from his back and pulled at his torn shirt. "At forty-three, I'm too old to play this game." He righted the stool and sat on it.

CHAPTER 25

G‍race R‍eme s‍hook her head. "Strikes me you came alone on purpose. It was a stupid thing to do. It really was, but..." She glanced at him. "I'm glad you did it."

His anger had burned down to dead coals. "I wasn't sure or I would have brought backup. The perp re'this'ed," he tried again, "*resisted* my invitation to accompany me downtown, thath's all." His split lip and mangled tongue had swollen and were obviously giving him trouble speaking.

The medical team hoisted the stretcher. Brian heard a deep groan and a gurgled protest. "My God, I can't breathe!" The face was fiercely distorted, "Get my hair!"

The Cuban Missile Crisis was now in crisis itself.

Gracie took statements and gathered up the equipment, carefully photographing Brian's back and face and the severed dressing table complete with the curved Turkish sword. Then she bagged it plus the silver cigarette holder. There was little doubt the perp's fingerprints were all over both pieces of evidence, and the dicer and slicer would show Father Kennedy's blood.

Darrel was eager to get the whole story. He walked beside Brian through the slime pit filled with shadow men, taking notes like a mad man. "Ya talk about a take down! One hell of a disguise, I'd say. What put you on to him? Care to comment?"

Gracie handed Brian a bag of ice wrapped in a napkin. He patted his busted lip with the bundle. "Darrel, I canh't talk too well righth now. I had a chat with a couple of folks who knew him in Ireland."

"Well, who *is* that SOB you squeezed?"

"Now, be kind, that'h SOB probably has'th a punctured lung and a couple of internal injuries yet to be diagnos'th-ed." His tongue began to feel like a dirigible. "Now lissen caref'lly 'cause I wath as gentle as I could be under the circumstath'nces. He'th the stepbrother of tonith's murder victim, Father Eamon Kennedy. I interviewed Kennedy concerthrn'ing another ma'ther. He menth'oned his stepbrother's name wa'th Sean Pedar McClintock. S'thaid' he wa'th an actor who smoked with a silver ciger'teth holder. We goth' witnesses who 'thaw 'em to'gther' in a silver Saturn. Grathie' will fill you in tho' mercy, you nu'th-hound! I've had a very bad ni-th'!"

As Darrel went off in a huff to file his story, he mumbled, "Hell, you want me to sit up and beg? Well, I will! In the morning!"

AFTER GRACIE LEFT to clear up the details at headquarters, Brian drove to Touro Infirmary to get his chin and lip attended to. His tongue also required a couple of stitches where he bit it. The ER doctor advised him not to drink any alcohol anytime soon. Hell's bells! The very thought gagged him.

After the doctor did his needlework and delivered his warning, the nurse on duty instructed him to return for a follow-up AIDS test. She volunteered the information that the "woman" he busted up was HIV positive and there was a slight possibility the artificial nails that punctured his back had passed the virus, but there were additional procedures to rule out infection. She handed him prescriptions for Percodan and an antibiotic. As she finished, she mentioned that she had recognized the individual as a woman who had visited the hospital earlier. The smooth-talking con person had attempted to visit the St. Denis boy just this morning.

Upon reflection, it was one of life's little ironies that this was the same hospital they had brought William St. Denis to after his episode with vodka. Brian laughed until it literally hurt when the nurse commented, "She had a lot of poise and was real pretty, but of course the boy was already released in the custody of his parents. I remember her because she was so unusual."

Novocain numbed his mouth and jaw, but he looked as if he had mumps on the right side of his face. Brian walked to the ICU's isolation ward to peer at the perp. The Cuban Missile Crisis looked sixty years old. IVs protruded from both arms, the narrow tubes like snakes curling up to bottles attached to the back of the bed. Behind Sean McClintock, machines beeped and hummed as they measured life signs. An oxygen mask covered his mouth and nose, but the patient appeared to be resting peacefully.

A doctor stepped into the hall and stopped to comment. "I'd say that he's a lucky man. A fractured rib perforated his lung, missing the aorta by an inch. The blow he received compressed the whole heart cavity, causing chest trauma called a surgical crunch. We worked on internal bleeding for an hour. He could have bled to death before he got here."

"He's gonna' make it, ri'th?"

Fascinated, the doctor couldn't tear his eyes away from Brian's mangled chin and blinked at the bloody front of his torn shirt trying to make out if he was also injured in the chest. "It's touch and go. BP's down to sixty over zip. I did a paracentesis for the blood in his abdomen. We've got a central line in, Ringer's lactate wide open, but we can't keep his pressure up. The preexisting viral complication makes working on him extremely dangerous."

"Oh, Doc tah'ths' not all tah'th mak'ths thi'sh bath'ard dangerous." The detective smiled what would have been a cynical smile if his mouth had cooperated. "I ju'th want him to live until we administer the needle filled with terminal sleep."

The doctor hesitated then his face tightened in disgust and he rushed away.

As Brian looked down at the tubes and machinery bristling around the body on the bed, he thought of the string of bodies left strewn across the country. Christ in Heaven, what makes a monster such as this? Is it only a cause thought to be righteous in a far-away Ireland? It has to be more that that. What? He turned and headed for his apartment and the long awaited shower and sack-time.

CHAPTER 26

His alarm clock jarred him back to the present at 7:00 a.m. He surfaced from a hideous dream in which he watched a bald woman dismembering a baby in a confessional while Eamon Kennedy smiled in an ironic way and chanted in a nasty-nice voice, "Aren't we having fun? He's fine, just fine!"

He sat up, exhausted, as if he had never even fallen asleep. His heart pounded as his nightmare faded. His right shoulder was sore like he had pitched a hard game, and the claw marks on his body itched like hell. He felt weak, oddly off balance, and could smell his sweat. He tried to move his mouth. It zinged with pain. He mumbled through a swollen lip, "I need a shower." He tried to call the office, but his mouth wouldn't cooperate. So he stumbled into the bathroom. The dream was still on his mind until he looked in the mirror. Eyes dazed with sleep, he stood motionless and stared at the reflection. His hair resembled a cornfield after a flying saucer landing, but that wasn't the worst half of it. His cheek and chin were blown up like a balloon and were bruised a slight shade of purple and brown. *Jesus, is that my face?*

The phone tore through the fog wrapped around his mind. Washing some water around in his soured mouth, he thought, *here goes nothing.* "Detetith Herlihy."

Gracie's voice was unusually businesslike. "Boss, you better sit down somewhere. There's more bad news. You ready for this?"

Brian shook his head and struggled to speak through a mouth full of cotton. "No, Grathie, I ain't up to th'th."

She continued brusquely, "Well, I can hear why, but you gotta know and I gotta be the one to tell you." There was a long pause and he could hear her taking a deep breath. "There's no easy way, so, I'm getting this over with."

Irritated, he sat on the edge of the bathtub. "Tho, do it!"

"Brian, the uniform on duty at Rebecca Webster's was relieved at dawn. Ricky Merriam, the rookie officer keeping an eye on her place, reported that Becky had a female visitor immediately after you left to meet me. He didn't think much about it because the woman was tall and swanky. It looked like some society dame from the neighborhood. He watched for trouble, but Becky let the woman in right away so he just noted it. The visitor didn't stay long and waved sweetly at him as she walked away, but without any sign of urgency. Just strolled away on foot like she belonged there.

"This morning when Officer Colette Couhig replaced Merriam, he told her about the visitor. Colette rang the doorbell but there was no answer. She tried to call inside on her cell phone but Rebecca didn't answer—the machine picked up. So, Colette called it in while Merriam went around the corner to her folk's house to get a key."

He heard another sharp intake of breath from Gracie's end of the line. "Jesus, they entered with her father! Her body was face up in the seat of a chair in her living room. Brian, Becky is dead. Her neck was broken."

He reached out to grab the edge of the lavatory with a trembling hand. His heart began rocketing, cold sweat rose on his neck. He was suddenly jittery. "Who?"

"No one was in or out of her place except you and the tall, brunette woman, if you can call her that. I figure you know who did it. Now, cool it! Remember, you already got the bastard."

Brian tried to unclamp his jaw and mumbled ferociously through a flood of feelings, "Noth' thoon enouth for Becky!"

Gracie knew this was not an ordinary murderer nor was the newest victim an ordinary homicide victim. She managed to say calmly, "I know. You need some time?"

"No!' He slammed down his phone. As he dressed, Brian thought about what Mona had told him about dreams and how closely one's dreams ally to one's fears. Dreams can be strong when you're weak. Dreams can be rich when you're poor. Dreams can have you climbing mountains when you deal with the masses scrambling about on the valley floor. Mona would tell him that his nightmare concerned his son. Only when he relinquished his fear and guilt would he relinquish his nightmare. A father's dreams shouldn't become his son's nightmares.

INSIDE THE STATION, Grace Reme stared at the phone for a minute and twisted her mouth. A bustle of activity surrounded her. Uniforms passed through the corridors. A three-piece suit carrying a briefcase announced himself at the front desk and demanded to see his client. A rambunctious reporter was making angry inquiries of the desk sergeant. A white faced woman keened demands for someone to locate her missing daughter. The *Vieux Carre's* unique wildlife was represented by a street character called "Ruthie, the Duck Lady." Ruthie was busy pushing herself against the battered counter, rocking back and forth on her roller skates, panhandling cigarettes with her famous line, "Hey, hows-bout some smokes—one for now and one for later." It was a usual morning at NOPD.

Ignoring the hubbub, Gracie pushed her way through the swinging doors into jungle of glass partitions, desks, file cabinets, computers, telephones, blackboards and TV screens toward Brian's office. She took the corridor covered in icky brown, indoor-outdoor carpeting and walked into his office. She reluctantly placed the coroner's report concerning Eamon Kennedy on his desk along with the papers she had hastily redeemed from the stacks of business materials brought from Mona's house. She had read them and had enough sense to recognize Brian would not want them newsed-about. They included an accounting of various payments marked as "contributions" to Catholic Children's Charity, but the reports indicated the checks were made out to Sean Pedar McClintock by Rebecca Webster and her parents. When added together, the sum was a staggering one hundred and twenty thousand dollars. Gracie was no fool. Nobody in the Webster clan had that kind of loose change. There was something else going on. Whose back were the Websters scratching and for what? The PI's report on Becky was missing—why? Trotter had brought that up at the end. What else was the dork holding back and why? Then there's the baby business with Becky. Maybe the Websters were being sucked at both ends. If Mona discovered the blackmail, what in hell kept her from telling Brian?

She called Touro Infirmary for a report on their perp. Nothing much had changed. He was in and out of surgery trying to survive the crunch with lots of troubles inside and bruises outside, plus injuries to his spinal column that might paralyze him, but AIDS was complicating matters. He was semi-conscious at times but not talking. She wrote up the medical information and placed it with the other papers.

She concentrated. What else? Car impounded, weapon in forensics, Eamon Kennedy in the morgue. St. Denis family guarded, Rebecca discovered dead at 6:00 a.m. this morning, her body not yet in the morgue. Miami informed, blood samples taken from prime suspects: the perp and Montz. Darrel Pitts stalled. Copies of the book's royalty release to John Warren still in Brian's pocket. She wondered why he wouldn't let her see who Mona Wright's heirs were. Could it be that Catholic Children's Charity in Ireland? If so, why wouldn't he let her see them?

She clicked her ballpoint pen against her front teeth then a light came on in her head. Her mouth twisted and her eyebrows arched as she thought maybe there is only one heir—Rebecca Webster. That would make sense. The two women had been like sisters, but then the prospect of a sizable inheritance made Rebecca a suspect in Mona's murder. Gracie wondered, hmm...there's dirty work afoot! Brian was close to both of the women. Could he be protecting Becky? That would be just like him.

Brian entered the office. His brow lowered and the swollen thrust of his jaw indicated that he was in a dangerous humor—like a bull that, before charging, backs up with its head down and paws the ground. She turned, catching sight of his hopelessly swollen face and gasped, "Wow! I don't have to ask what the other guy looks like!"

Grief melding with irritation on his face, he shot her the finger and exclaimed, "Nu'fing! Underthand?" He gestured for a note pad and pen. He wrote on it in big letters: *I WILL NOT BE TEASED BY A BITCHIN' WOMAN TODAY!*

She grimaced, "Ooo-kaaay, Officer Mad-at-the-World, if insulting me makes it hurt less then go for it. I'll get you a snowball for lunch. Here's some stuff you want to look into. No need for dialogue. I confiscated the reports and bank records from Mona's before anyone took a gander at them. You might start with those items. There are several peculiarities that need some explaining concerning the Websters. You may be able to shed some light on it."

She waited a second to see if he'd give her some reaction. He simply nodded. She sighed, "Our beloved perp is gonna live. Curse the luck of the Irish! Should I arrange for legal council or contact the Irish Embassy that he is under arrest?"

He wrote: *NOT YET let the SOB ask for a lawyer. The Irish will contact us.*

She asked him for the heirs' release to send to Warren.

His face was carefully blank. He wrote: *I'll handle it.* Then he scribbled: *clues at Becky's? Info about Miami, car, body from last night, the dead.* He wrote *PRIEST* then scratched it out and wrote *IRISHMAN? I want a giant Technicolor snowball ASAP. My mouth hurts like HELL!*

She saluted. "Right on, Boss, Sir! Nope, not much. Of course we have the ill-fated sighting of Officer Merriam plus the fact no one entered or left after the perp and we have some deep, high heel indentations in the thick carpet. They gotta be Ms. Kick 'em to death, Ou'-La-La's' because Rebecca was barefooted. We are making plaster casts and should be able to match the marks with McClintock's heels. Maybe it's the same ones that smacked you in the jaw. All the rest of the stuff is covered except the snowball and I'm leaving as we speak, or as I speak, rather."

With a knee, Brian nudged his wooden armchair closer to the side of his desk, sat on his spine and stretched his legs out. He sat quietly and read the financial reports. They corroborated what Becky had told him except for her parents' payments. Apparently she knew nothing about Eamon's double dipping. What webs we humans weave! It wasn't often he misjudged a man's basic character to this extent. He wished he could speak to the old dog. The gentle Father Eamon Kennedy he had known must have suffered bullets over his part in the intrigue. A priest caught between his family, country, and his friends, not to mention his church. Not a pretty picture. Brian wondered how many other families the priest had scammed for the cause.

He shifted restlessly in his chair and pressed his aching chin. Well, it would all come out soon that Rebecca and he were definitely implicated. Wonder what the sentence is for complicity in murder plus blackmail and money laundering for the IRA? He'd handle that when it happened—kid and all. *Thanks a lot, Eamon! You knew all along even before Rebecca came to you for help. I told you I screwed Mona's best friend that Mardi Gras night. I told you in confession, for God's sake! I should have had my tongue cut out. Ouch, that hurts in more ways than one!*

He pulled out the heirs' release that he and Becky had co-signed and copied it three times. He faxed copies to Warren. He knew trouble was coming his way. He enumerated the choice bits of circumstantial evidence against himself. He is Irish, the perp is Irish. And now he, Brian David Herlihy, is Mona's only heir left alive plus he is the father of Rebecca's illegitimate son, potentially her only heir, and a jailbird in Ireland. He sighed. Oh, yes, he was implicated all right! He would have to explain a lot of things best left alone. Christ, he hoped there was some other reason why that psychotic went on a killing spree. He needed to speak again to Mona's editor, but his tongue needed to subside a bit before he could speak with any dignity.

He thumbed through the excellent reports Gracie had accumulated. *What would I do without her? What is she gonna say when all this shit hits the proverbial fan? One consolation: Darlin' Darrel will have a ball! Ah, well, enough of this private pity-party.* He was stuck inside his own head. Now he understood why Mona insisted that verbalization was so damn important to sanity.

He signed the extradition forms for Julien to be hauled to Florida. He noted Gracie had included a clause stating Julien Montz must be available to NOPD as a possible witness and/or accomplice in the homicide of Doctor Mona Wright Montz.

It was going to be tough to tie Julien to the drug money, but Florida had him on the murder rap for sure. Sean Pedar McClintock was a pretty sharp cookie when he left some evidence under the bed, but there were no fingerprints, markings on the box—nothing tied Julien with Sean, except the Saturn. That connection was weak because the only witness was now dead.

He was about to leave and go back to his pad to read Mona's manuscript when Grace bounced though the door. "Big Un! Guess what we found in the perp's stuff besides pasties and panty hose? He had narcotics galore! We've sent samples to Miami. I'd take odds on the crap being from the same lot as the stash you uncovered. Sean also has some of the wrong size costumes, like maybe for Roxy or the Silver Saturn. Seems he just couldn't throw away a perfectly good G-sting! There are hairs all over the interior of the Saturn. Some are from the black wig you jerked off of the Cuban Missile as well as the red one he wore as that Spanish opera star. Forensics got some foreign hairs—maybe they belong to the sisters. And if we're lucky some may even be Montz hairs. They are checking his high heels for carpet fibers from Becky's house, the shoes are already covered with mud from the park. But that ain't the best part. He has IRA papers. And listen to this—he has Mona Wright's laptop containing her novel. He sent the manuscript to John Warren under the name, Peddler. There is an e-mail record showing he was arranging to meet with Warren to finalize a fabulous book deal. What a greedy, greedy man! Take her life and take her book! Is that a motive for murder or isn't it?"

He slashed across the page: *GRACIE, I COULD KISS YOU! LATER!*

CHAPTER 27

DETECTIVE HERLIHY HUNG up after speaking to John Warren. He had assured the editor that he would be on an extended leave after the upcoming trial. Yes, he would begin pulling together some ideas for a sequel to Mona's book while he was visiting in Ireland. He had laughed when the publisher had quipped that he had never had a writer who had literally 'taken it on the chin' so to speak. Mona's book had been published with as much fanfare as John Warren could muster which was considerable. The editor and publishing house agreed with the courts that the previously signed releases giving over the rights for royalties to Mona's murderer were null and void. Brian was interviewed until his tongue hung out, stitches and all. But the real challenge was a special interview yet to come.

Brian nudged the assortment of legal forms and papers from the center of his desk. Then as an afterthought, he made a futile attempt to arrange them in some sort of order, mostly for Gracie's benefit. He flopped the morning's edition of the *Times-Picayune* in front of him and read the headline: UNEXPECTED STRATEGY LEADS DETECTIVE TO SERIAL KILLING MACHINE! His buddy, Darlin' Darrel Pitts was still aiming at a Pulitzer. The news-hound made the crime scene evidence public and made the lakefront strip joint encounter read like a Mickey Spillane novel as if he had been an eyewitness to the whole thing. But Pitts didn't know how all the cards were dealt. Yes, the article reported that Sean Pedar McClintock would be standing trial in a wheelchair unless AIDS sentenced him to death before the state could.

But what Darrel didn't know was that the Irish police had arrested Padraig and Sean's mother. However, the authorities didn't seem particularly concerned with the fate of a "son of the Emerald Isles" named Sean who happened to be a psychotic serial killer. They had promptly waived extradition and requested that Sean be tried in the

States. Seems the Irish government didn't want sensational press or demonstrations of sympathy for a paralyzed AIDS patriot. Plus they deemed it wise not to air the church's dirty laundry. It was not nice to be implicated in a blackmail scheme concerning sweet little babies of good Catholic girls so they had brushed that detail under the carpet as well. It was arranged for him to be deposed in Louisiana concerning his IRA activities. Both the government and the IRA gambled on McClintock's silence. They needn't have worried. Sean wasn't telling anyone anything. Pitts quoted the district attorney: "He told us that we wouldn't be getting anything from him."

In exchange for a minutia of leniency, Sean's father, good ole' Paddy, cleared the adopted son of Fergus and Deirdre McGlynn of any involvement in resistance activities. Padraig swore that Branden Michael McGlynn was an innocent bystander. The boy was released into the custody of his adoptive parents and returned to Dingle Bay.

The lead story continued as Darrel Pitts delighted in anticipation of covering the trial of Mona and Rebecca's killer plus that of Father Eamon Kennedy. "The crime case grows more complex. The district attorney's office discloses that Sean McClintock is also a suspect in the killings of Rebecca Webster and the vicious mutilation slaying of his own step-brother, Father Eamon Kennedy." Then he feasted upon the inevitable conspiracy to commit murder in the trial of Julien Montz.

The week before this present great piece of reporting, Darrel Pitts had exploded another bombshell. The headlines had read: *DOCTOR MONA WRIGHT'S WILL MAKES POLICE DETECTIVE RICH*! Brian's relationship with the famous woman was exploited to the fullest extent. The water cooler conversations were reenergized all over the city when it was revealed Mona's estate was left to the deceased Rebecca Webster and Brian Herlihy. The innuendoes followed him wherever he went. It seemed practical to just tough it out, so he affected vague tolerance instead of the irritation he actually felt.

Brian thought it was a blessing that the Catholic Church had managed to pull some strings and protect their priest's involvement in the murders and the blackmail scheme. The church fathers were busy with a score of altar boy incidents and certainly weren't interested in any more public scrutiny. The official response was: *Out of concern for the bereaved family of Ms Rebecca Webster, the fact of her pregnancy and surrounding information were deemed irrelevant to her murder.* The public readily accepted that her murderer had killed her to eliminate any possible witnesses who might have known his relationship to Father Eamon Kennedy. The church certainly didn't want to be mentioned in connection with Dr. Mona Wright's expose of the IRA and the assassin's inaccurate revenge.

All press releases from the church simply stated: *Rebecca Webster attended Galway College. She was a close friend of the recently deceased Mona Wright, Ph.D. Father Eamon Kennedy arranged for both women to reside with the McClintock family during their several trips to Ireland. The women's deaths and that of Father Eamon Kennedy are judged to be regrettable aftermaths of Sean Pedar McClintock's homicidal rampage."*

Brian figured he hadn't heard the last of Darlin' Darrel. Maybe he could offer Pittzy a piece of the action. After all, he liked the reporter's style. When the damn trial was over, he might explore the idea of getting Darrel to write the book with him. But, that would have to wait until he pulled some slight of hand concerning his son's part in the IRA business. Right now, he had to deal with Darrel concerning other matters.

Gracie ushered someone through the maze of outer offices and opened Brian's door.

Darlin' Darrel Pitts eased into the only available chair in Detective Brian Herlihy's cluttered space. The slight smile on the man's lips masked a steely resolve forged in his college days as quarterback and honed by the challenges of his profession. His combativeness was a trait left over from years of racial injustices and one day it would get him killed. But not today. Today, there was a pleasant haphazard look about the ace reporter that belied his instincts. The man with the small, white teeth showing in his predatory smile was round—round in the way an ex-athlete was round. His battered pants had shiny spots at the knees. He casually rolled the sleeves of his plaid shirt halfway to his elbows while swearing softly under his breath, "Damn prickly heat!" Then he pressed the detective for answers to several questions. "And, now that you are to inherit a considerable fortune plus a sizeable chunk of change from your half of the royalties from Dr. Mona Wright's most recent bestselling novel, Detective Herlihy, would you care to speculate on your future?"

Detective Herlihy felt a muscle twitch behind his left shoulder and shrugged. "I don't care to speculate on anything at all."

"Will you be retiring from the New Orleans Police Force? Tell me about your situation. I have heard rumors that you and John Warren are considering a sequel to Dr. Mona's book. It is to be a pot-boiler concerning a New York editor's collusion with a New Orleans detective? A member of John Warren's staff informs me that the consequent collaboration was your suggestion. Don't you think exploiting the circumstances surrounding a case in which you have been personally involved and becoming a consultant on such a project is rather callous?"

Brian leaned back in his office chair and closed his eyes. He looked perfectly relaxed except for the little knot of muscle at the corner of his jaw. "Why, Mr. Pitts, you of all people know that there is no such thing as a literary agent—especially since this is an inside story—that is also simply a rumor—that your novelistic efforts have been turned down repeatedly by the publishing world. No? Not even a nibble from that anomaly you refer to as a literary agent? Ah, then we must render a decision that literary agents are a fiction, pure and simple."

Pitts raised his chin a smidgen, as though his tie was too tight. But he wasn't wearing a tie. "Well, fact or fiction? Is it true?"

The detective's lips pursed as he shook his head sadly. "Like it or lump it, there is no juicy scandal. All we have here is just an ole' fashioned cop, some robbers, some killers and some diehard newspaper reporters. To imply there is more would be distasteful."

Darrel frowned. "I expect you know that the incidence of homosexual serial killers is rare. You're going to have difficulty persuading a jury that 'The Peddler' is a good candidate in this case."

"Doesn't matter. We've got all the evidence we need plus an eye witness or six or seven. Besides that's the D.A.'s problem, not mine. Remember, Darlin', none of the victims were actually sexually assaulted."

"What about the good doc that you inherit a fortune from?"

"Mona was a put-up deal meant to throw us off the track. Need I remind you, Mr. Pitts, I have three close friends seriously dead? Dr. Mona Wright is dead, Rebecca Webster is dead, and Father Eamon Kennedy is dead." He thought, *you schmuck, the world that is left to me is ugly and terrifying. Money be damned!* But he continued smoothly, "I ain't gonna lie about it. But your asinine, emotionally loaded questions seem premature and, I might add, a bit crass at a time when I am trying to convict a discontented Sinn Fein, clever sonovabitch, cold-blooded, psychopathic, serial killer of several vicious premeditated murders."

"Could you be a little more explicit?" The reporter said with a dry smile.

They both laughed, relieving the tension that had built up in the room. Then Brian pulled a big, fake smile and that was the end of that interview.

CHAPTER 28

WHAT DARREL PITTS, ace reporter, didn't know was that two days before, Brian had one last try at persuading Sean Pedar McClintock to confess. They had come face to face in the prison hospital—a place that was no more appetizing than the cells themselves. The first thing that struck him when he walked into the stuffy isolation unit was the thin, acrid smell, an odor quite distinct from the smell of a hospital. It came from the cheesy, unwashed reek of the narrow body on the bed. Brian was pleased to see that McClintock had lost weight and his jaundiced face was shiny with a bloodless pallor while his shaved head was lumpy with inflamed pustules. AIDS was rapidly making its own inroads into this man's system. Even though the civilized part of Brian objected to the idea of Sean never making it to a trial date, the prospect of the rapist-murderer dying evoked no sympathy from him.

They had eyed each other across the space between the bed and the chair. "Did you bring some cigarettes?" The patient's red-rimed eyes narrowed as his lips, so chapped that they looked like scales were growing on them, demanded, "You got smokes?"

Silently, Brian shoved a pack of Menthol Light 100's and a lighter on to the bedside table. A thin hand snaked out and grabbed them. McClintock snatched one up greedily and lit it with a shaking hand. He drew in the smoke and hacked violently through blistered lips. When the spasm ceased, Brian saw white spit flecked with blood at the corners of Sean's mouth as he wheezed, "I'll be outta here for the trial. You bastards think I'm gonna croak, but I am gonna tell the world how bent the IRA is! I don't confess to any killins! They fitted me up, I tell you!"

Brain shook his head, almost admiring the dying man's defiance. "You're whistling in the dark, Sean Pedar McClintock," he said, his voice deliberately condescending. "However you try to make the world believe otherwise, you know that nobody has framed you. Nobody had to. You did the deeds yourself and I caught you. But listen, you still have a choice about eternity so how about you clear this up before you meet God."

McClintock twitched, his face clinching round his cigarette in a tight spasm then he sneered, "Stuff it, copper! I heard you kicked off being a priest. Is this part of the drill? Okay, Father, I confess, I never off't nobody so ya' just as well fob off!"

Brian jerked forward, his gaze locked on McClintock's red-rimmed eyes. "It's a good act, Pusface-Pedar, but your acting days are over. Look, do yourself a favor, tell me how did it happened that you chose Mona Wright as a victim."

A smirk crept over Sean's face.

"What's so bloody funny?"

The patient shook his head and moaned with a ghoulish wink. "You ain't heard proper, Detective Herlihy," he said, turning the name into an insult. "I'll not be givin' you shit! There are bigger, deeper battles going on here on earth, so just bugger off. Pin a frigin' red rose to your arse!"

Brian did a double-take at the subject of roses as he flashed on the Valentine's Day event. "A rose? Thanks for reminding me. Who sent the Valentine roses? Why? Did Julien Montz send those Valentine roses to warn her that you were on your way?"

"Ain't roses a sweet gesture, now? God, Yanks is a sentimental bunch of nutters! Perchance, whoever sent them shoulda made it a funeral wreath." His eyes closed. Sean McClintock seemed to fold in on himself and sink onto the stained pillows as if he knew that death would not end his renown but extend and complete it. As if to emphasize his decision to die in silence, he wheezed, "Bugger off!" Coughing like an asthmatic popcorn popper, his lips moved forming words. He began to sing "My Wild Irish Rose, sweetest flower that grows..." and blew smoke at the ceiling.

Brian drew in a slow breath. One of his hands balled into a fist. The other hand reached to cradle it. He got to his feet, sweeping the pack of smokes into his pocket. He looked at McClintock then gave a knotted shrug. He walked towards the door, hoping his voice didn't sound as weary as he felt. "Suit yourself, cock-suckin' barfbag. I'll get a verdict of guilty while you rot in this bed."

CHAPTER 29

AN ENTHUSED OPRAH Winfrey did a segment on the murder, the book, and the IRA. Salient portions of Dr. Wright's book were quoted and praised for their insight and impact on the nation and the readers. Mona would have loved the fact that so many people were enthralled with her efforts. It would have amused her to watch as fascinated readers toyed with the psychopathic ravings of the desperately cruel, misguided, bogus author, calling himself Peddler. John Warren, with the usual publisher's finesse, had skillfully added her killer's notes as an appendix to the book.

The awesome marathon of political debate and press coverage only helped sell the book as a sensation. Psychiatrists and forensic commentators had a ball with Peddler's unbalanced mental state. Every prominent mental health professional seemed to have an opinion. Naturally, they all claimed to be collaborators of the famous Dr. Mona Wright and to have been consulted by the author for assistance in writing the book. They got busy analyzing every detail of her sad and pointless death, and also the Peddler's babble. Every author was preoccupied with drawing conclusions about serial killers and their personalities.

Unhappy with the peace process and thinking the Sinn Fein had sold out, Sean had written a bunch of twisted slop from the heroic literature of Ireland. He expressed the belief that he was a part of the great cycle of Irish writers. He even quoted passages from a tragedy called *The Ulster Cycle, a story of the northern peoples and the mythological god, Lug of the Long Arm.* Sean mingled the epic with the ongoing Irish troubles and warned of coming doom. He had discovered that the armies of the ancient Ulstermen were stricken with a mysterious illness, the result of a curse laid on them by a boy baby. Sean Pedar, calling himself Peddler, equated this disease with the AIDS virus.

In the epic, the ancient hero eradicates men with his curved sword and disembowels his mother with an empty, broken wine bottle. Sean Pedar, as Peddler, added for effect some lines from the old legend. *"Do not break my heart. Soon I shall die. Grief is stronger than the sea, if thou dids't know it. The good spear drinks good liquor. Though it be he of the church, said he, "I will kill him for the honour of Ulster. Thou shalt die, if thou doest tell thy name. Be it so," said the lad. They smite each other. The boy shaves his head by measured stroke. "We killed for truth that was in our hearts, and strength in our arms, and a peddler's fulfillment in our tongues."*

CHAPTER 30

DETECTIVE HERLIHY AND Officer Grace Reme were relishing the trout dinner they had been forced to abandon the evening Eamon Kennedy was murdered. Above the bar, a phenomenon was going on. The television screen wasn't covering a sports event or a political race. Brian watched the national media feeding frenzy complete with the learned commentaries concerning Sean Pedar McClintock. The press was already dubbing him, *Peddler of Death.*

Trying to calm himself, Brian scoffed to Gracie, "What tommyrot! They're scaring the wits out of everyone. He was obviously Gaelic crazy! Shrinks will be studying those damn notes for years. Sean thought he was another Yeats or John Synge or a kind of avenging Celtic angel of death when he was nothing but an Irish terrorist, drug-dealing, blackmailing, sociopath who wanted to be known as a literary genius.

"It's an irony that Sean swore the drug shipment from Cuba was to be his last. And in all likelihood, that would have been the end of it. He was still casting about looking for some way to revenge himself for being dumped by the IRA. Julien must have had to settle his gambling debts or end up on a one-way ride to the desert with a couple of busted kneecaps. I figure it was Sean, dressed as the Wicked Witch of North Ireland that Bulldog saw out in Vegas. Montzy must have given the nutzoid Mona's damn laptop and included her incredible manuscript. Probably just for spite. Sean began reading it to dig up something to damage either Rebecca or Mona or maybe Julien himself. Then he hit on the idea that Mona's book could provide the catalysis for his revenge. But if he wanted to be the source, then he had to eliminate the author. Crazy how things worked out. If Julien hadn't lifted her computer and floppies, Mona would still be alive."

Grace said softly, "Brian, you don't know what was going down. The contract might have already been out on her."

"Maybe. But I think the sleaze saw publishing the book as more than a chance to join the wannabes attracted to the sweet promise of fame and fortune. His desire to expose Sinn Fein and the IRA for selling out overpowered him to the point that he was willing to risk being exposed just to get credit for that book." His lips flattened to a thin line. "Well, he's as famous as Jack the Ripper now."

They were in the easy going back and forth of an ongoing case. But he was slightly defensive, his shoulders tense, and she was slightly brittle. Both were pretending there wasn't a big swamp of emotions swimming around beneath their conversation.

Gracie touched his hand. "It's a shame Mona wrote such a fine book about the IRA and accidentally discovered the blackmail scheme. How do you think she got on to the church's involvement in the first place?'

Brian shrugged and laughed uncomfortably. "Hell, no tellin'. Maybe she figured out something about Rebecca's trip. Becky never could keep her mouth shut—especially if she was drinking. I know she was pissed about the money the McClintocks were extorting to hand over to their favorite cause. Mona was a damn intuitive woman as well as a professional. Knowing stuff was her specialty. But some things, once they are set in motion, are difficult to stop." He gazed at the TV. "She was always skiing rainbows, but this one didn't end in a pot of Irish gold."

Gracie asked the question that had been nagging her since she first sensed something was being withheld. "Who's this kid, Branden Michael McGlynn?" She'd meant to be a little more smooth, work up to it with some finesse, but the name just popped out.

Brian's jaw dropped. He lowered his glass, leaned back and sighed, "Gracie, my brown-eyed buddy, remember, don't ask, don't tell?"

She stared hard at him, making her eyes wide and unblinking. "I will ask and you will tell me!"

He winked at her. "Third degree, is it?'

She did not laugh. "I'm not going to be put off by the Irish shtick, Brian."

He made a sound, half laugh, half snort, and grabbed his chest, as though mortally wounded. "Well, that's it for all my best lines." Then he smiled tiredly. "Okay, since you seem determined to pry into my personal affairs," he said, lowering his voice, "hold on to your hat—here goes. Branden Michael McGlynn is my son."

Gracie ducked her head and murmured, "Oh Christ, I asked for it, didn't I? Sorry, it's none of my business."

He laughed loudly, "And when has that ever stopped you? No, I'm grateful you pushed me. I couldn't get up the nerve to tell you. Well, at least not before my mouth and chin healed. I don't want any new stitches."

Gracie's eyelids lowered as she fingered her glass. "Look, if it's too painful for you, I'll just back off."

"No, you won't. You'll chew on it forever." The look on his face was sober but decidedly settled. "I've come to terms with it as best I can. Remember when I ditched everything and tried to do the priest thing?" He took up his Scotch glass and swirled the remainder of the amber liquid around. "You see, once upon a time," he said, "long, long ago, I was a nasty little boy one Mardi Gras and took my fiancée's best friend to bed. In Mona's house, no less! I guess I could say the devil made me do it, but actually it was booze that made me do it. We were a couple of kids and she thought I needed my sexual horizons expanded. I thought—hell, I don't know what possessed me to start chugging down shooters of tequila. I don't even like tequila. But she was ripe for the plucking and determined. Plus I was so smashed that screwing seemed like a good idea. It turned out we were both wrong. I think it was Rebecca's malicious game—the idea of wrecking my relationship with Mona was a result of her sadistic, twisted jealousy. She never told me there was a kid and swore she never told Mona. Jesus, she erased Mona's voicemail messages after she died and for a while there I suspected her of arranging to have Julien steal the manuscript to protect her reputation—or what was left of it. She could be as spiteful as they come. Gracie, I think she may have even seduced Julien or he seduced her. I've had my share of poor judgments, and the way I handled booze, Rebecca, and sex were the worst. I guess Mona knew something was different after that night. My God, everything was different."

Gracie's eyes flashed darkly at Brian and seemed to say that she did not approve. She couldn't let it hang there. "I hear that you are sorry that you couldn't keep your pants zipped. Or maybe you're just sorry she brought it up and tried to get her sticky claws into you."

"Don't be snide, Gracie. You don't do snide convincingly." There was that edge to his voice she didn't like.

Noticeably more pale, she set her drink down, and said sharply, "You must really trust me!" Staring at him, she added, "It seems like you could have mentioned it to me. It *did* have to do with the case."

Brian took a breath, let it out. "Ah, that's just what I mean! A little prickly, but an amazing woman. It's what I like about you—that probing mind! Hey, I'm groveling at your feet, what more do you want? I told you my fall from grace with Rebecca just happened. Ascribe it to excessive drink and more excessive randy-ness. You didn't know her. She'd tell me whatever suited her fancy at the moment."

"In bed, maybe?"

He ignored the comment. "Gee, Gracie, cut me some slack, will ya? I was completely out to sea at that time, so I simply waited to see what turned up. Hell, it was an awkward fact to just drop into the evidence pile. Like, oh by the way, I have an illegitimate son left over from a one night stand with Rebecca Webster, the victim's best friend and heir. Nothing like a soap opera lover's triangle to muddy the waters."

"Yes, and any normal person would have shared the information." Gracie felt a heavy lump in her throat. "Especially after your frigin' priest who handled the matter was murdered by his co-conspirator. I understand what you did and why you did it. In your place, I might have done the same things—"

"Is there a 'but' at the end of that sentence?"

"There is. It's a matter of trust."

Brian caught the hint of hurt in her voice. He sat quietly and rubbed a thumb through the condensation on his glass and took a quick swig. His voice was flat. "Gracie, don't. I found myself in a very difficult position and time was of the essence. I had no choice. This case was going to be a bitch no matter how I worked it. I knew it was going to take a lot of working out and involving you was the last thing I wanted to do. Mostly for personal reasons." He rubbed his hand over his scarred chin, "I realized that I might be the intended target instead of Mona. And I didn't want you to lie for me. I wanted you to play it absolutely straight, as of course, you did. We all know that there are leaks in our office. All this personal stuff might get back to Darrel Pitts through someone who couldn't keep his trap shut. I couldn't afford to tell anyone."

Gracie hesitated, but continued while trying to keep her voice calm and low with no hint of a challenge. A challenge might send him to the moon like a rocket. She shook her head slowly. "If it was only personal, I could drop it, but deaths occurred. I can't just ignore the fact that we had an investigation going on. Technically, you were involved simply by your relationship with one of the victims. Now I find out you were involved with all three! I can see this is stuff you would have rather not had gone into with others. Procedure says you would be considered a suspect. But me—I would have respected your wishes. At this point I don't even know which side of the fence you're on. Does the word 'suspension' mean anything to you? Or how about the words—'suspension without pay'? How about an I.A. investigation with you as their target? If I told the brass what you covered up, they could bury you! You'd be on suspension so fast we could send eggs to market on your coattails!"

He looked at her calmly.

She cocked her head at him. "Now what is *that* look? You know how it works!"

Her eyes were full of unasked questions and he remembered what Rebecca had said about never knowing what was in the bottom of a Cracker Jack Box. He answered in a deadpan voice, "Yeah, I realize we never know what is in the bottom of the Cracker Jack Box, but I'm the boss."

"Yes, and I don't like hearing *that* response. You think I'd just drop it on the chief's desk? Bad idea. Ratting is not my style. We're a team, Goddamn it!"

He continued to look at her, and then to her great surprise, he smiled a quick, apologetic smile and said, "Message received! You're right. You didn't question my investigation for a second, did you? Besides," he offered, "it was *my* risk, not yours. If it backfired and I got caught, I acted alone. You did nothing but what you were supposed to do in any investigation." His heart was beating fast. His drink sat in front of him untouched. "And life's a pie in the face."

Gracie shook her head in amazement and laughed quietly. "Okay, the one thing I could always count on was your honesty. But I feel betrayed as a...friend. So I'm angry." She flushed and said, "and maybe a little green-eyed. So, let's have it—better late than never, as they say."

Brian sighed, "Gracie, Rebecca told me the morning after that we had just rolled around, petted and hadn't played a round of 'stick-in-hole.' In my gut, I knew she was lying. I was so angry about the whole sordid affair I came close to hitting her, close enough that it scared the shit out of me. I have a temper, the family legacy from a drunken father. At that exact moment, my mind flashed on my old man, face red, fists raised. There was something about his rage. He sure as hell knew what to do with it. You hit someone. If I became my old man I would batter my wife and children. If you had been one of his children who got beat up a lot, you would tell yourself that you were better than he was. Then a Rebecca comes along and reminds you that you aren't better. You're simply a drunk with no control. I could never let it happen again. I would never get that close to becoming my father. The only answer seemed to be my mother's way to solve every problem—the church."

Gracie asked, "What did Mona do?"

"Oh, we stayed together a few more weeks during which we inflicted pain on each other. Mona and her parents tried to reason with me, but there was no way I could tell them the truth. I was rudderless so I lied. 'It wouldn't work out...I need space to consider the calling of the priesthood...I realized I wasn't ready for a long-term commitment like marriage.' Blah, blah, blah! Feelings ran pretty high and through it all, I had the feeling Rebecca was standing on the sidelines observing the moves in a game. It was like she was enjoying it all and giggling, 'See, this is the way tragic, doomed love is played.'"

She shook her head grimly. "Well, Brian, Rebecca has always been a bit odd, but she didn't deserve what she got. Do you figure Mona found out about the baby while she was researching her book in Ireland?"

He rolled his eyes and leaned back a little. "Rebecca kept harping on that, too. I think she knew even before those trips. She could make a good guess after the way I upped and changed our entire lives. I'd sooner say her suspicions were the reason she decided to write the book about Ireland. Jesus, what a terrible punishment for that decision. In a way, that makes me responsible for what happened to her."

Gracie's eyes flashed. "That's a crock!"

His eyes teared and he said softly, "Thanks. It's a big relief to know only me, myself, and I question my sanity. Okay, I know the facts, but it's the feelings of guilt I can't shed. I am so frustrated at the outcome of my fiasco. I caused as many people as possible unhappiness, embarrassment and heartache, then disaster. I find myself the most convenient person to blame. I'm sorry it ended this way. I took no responsibility for the child. I ran from everything."

"Stop blaming yourself and go find your boy, Brian. Don't be a cop! Jesus, just be human and finish this business."

He nodded to himself and seemed to drift for a minute. His eyes floated across her face then around the crowded room. Eventually he looked back into her eyes as if he had made some kind of decision. He spoke dully, "Gracie, I can do this alone but I thought I'd ask you. If I'm pressuring you then let's just drop it. Will you provide backup?"

She put down her fork, pursed her lips and looked at him quizzically, skeptically, squinting in a way that felt as if she was measuring him. Testing him. Then she cocked her head and put her hand to her ear.

"Please?" he said.

She smiled and saluted with two fingers. "You better believe it, Big Un! When do we leave?"

EPILOGUE

Either Brian had never had the guts or, as he told himself, actually never had the time to read Mona's novel, *Skiing the Rainbow*, even though he had signed enough copies for everyone in Christendom. When Gracie and he left in September of that year, he took his copy along. He settled in first class for the first time in his life and opened the colorful book with his beloved's picture on the back. He sat for a moment listening to the plane's jets revving up and had a sudden vivid memory of the last time he'd seen Mona. It had been a brief meeting at Morning Call for coffee and beignets. They had made love with their hands and their eyes. He remembered how she was always in motion, her long blonde hair catching the light and the big green eyes alive with excitement. *Why didn't we enjoy each other more than we did? I guess we thought we had forever.* Pain etched lines in his face.

He rubbed the tender scar on the underside of his chin and turned to the flyleaf. He felt a surge of resentment as he read the tragic event of her murder. *Mona, Mona, I'm so lonely for you.* With a heavy sigh, he turned to the last thing she had added before her murder and read:

DEDICATION

Human beings are unable to be totally truthful about themselves. Therefore, in the end, the reader will know more about the author than the author knows about herself. The human heart dares not stay away too long from that which hurts it most. There is a return journey to anguish that few of us are released from making. I dedicate this book to Brian, in his joy and pain at being Irish—and also to the son we never had.

"Out of love you can speak with strong fury."
Author's favorite quote from Eudora Welty

Brian stared at the words until they were nothing more than a blur through his tears. He leaned against the window and watched as The Crescent City disappeared below him. *Thank you, my love—thank you for peace.*

Photo by Carlton Mickle

About her life, Jane Stennett, Ph.D says:

"After growing up in Midland, Texas, I was transplanted by marriage to fascinating New Orleans. I had a bachelor's degree from Baylor in drama, education and English that equipped me to act in community theaters and teach school. After marriage, I taught and raised two children while earning my master's degree from Texas Technological University and eventually added a religious counseling certificate.

In the eight years that followed, I decided that a new definition of infinity was found in the time it took me to earn a Ph.D. Before the ink was dry on the sheepskin, I became New Orleans' 'Dr Jane' on WGSO radio. I helped people solve problems for four years at three radio stations during which time I also directed a counseling center for agoraphobics and went to China for six weeks with the US government. When I returned from serving my country, I learned the true meaning of the painful concept that 'good things often follow bad things.' I had to put my dishonest secretary in jail!

This event necessitated my learning to use the office computer myself in order to write journal and magazine articles. The wonder of writing soon led to the fun of entering writing competitions. I was frequently recognized for my writing, but no editors were forthcoming. Largely as a joke, I entered my first murder mystery, a 'tongue-in-cheek' New Orleans slasher that stars a version of myself and loads of cool-weird New Orleans characters. The effort resulted in "There Is No Such Thing As A Literary Agent."

Since then, I have survived Katrina and begun a sequel set in Ireland, written children's stories and two historical novels, plus ministered to the elderly. I'm having a fun life."